"Get him, he's a thief," the librarian screamed.

The priests moved forward, hesitantly. The librarian, exasperated, lunged forward to try and grasp Ian with his long bony fingers.

Ian had been standing there, in shock. He lurched back, barely avoiding the hooked talons of the librarian. He swiveled. Leaping to the right, he soared past the startled group of priests who had been slowly converging on him. Several giant bounds brought him to the doors. As the doors closed behind him, the shrill sound of the librarian's screams were mercifully cut off.

Leaping down the wide steps, he sprinted across the road behind the library, the late afternoon light splashing on his head. Behind him, he could hear a loud commotion. Twisting his neck, he looked back. There, outside the doors, stood the librarian, gesticulating wildly with his arms to the group of younger priests that surrounded him. The librarian looked across the way with the all-seeing glare of a wrathful god. Catching sight of Ian, his malevolence concentrated itself.

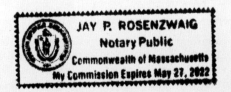

## Acknowledgments

Thanks go to all those who gave me encouragement, or helped in proofreading and critiquing the manuscript. They include my dear wife, Marcia, Dr. David Sanders, Debbie Klahr, Sarah and Stephen Craimer, Doris and Jay Hartman, Sam Reiken, Kate Blackburn, Steve Faiwiszewski, and my mother, Beatrice Sanders. For their help, thanks also go to my entire Thursday night class, especially, Marc Kaye, Michael Luxenberg, Josh Marcus, Dr. Jeffrey Raskin, and Barry Schwartz.

Most of all I thank the Holy One, blessed be He, who guided my hand. May this work be found pleasing in His Eyes.

---

All rights reserved.

**ATTENTION: ORGANIZATIONS AND CORPORATIONS**

Olive Press paperbacks are available at special quantity discounts for bulk purchases, for sales promotions, premiums, or fundraising. For information, please write:
**Special Markets Department, The Olive Press, P.O. Box 7077 W.O.B. West Orange , N.J. 07052**

# Menorah

|||||||

## Daniel Sanders
. . . . . . .

♣

The Olive Press

*New York • New Jersey • Jerusalem*

If you purchased this book without a cover, you should be aware that this book is stolen property. It was reported as "unsold and destroyed" to the publisher and neither the publisher nor the author has received any payment for this "stripped book."

This is a work of fiction. The characters, incidents, and dialogues are products of the author's imagination and are not to be construed as real. Any resemblance to actual events or persons, living or dead, is entirely coincidental.

*The Olive Press* ♣

Published in association with
Tree of Life Productions
"It is a tree of life to those who seize it."

Copyright © 1997 by Daniel Sanders
All rights reserved. No part of this book may be reproduced or transmitted in any form or by any means, electronic or mechanical, including photocopying, recording, or by any information storage and retrieval system, without permission in writing from the publisher, except in the case of brief quotations embodied in critical articles and reviews. For information address:
The Olive Press, P.O. Box 7077 W.O.B. West Orange, N.J. 07052

Design and typography by Eileen Panepinto

ISBN 0-9655905-7-7

Printed in Canada

10 9 8 7 6 5 4 3 2 1

*In memory of my father,
who showed me the beauty
of the "Song of Songs."*

*And with deep love
to my wife, Marcia,
and our sons, Jonathan,
Ian, and Noah.*

# PROLOGUE

…He changes the times and appointed moments, He removes kings and He sets up kings; He gives wisdom to the wise and knowledge to those who have understanding. He reveals the deep and secret things, He knows what is in darkness and Light dwells with Him.

Daniel 2:21-22

## 70 COMMON ERA

Black smoke rose heavenward in great roiling billows, spreading out over the scene of carnage. Warm dry air coming off the desert mountains lifted and swirled the ashes. To his nostrils came an oversweet smell, as of fat burning. Tears ran down his soot-covered face. He knew this smell well. His family house was located very near to the Chamber of Hewn Stone, the meeting place of the Great Assembly. Here the luminary sages and their disciples would gather twice weekly to adjudicate those cases brought before them according to the living word of God. This chamber directly adjoined the Temple courtyard where the priests performed the daily burnt-offering.

One family guarded the secret to mixing the fragrant spices of the holy incense that was burned every morning and evening. The smell that came to him that day, though, was of a different burnt-offering.

He had awoken early that morning. All night they'd hidden in the wine cellar: his mother, his brother, and himself. The hunger in his belly only bothered him on occasion. He awoke, not out of hunger but out of fear. The fear was a living thing inside him. He feared the enemy. Where were they, and what would they do if they found them?

Joseph ben Israel had reached fifteen years, four months earlier. His father was of the illustrious house of Bezalel.

He spoke to his younger brother Yair in whispers so as not to disturb their mother. They were alone, but he knew they could find them easily. So he told Yair that he would go out and see if there might not be any chance for them to escape. At the least, he would try to find them something to eat.

As he rose to leave, Yair pressed his small, thin body against him and said, "May the Lord protect you from evil."

Joseph answered, "May He protect your soul."

Yair was seven, very handsome, always with a smile. Joseph loved him with all his heart. He could feel Yair's body trembling with hunger and fear as he pressed against him. Joseph swallowed the lump that rose up in his throat.

"Don't worry, I'll be back before mother wakes."

He hurried up the cold stone steps with only a

quick glance back and a wave of his hand. He passed through several empty passageways that had once bustled with activity. Silk curtains hung in tatters in the open windows. The wooden shutters that normally enclosed them had long ago been taken for firewood. He turned right under the large arch and took the passage that led to the side alleyway door.

Joseph came out onto the alley, and looked to the right, then to the left. The alley was deserted as far as he could see, until the curve of the buildings on either side obscured his view.

The alley was filled with the stench of dog excrement. Ten cubits away, a swarm of large black flies hovered above a rotting corpse. Such sights and smells were commonplace. His gaze was fixed upon the massive stone blocks of the wall before him.

This was the outer side of the great perimeter wall that enclosed the Temple courtyard itself. The stones were very large at the base, smaller as the wall rose. Joseph was strong despite his hunger, and it took him but a few moments to reach the top. He hooked his legs over the top and flattened his entire body down in the hope that no one would see him. Slowly, he lifted his head.

He smelled it first. Thick black smoke stung his eyes, making it difficult to see. It billowed in clouds, occasionally leaving his view almost clear.

In the distance he could see a great cloud of smoke and dust; to his ears came the clamor of men at war. He could hear the muffled screams of the combatants. Shouts rang out in the direction of the main Temple gate.

Blinking from the smoke, he stared down at a sight few mortal eyes have beheld. The Romans had set the huge Temple doors on fire. The defenders had held out for so long. And somewhere deep inside, he had held on to the hope that they could somehow outlast the brutal invaders.

A great booming sound rolled through the air, jolting him, and he knew that the enemy had breached the massive doors. They had penetrated the Temple itself. Joseph felt sick inside.

The immense Temple courtyard spread out below. Not far off from where he lay atop the wall sat the massive stone outer altar. There, on the north side of the altar, stood a long line of men, robed in the white linen garments of the priestly tribe. A red flame burnt atop the altar and on its face stood a lone priest. Strapped to his chest was a golden breastplate.

A cloud of smoke blew by, stinging his eyes again. Blinking away the tears, he gazed down at the scene below. The priests' lips moved slowly, deliberately. Around each neck hung a gold key on a gold chain. These were the keys that were the priests' sacred trust. They unlocked the secret subterranean crypts that held the Ark of the Covenant and Aaron's staff. Joseph did not have to hear the words they spoke. Somehow he knew they were reciting the Shema, the words uttered by every Judean as he affirms his life at the moment of death.

"Hear O Israel the Lord our God, the Lord is One."

Their faces were so peaceful as they walked into the flames. Their white robes fluttered slightly in the desert wind as they were consumed. Tears flowed from his eyes and he felt a strong constriction like a metal band being tightened around his chest.

The last priest stood alone. Joseph felt a shock. He recognized this man. It was the High Priest's younger brother who had been his father's friend for many years. The priest looked up to heaven, as if he expected the Messiah to come riding down on a cloud, an army of angels at his side. Joseph tried to call out to him, but no sound issued from his throat. The priest lowered his eyes and said something, but he could not hear the words nor read the expression on his face. Then the priest leapt into the flames. Joseph could not move; his body would not heed his command.

A column of pure light broke through the leaden sky, which had turned almost black. The exquisite light drove downward, straight into the flames. The gold keys that had hung around the priests' necks flew heavenward, held within that light. Then, as suddenly as it had appeared, the light was gone.

Joseph's heart had stopped beating. He felt his mouth open, air rushing back into his lungs. He lived again. It was several minutes before he could command his body once more.

The fire had died down to a sputter on the altar and the sky seemed to open up, as if a giant hand had parted the clouds. Rays of sunlight slanted down upon the altar top, striking something shiny on its face. It shone with brilliant points of fire. Squinting, he realized that he was looking at the golden breastplate, the Tablet of Truth. It had been left behind by God's hand. Almost without thinking, he swung his legs over, and scrambled down to the flagstones of the Temple courtyard.

He was standing on holy ground. Dazzling sunlight reflected off the bone-white Jerusalem paving to create shimmering waves in the hot summer air. He looked up, shading his eyes with his hand, and saw the sun was near its zenith. Too much time had passed, and now he was exposed. Joseph started to turn back to the wall, but he hesitated.

The altar was but fifty cubits away and he thought: How can I let the Tablet of Truth fall into the hands of the Edomite?

An instant later he was streaking toward it. He left no shadow on the stones as he bolted up the ramp to the top. Here, he paused, his heart racing as he gazed into the sputtering flames.

There it was, right before him. Twelve precious stones set in a rectangle of beaten gold in four neat rows, three to a row. Each jewel was engraved with the name of one of the twelve tribes of Israel. Joseph's great ancestor Bezalel had beaten this metal and inlaid these very stones with his own hands for the tabernacle, in the wastelands of Sinai.

Ashes swirled above the breastplate and he saw that the gold had become dulled and blackened from the intense heat. Stripping off his upper tunic and wrapping it around his hand, he pulled the heavy breastplate from the ashes. He held it away from his body. He spun around, just as a large detachment of Roman soldiers entered the far end of the courtyard. They had not yet spotted him. Terrified, he bounded down the ramp.

He reached the ground and took off for the far eastern wall. Should they catch me, he thought, let them not take me near my family home, where my mother and brother still hide. His sandaled feet seemed to soar over the hot stone slabs. Nearing the eastern wall, he heard a shout off in the distance, like the cry of the condor. He had been sighted.

With a last burst of speed, Joseph leapt to the wall face and began to climb. The stone blocks were more closely set here, leaving him less purchase for his hands and feet. Still clutching the breastplate, he continued to climb with one hand. Suddenly, he lost his handhold and nearly fell, slamming his body against the rough stone as he scrambled for a grip. Twisting his head back, he gauged that he was close to halfway up, but the stones were even smaller and more tightly fitted near the top. He knew that if he lost his grip, he could easily fall and the enemy would surely have him.

He had to make a choice. He couldn't risk using only one hand. He could drop the breastplate or could climb back down, re-wrap it, and tie it around his neck. He cursed himself for not having done so right away. Holding on with one arm and leg, he swung about to look behind him. The soldiers were coming up too close for him to go back down.

His vision sharpened, all his senses becoming more acute. Everything went into slow motion. The lead soldier ran toward him, every detail of his armor so clear he could almost touch it. He saw the sweat drops beaded on the soldier's forehead, the cords of muscle around his mouth and cheeks stretched taut. Joseph's mind raced with a jumble of thoughts.

Inside him, something snapped. A great surge of power coursed through his limbs. Turning back to the wall, he quickly scaled its rough surface, willing his body up and over the lip. He could hear the hoarse cries from the other side. He could not yet understand their strange tongue, but he knew they seethed with frustration. He rose up, looking right then left.

Joseph had come over onto a wide street not far from an intersection that opened onto his own house's side alleyway. Seeing no one about, he sprinted towards the intersection and collided head-first with a Roman patrol. His head struck something solid.

---

He awoke to find himself shackled by heavy chains, a thick iron collar fastened around his neck. He had been taken captive along with the Tablet of Truth. Only once again would he see it. What had become of his mother and brother he never learned. From others he heard that most of the people had died either by the sword or the flames when they torched the city.

He was taken, along with several others, to a large courtroom in the Temple where the Romans had gathered many captives. As he was tall and fair, he was selected with other young men and maidens, along with other spoils of war, to be taken by ship to the heart of their evil empire, Rome. Much evil befell them on that long journey.

Almost a year later, shackled in two long lines, Joseph, amongst a select few, was marched along a wide avenue in the center of the Roman's great city to celebrate their triumph. They were made to carry the holy vessels of the Temple as drunken crowds lining the avenue cheered. He was one of six boys, three on each side, who carried the sacred Menorah by two wooden poles set through large rings in its base.

It was here that he saw for the last time the golden breastplate. They had tied it by a chain to the naked breasts of a young girl who was just becoming a woman. So the Romans thought to shame them.

He was taken as a slave along with another boy into the house of a wealthy patron of Rome. There he became a scribe and won favor in the eyes of his master, a wealthy merchant. Joseph discovered new ways to keep his master's books so that he paid fewer taxes. He was treated well, and given many liberties not afforded other slaves of the house.

Still, he was far from content. His heart longed for his family and the beautiful city he loved: Jerusalem. How his soul ached to be there again, among its white towers and walls. Each night he would cry with a deep longing, and pray before he slept:

"If I forget thee O Jerusalem, let my right arm lose its cunning."

# CHAPTER 1

And the land was desolate and void, and darkness upon the face of the deep…

Genesis 1:2

desolate… this is the exile of Babylon,
void… this is the exile of Persia,
darkness… this is the exile of Greece,
the deep… this is the exile of Rome.

Genesis Rabbah 2:5

---

## NEW YORK CITY
### Present Day

It was mid-morning. Bright sunlight streamed in over the tree-tops. The white bed sheets nailed to the tall window-frames billowed outward in the freshening breeze off the river, spilling sunlight into the room at intervals. It was too bright to sleep any longer. Ian stretched out his long muscular frame on the queen-sized mattress that lay on the bare wood floor in the middle of the room.

A deep drowsiness clung to him. He shifted lazily over on his side but was stopped by the shapely form that lay there, wrapped in a white bed sheet. Rolling off the other way, he landed with a soft thud. Getting up slowly, Ian searched for the sweats he'd tossed somewhere the night before. There they lay, crumpled by the chair leg, near the battered wooden desk piled high with all his papers. He slipped into them and plodded across the apartment.

He'd met Jessica just a few months earlier, at a New Year's Eve party at Columbia. Ian had noticed her on the dance floor with a group of her girlfriends, and he hadn't been able to take his eyes off her. That night she'd worn an off-white silk blouse with a short, dark green skirt that showed off her long, bare, athletic legs. She was tall even in her matching green flats. One thing had led to another, and they were seeing each other now on a regular basis.

The one thing they didn't speak much about was their relationship, as if it were some unwritten rule. Maybe they were both afraid to discuss it for the obvious reasons. Ian's father had been an orthodox pulpit rabbi until he'd died two years earlier, and Jessica's family were practicing Irish Catholics from Chicago, though she hadn't been inside a church in years.

Entering the kitchen, he filled the kettle with water from the stained porcelain sink and put it on the old gas range. Plopping himself down on a rickety wooden chair by the table, he leaned the back against the wall and yawned, waiting for the water to boil.

He'd inherited the rent controlled apartment less than a year ago, after his grandfather had died. Ian had been having some of his mail and bills sent to the apartment for years to establish tenancy in his name. He hadn't really furnished it yet, but then he didn't have the money for that right now. His mind began to wander, back to earlier days, and his father.

They'd fought many times about religion. His father had received his rabbinical ordination at Yeshiva University. The University seal had the guiding slogans written in Hebrew: Torah and Science. They had been very close when Ian was young. Before going on to his rabbinical studies, his father had majored in mathematics, and was an avid chess player of tournament quality. On many Sabbath afternoons they had set up chess pieces on the simple black and white checkered board, after coming home from synagogue and finishing the traditional Sabbath meal. Ian had loved the game right from the beginning. His father taught him well, but it was their discussions on philosophy and religion during the games that Ian enjoyed most.

In the beginning he had mainly listened, but as the years went by and he grew older, the discussions had become more lively and eventually turned into heated debates. His father had been very open-minded at first, but when Ian stopped putting on tefilin in his sophomore year at college, their discussions had taken on a different quality. The break came in Ian's senior year. His father had found out by accident that Ian no longer kept the Sabbath. His mother had called him on the phone one day in his dorm room and asked him to come home for dinner.

He could tell that something was up by the sound of her voice and when he asked her if anything was wrong, all she said was, "Just come home."

About a block from his house, Ian fished into the front pocket of his worn jeans and pulled out a crumpled, hand knit yarmulke. He smoothed it out, affixing it to his head with two black bobby pins. Stepping into the house, he immediately sensed tension. His mother greeted him at the door and kissed him on the cheek. His younger brother Jonathan was still away at yeshiva in Israel.

It was early October, and the weather was beginning to turn cold. All meals had to be eaten in the succah, as they were in the intermediate days of Tabernacles. Theirs was a light metal pole and canvas affair which they'd used every year for as long as Ian could remember. Ian walked through the house, his mother trailing behind him. In the tiny backyard, the faded yellow and blue canvas hut stood with the traditional bamboo poles jutting irregularly out on top.

Ian stooped down to enter through the narrow flap. His father rose up from his seat at the head of the table. He had been reading a religious text that lay open in front of him. Ian rushed over. His first thought was, God, I can't believe how the dark blue suit hangs on his big frame. Rabbi Charosh had been a diabetic for many years, but it was only in the last few that the damage from the disease had become obvious. He had lost several toes on his right foot last summer, and his eyesight was failing.

Still, he smiled broadly, managing to squeeze Ian's hand with a faint echo of his old vise-like grip.

Ian hugged his father. "It's good to see you. I see you still have your grip."

His father smiled warmly. "Come, let's go wash. I'm hungry. Your mother has prepared a delicious meal for us."

Later, standing by the sink in the kitchen, Ian asked, "What did you want to speak to me about?"

"Let's first wash and eat and then we can talk," replied his father as he picked up the silver laver.

His father spoke of many things while they ate. He spoke most of how well Ian's brother Jonathan was doing in yeshiva in Israel.

"All his teachers tell me that he is a genius and that he has great insights into the gemara. It's a shame that you haven't applied yourself similarly, but no, everyone must follow his own path to God. Tell me, how are your courses going? I hear from your mother that it's likely you will graduate with high honors. That should ensure you a place in the graduate program, no?"

Ian nodded. "Yeah. I should graduate summa cum laude as long as my final grades this semester hold up. As to my spot in the graduate program, that's already a definite, so there's nothing to worry about over that."

"I see," answered his father. Pausing for a moment he said, "There is something else I wanted to discuss with you. Tell me, where were you last Shabbos?"

Ian's face turned slightly red. "Why?"

"You know why," said his father. "Tell me, when were you planning on telling me you were a desecrator of the Sabbath? Or were you just going to sneak around and lie to me? I can't believe this is the son your mother and I raised. Master of the Universe, if you're going to deny God at least have the honesty to tell me!"

Ian sat there, stunned. Unable to look his father in the eye, he replied in a quiet voice, "I didn't tell you because I didn't want to upset you. You haven't been well, and I knew you would never accept it, so I thought it was best not to say anything."

"You don't understand anything, do you? Do you think you were doing me a favor? I'm your father. If I died tomorrow and never had a chance to help you, do you think I would want it that way?" he cried out. He paused, and then in a small, still voice he said, "Do you really no longer believe in God?"

"Why can't you leave this alone?" Ian said. "How am I supposed to answer that? We've been over this before. I don't know if God exists. Maybe he does and I sincerely hope so. But I don't see how keeping the Sabbath helped any of the six million who perished in the Holocaust. I still can't understand how an All-Merciful God could countenance the brutal murder of one and a half million innocent Jewish children for any kind of higher purpose. Why? So the world would finally let us have the State of Israel?"

His father shook his head sadly. "The world didn't give us Israel. The other nations have never given us anything, except hatred and death. We created the State of Israel. With our sweat and blood, and tears. Only God helped us. No one else! And who are you to judge God? His ways are not our ways. He cries when every Jewish soul leaves this world. Do I understand his plans? No, of course not. But does that mean that I reject Him because of my own limitations?"

Ian was silent. Taking a deep breath he said, "I can't keep the Sabbath or any of the other rituals if I don't fully believe in them. I want to be honest to myself and I see it's better that I be honest with you as well."

"I see," his father said. A short sigh filled with melancholy escaped his lips. "I don't know what else to say, except that I pray God will show you loving-kindness and help you back to the right path. Now I need to rest. I fear that your ego has gotten in the way of your seeing clearly. Come speak to me again when you are maybe a little more humble."

The words stabbed like sharp arrows of ice through Ian's heart. As he got up to leave he bowed his head in silence, struggling to fight back the tears.

His mother had hovered silently just inside the kitchen door during their argument, but as he came in to get his jacket she said, "Ian, you have to understand how much you hurt us both. We raised you to be a good Jew. Not to be this way. Please think over what your father has been telling you."

Ian stepped forward to hug his mother. Pulling away, he said, "I will Mom. I have to get back to school to study, but I promise I'll call you soon."

He kissed his mother good-bye and left, not having the courage to go back to say good-bye to his father. Staring down at the cracked sidewalk pavement on his way to the subway station, he felt hot tears well up inside him again, blurring his vision.

That week he had two exams, and being caught up with them, he forgot to call. Or maybe subconsciously he put it off. In the middle of the following week, laying on his bed in his dorm room, idly thinking about his next exam, the phone rang. He let it ring. Groaning, he pushed himself up off the bed and picked it up in the middle of the next ring.

"Hullo…who is it?" he said, puzzled by the silence on the other end.

Then he heard his mother's voice. It sounded strange, muffled, like she was talking through a sock. "You have to come to the hospital right away. Daddy almost died this morning."

Ian froze for a moment, his mind trying to grasp the enormity of her words. He finally blurted out, "Where are you?"

"We're at Columbia Presbyterian, in the Intensive Care Unit. It's on the third floor of the big new building."

"Yeah, sure, I know which one you mean. What

happened?"

"Your father caught pneumonia taking down the succah."

"I'll be right over. Don't worry. Dad's very strong. I'm sure he'll make it through this also."

"I hope so… I'm very worried. You know how much I love you," she added, almost breaking down once more.

"I love you too," Ian said, before hanging up.

He opened the door. Several knots of people sat or stood around the various low soft couches and chairs scattered about the room. A few looked up for an instant and then looked away. None of them was his mother. Scanning the room, he noticed a hospital phone on a nearby wall. He picked it up.

A female voice on the other end said, "Intensive care unit. Can I help you?"

He asked, "I'm hear to see my father, ah…Rabbi Charosh. Can I see him now?"

The disembodied voice said, "One moment."

Ian stood by the wall, cupping the phone by his ear as he twisted around to see if his mother had come in. There was no sign of her. Impatiently, he waited, listening to the slight hiss on the line.

He was just about to hang up and try again when the voice said, "You can come in now. Just go through the doors marked I.C.U. Your mother is in there now."

Eagerly he entered, anxious to find her. He stopped to look around. He had stepped into another world. The ward was dimly lit, the large rooms separated only by glass walls with curtains for partitions. The rooms had no doors and as he passed down the center aisle, he could see right into each one. Glancing with morbid fascination at the inhabitants who lay hooked up to complex machines, Ian suddenly felt sick inside. He wondered, God, is Dad going to look like that?

Down near the other end of the aisle he caught sight of his mother, talking to a doctor in a long white clinic coat. He approached, hearing the doctor in the middle of answering one of his mother's questions.

"…he appears to be stable now, but the next forty-eight hours are very important. We have to see how well he responds to the antibiotics we're giving him, and we have to get his fluid retention under control. His kidney function is low, being a diabetic, so we have to be careful not to strain them."

"When are you going to get back the culture results they took earlier to see if you're giving him the right antibiotics?" his mother said.

"It takes a few days to get back all the cultures, but right now we have him on two different broad spectrum antibiotics. That should cover him for basically all the strains we would be worried about."

He seemed to be finished, so Ian took the opportunity to make his presence known.

Coming forward, he hugged his mother as she whispered into his ear, "I'm so glad to see you."

His mother introduced him to the doctor and after exchanging brief pleasantries, the doctor excused himself.

"How is he doing?" Ian said.

"He seems to be a little better. I saw Dr. Feldberg, his regular internist, about half an hour ago. He didn't seem to be too concerned about the pneumonia. He says that they can usually get that under control in a few days. He's more worried about Daddy's kidneys failing because of all the fluid. The fluid puts a strain on his heart too, but his blood pressure is pretty stable right now," she said in a rush.

Ian looked into the room. There was his father, his thin frame dressed in a hospital gown, laid out on his side on the hospital bed. A blue plastic breathing tube was taped to his mouth. Thin clear tubes from several hanging I.V. bags led into one arm. He was facing Ian, his eyes closed.

"Is he sleeping?" he mumbled.

---

The shrill whistle of the kettle cut through his thoughts. With a start, he banged the chair forward onto the cracked linoleum floor, jumping up to pull it off the burner. Not paying attention, he sloshed some of the boiling water onto his wrist.

He cursed, dropping the kettle on the counter-top. He twisted the cold water faucet on full, plunging his burnt wrist under the soothing ice-cold stream. Relaxing in relief, he slumped forward, leaning his body against the sink cabinet. Gazing at the bubbly stream, he allowed it to lull him into a light trance.

Sharp pins and needles stabbed into his flesh. Jerking his arm away, he turned the water off. He shook his head. I'm not starting today off very well, he thought.

The pain of the burn began to return as the coldness faded. Consciously ignoring it, he made himself a cup of instant coffee with a lot of sugar and a little milk. Sipping from the rim of a chipped porcelain mug, he trudged down the long hall to the living room. He sank back into the soft cushions of the frayed old lounge chair. The sunlight, filtering in through the tall windows of the apartment, bathed him with its warmth. The heated liquid warmed him inside and he quickly began to feel more alert.

"What am I supposed to be doing today?" he mused, talking to himself in a mocking tone.

He looked up. Framed in the doorway stood Jessica, wearing only a long tee-shirt that just barely covered her hips. Ian quickly abandoned his mental search.

"Good morning, how'd you sleep?" he said.

Jessica smiled, coming toward him. Perching herself on the padded arm of the chair, she stroked his arm absentmindedly as she answered, "I slept really well. What time is it?"

Ian looked at his watch in surprise. "It's ten to eleven. Do you want some coffee or tea? I think there might be some orange juice left in the fridge."

"Okay. Do you want anything?" she said.

He shook his head no. As she got up to go, he swatted her playfully.

Letting out a squeal, Jessica headed down the hallway, rubbing her bottom.

"Watch it," she called out behind her, padding into the kitchen.

Ian saw her returning out of the corner of his eye. Before he could move, she tipped a mug on him, ice-cold water splashing onto his face and bare chest. Laughing, she danced about the room.

"Gotcha," she cried, dashing into the hall.

Ian lunged out of the deep cushions after her retreating form. He chased her several times around the apartment as she shrieked, finally catching her in the dining room. She struggled to get loose, flailing her arms ineffectually against his broad back. He lifted her up easily onto the heavy oak table, kissing her neck and throat. Her arms slowed their frantic movements to clasp his shoulders. He started to lift the tee-shirt up over her breasts. The phone rang. Ignoring it, he kissed her neck, working his way down. She arched her back and moaned.

The phone kept ringing. The strident ringing held his attention, breaking his mood.

"Don't stop," she said into his ear as she leaned her body forward. The phone rang insistently. Annoyed, he pulled away.

"I'll be right back," he muttered, heading for the phone.

As he walked barefoot across the apartment he thought, I'll bet the answering machine is screwed up again.

"Hello?"

"Is everything okay?" his mother's voice came over the line.

Ian cleared his throat. "Yeah, everything's fine. I just slept late. What's up?"

"I knew you'd forget."

"Forget what?" Ian said, rubbing his scruffy chin.

"Jonathan's coming in today, and you promised you would come with me to the airport."

"Oh, right. When's the flight supposed to come in?"

"Two o'clock on El Al."

"Well, that means he'll be at least two hours late," he said.

"No, they're really much better now. Besides, I called up and they said the flight was on time."

"So when should I be there?"

"Well, I figure we should get to the airport by three, since it'll take him about an hour to get his luggage and go through customs. I guess you should try to be here around two, just in case we hit some traffic."

Ian turned to see Jessica standing silently behind him. Cupping the receiver with his hand, he raised his eyebrows apologetically as he mouthed, "It's my mother."

Taking his hand away he spoke into the receiver. "Okay. I'm going to take a shower right now. I have a few things to do here first, but I should be there by two no problem."

"Good, I'll see you then. You know I love you, don't you?" she said.

"Yes I know. I love you too. I'll see you soon." He hung up the phone and said, "I knew there was something I had to do today. I promised her I'd go with her to meet my brother at the airport."

Jessica nodded. "You should go. You haven't seen him in a year, and your mom must be very lonely. You should spend more time with her, you know. She doesn't live so far away and you almost never go to see her."

"Look, I didn't ask for your advice about my mother," he said. Seeing the hurt look on her face, he softened his tone. "Sorry, I didn't mean it," Ian murmured softly, leaning over to wrap his arms around her slim waist.

Jessica pulled away. "You're right. I wouldn't want you to tell me how to be with my parents."

Ian nodded. There was an awkward silence. Ian stared down at the small, battered machine on the floor. A blinking red light winked up at him. Tapping a button with his big toe, he waited. There was an audible click, followed by a whirring sound, followed by a second click. Then a man's voice came on.

"This is Dr. Berluonti. Come see me first thing Monday morning before class. By the way, how is your Latin?" The line went dead but the tape kept playing.

Frowning, Ian tapped another button repeatedly. The machine let out a high-pitched whine, followed by a grinding sound. He quickly stooped down and pulled out the plug.

Looking up, he said, "I think it's had it."

Jessica stared down, a quick series of emotions

playing across her face. She said, "Who was that?"

Ian straightened up. "My thesis advisor."

"What does he want?"

"I have no idea."

At 2:06 p.m. Ian strode up the walk to his mother's house. The bushes were budding nicely and would soon need to be trimmed. He noticed that the flower beds were crying for attention.

Since Dad died, he thought, she no longer seemed to care about gardening the way she used to. He knocked loudly on the metal security door. A moment later the inner door opened and his mother stood in the doorway.

"One minute," she said, muffled by the thick glass and bars. She pulled out a key and opened the heavy door.

"Hi, it's good to see you," she said as they embraced. "How have you been?"

"I've been okay," he said.

"Come, we'll talk more in the car," she said.

Ten minutes later on the Van Wyck Expressway, they hit some unusually heavy traffic.

"There's probably an accident up ahead. Once we get past it, it should get much better," he reassured her.

She tapped the steering wheel, flicking the radio on to hear a traffic report.

"Don't even bother," Ian said. "Those reports are half an hour behind, and anyway there's no other way to go. Don't worry. The flight's going to be late. We're going to have to sit around waiting for him anyway. This way we wait in the car. The other way we wait in the airport. What's the difference?"

"Very clever. Is that the kind of logic you use in your philosophy thesis? If you don't mind, I'd like to hear the traffic report, shh…wait, I think it's about to come on," she said as she raised the volume.

They listened for a minute to the announcer drone on about the Hudson river crossings and a three car accident on the Saw Mill River Parkway. No mention was made of the Van Wyck. The report ended with, "More traffic and weather in ten minutes."

A particularly annoying commercial blared forth. Ian reached forward to shut it off. "Well, tell me what's going on at school these days?"

His mother glanced at him as she inched her car forward behind a taxi. Turning her head a little she said, "We're off next week for Easter. The kids are pretty good this semester."

Ian's mother was a special-education teacher in the New York City public school system. She'd gone back to work after his father had died and though she complained at times, she admitted that it was good for her to keep busy. The money wasn't much, but it helped her avoid dipping into her savings.

The traffic began to move. Off to their right, a Pakistani driver stood by a tow truck that had just hooked up his broken down livery cab. Ian caught a brief look at the driver's exasperated face as they slid by, their car accelerating into the suddenly clear road.

"Well that was it," Ian said. "It should be clear sailing from now on."

His mother glanced at him a moment. "What time is it?"

Looking at his watch he said, "It's five to three. Don't worry, we'll be there in ten minutes. I'm telling you, if we're lucky the plane probably just landed and we're going to have to sit around 'til he gets out."

"I hope you're right."

# CHAPTER 2

That night sleep eluded the King so he ordered that the record book, the annals, be brought and be read before the King.

Book of Esther VI:1

---

## VATICAN CITY, ROME
### Present Day

Undersecretary for the Sacred Office Alberto Maglione leaned his body to the side. His impeccably manicured hand closed around the soft petals, cradling the bloom near its base. With a flick of his wrist, he plucked the lush flower, carefully avoiding the small thorns embedded a scant few millimeters away. He lifted it delicately to his long aristocratic nose, breathing in deeply the heady nectar. Warm sunlight splashed on patterned scarlet silk robes, bathing him in a soft red glow. Around him grew all manner of exotic tropical vegetation, pruned to perfection.

Thoughts came to him, dark memories of times long past. As he stared up at the brilliant azure sky, they came again, only stronger. They seeped forth from some deep, hidden well, forced to the surface by an undefined pressure, unbidden, unwanted.

"Oh, Gabrielle," he groaned. "Why? Was I so wretched?"

Her beautiful face swam up, blotting his vision. He could almost feel her full, sensuous lips, the fragrance of her body. *Why do I still think of her?* He silently rebuked himself.

A hand tapped his shoulder. Startled, he spun around, his long silken garments swishing in a small circle on the ground.

Secretary Karocyz stood before his underling, fairly bursting from the blood-red silk garments that swathed his impressive bulk. Trimmed in thick gold braid, the robes hung in broad folds on his chest. From a heavy gold chain hung an ancient gold cross, its surface studded with huge emeralds encased in mother of pearl.

In carefully modulated tones, the large man spoke with just the right amount of condescension in his voice. "I was told that I might find you here."

Undersecretary Maglione stood awkwardly before his superior, a tremulous smile on his lips.

His head cocked at a respectful angle, he said, "Yes, your Grace. I enjoy walking in the gardens, especially at this time of year."

The Secretary's thick lower lip quivered almost imperceptibly as he continued, barely taking note of the reply. "As you may know, each year the Holy Church invites a visiting secular scholar on a six month scholarship."

Maglione nodded.

Sniffing daintily from the bouquet of an exquisitely

pale rose on a nearby bush, the Secretary rumbled, "Yes, well, you of course heard of the untimely death of Secretary Fouchere last month?"

"Yes, your Grace," he replied. "A terrible tragedy. I have heard that, under the circumstances, acting Secretary Monterosso is doing an able job over at the Office of the Propagation of the Faith."

"Just so," said the Secretary. "Yet just yesterday he asked me, due to the overwhelming nature of his new duties, if our Office could assist with some of their usual duties. Only in the short term, he assured me."

"I see, your Grace."

Secretary Karocyz stopped to turn his vast bulk and face the smaller priest. "Do you think you could handle the process of selecting a proper candidate for the scholarship?"

"Of course, your Grace," Maglione exclaimed, his face the very picture of sincerity.

Inside, he seethed. *Always, I am the one he picks for these meaningless tasks,* he thought bitterly. *Only last week I asked him to authorize my plan for the mass distribution of leaflets on the sanctity of the family, but of course he didn't even look at it.*

Aloud, he added, "I will take care of it personally, your Grace."

Secretary Karocyz smiled benevolently. He plucked a fragrant young bud, lifting it to his nose. "You should know that this year the candidate is to be chosen from America."

He let the flower fall to the ground, as he strolled away in the halcyon light of the garden.

*What a pompous, bloated fool,* Maglione thought as he watched the red bulk of his superior's body recede down the lane, to be swallowed from his view by the lush foliage.

An hour later, Undersecretary Maglione lined up the pile of papers nearest him with the right border of the massive desktop. He paused to stare at the age-darkened walnut burl of the thickly waxed surface. Absentmindedly, he stroked the large red ruby he wore on his left ring finger with the soft pad of his right index finger. An annoying thought disturbed the even flow of his mind.

The Secretary wants me to be personally responsible, he thought. He stared up at the frescoed ceiling high above, barely noticing the work a master artisan had devoted half his life to complete. "Where am I to find a scholarship student from America?" he said aloud.

# CHAPTER 3

And behold a ladder standing on the ground, and its top reached towards heaven…

Genesis 28:12

---

It was a 747 wide-body direct flight, from Ben-Gurion to JFK. The heavy machine flew smoothly, pushing through the thin air like a great beast through water. It was just over an hour into the flight and Jonathan Charosh sat silently, immersed in study. An open book lay on the small tray in front of him. Looking up, he took a short break to shift his legs. He had stretched them out as far as he could under the seat in front of him. At six feet two inches, his lanky frame barely fit into the space provided.

He wondered why the space between the rows of seats seemed to get smaller and smaller each time he flew. He shifted his legs again. As a child he had suffered from arthritis in the knees and he still seemed to feel it at times. Two rows behind, a baby started to cry, its piercing screams audible above the surrounding din. The lights had been dimmed for the in-flight movie he had been ignoring.

Jonathan had just recently turned twenty-four. His light complexion and fair hair contrasted starkly with his almond-brown eyes. His hair was cropped short, except for two long payos tucked behind his ears. A black velvet yarmulke covered most of his narrow skull. He was clean shaven and dressed in a plain black suit.

His unassuming appearance excited no particular attention. A young American talmudic scholar, studying in the renowned Aish Yosef yeshiva in the Old City of Jerusalem, he was returning home to spend the Passover holiday with his family. The yeshiva, located a stone's throw from the Western Wall, the last remaining section of the outer wall of the Second Temple, housed more than a thousand full-time students.

His father had died nearly two years before, but he still went back to be with his mother and older brother each year for the seder.

"Excuse me," the passenger seated next to him said in a thick Israeli accent. Turning his head, his eyes met those of the burly man seated a few inches away. The older man's sparkling eyes crinkled in a smile as he remarked, "I couldn't help notice that you were learning."

"Yes," Jonathan said. "I'm reviewing the gemarah in the tractate of Sotah."

The man appeared to be in his late sixties. Shifting awkwardly in the cramped space to face Jonathan, the man said, "Shalom Aleichem. My name is Yitzchak Harel."

"Aleichem Shalom. My name is Jonathan, Jonathan Charosh," he replied, smiling warmly, as they turned to shake hands.

Yitzchak smiled back. Motioning to the open text

on Jonathan's tray, he remarked, "Eh, I'm not as religious as I used to be, but when I was very young, I learned some. Maybe you wouldn't mind to show me what it is you are learning?"

"Of course not," came the reply. Jonathan inched the book over a little. Swallowing once, he began.

"I'm on page eleven-b. The gemara is discussing a passage in the Torah. Right here," he pointed with his finger.

Yitzchak nodded.

Jonathan continued more confidently.

"It speaks of the reward God gave Yocheved and Miriam, who, as the midwives in Egypt, refused to obey the Pharaoh's edict to kill all the Jewish male children on the birthing table and instead let them live." Pleased to have such a receptive audience, Jonathan went on, a slight lilt creeping into his voice. "The gemara discusses what reward they received from God for risking their lives to defy the Pharaoh."

"Go on," said Yitzchak, warming to the subject. "What does it say?"

"Well, starting here, there is an argument on this very point by the two great sages Rav and Shmuel." Jonathan's voice began to take on the characteristic sing song chant of those accustomed to learning the Talmud.

"Rav says that God gave Yocheved and Miriam the houses of the priesthood and the Levites. But Shmuel says God gave Yocheved the houses of the priesthood and the Levites through her son Aaron. And God also gave Miriam the house of royalty through her descendant, King David. The gemara tries to bring as a proof to this the following. We know that Miriam married Caleb Ben Yefuneh, who was the leader of the tribe of Judah. But, the gemara adds, Caleb's father's real name was Hetzron who we know is in the direct line to David. God bestowed on Caleb the name Son of Yefuneh to commemorate his role in the episode with the spies." Jonathan paused for effect. "And that's what's been bothering me."

"What?" Yitzchak said.

"Well, something just didn't seem right to me. So I went back and traced the line from Judah to David."

"Yah, so what did you find?"

"I found that Hetzron had two sons. One was Caleb, but the other was Ram. The problem is, the line to the royal House of David goes through Ram, not Caleb. I looked further and found that Miriam and Caleb's son was Hur. The people stoned Hur to death for trying to stop them from sinning with the Golden Calf, but he'd already had a son before that, named Uri. And Uri's son was Bezalel, the master craftsman who fashioned all the holy vessels that were lost long ago along with the Menorah after the destruction of the Second Temple by the Romans.

"So, you see, if the line to the House of David goes through Ram and not Caleb, how could Shmuel say that Miriam received God's reward of kingship?"

Yitzchak thought in silence. "Mm...that's a good question. But do you have an answer?"

Jonathan shook his head. "No, not yet."

"Tell me, you mentioned the Menorah a moment ago," Yitzchak said.

"Yes."

"Well, I was wondering. Does anybody know what happened to it?"

Jonathan thought seriously about the question the older man had posed. Furrowing his brow, he said, "I remember seeing once, a long time ago, a picture of the Arch of Titus in Rome. Titus was the man who commanded the Roman legions that destroyed Jerusalem and burned the Temple. Carved on the arch in stone is a representation of Jewish captives carrying what looks like a Menorah and some of the other holy vessels in a Roman victory march. I don't think anyone knows for sure if it depicts an actual event, but I do know that nobody knows where the Menorah is now."

An enigmatic smile had spread across the older man's face, prompting Jonathan to ask, "Forgive me, but if you don't mind, may I ask what you find so amusing?"

Yitzchak's smile evaporated as he leaned in close to say in a soft but intense whisper, "You may not believe this, but I know where it is!"

"Where what is?" Jonathan said innocently.

The older man leaned in even closer and whispered, "Where the Menorah is!"

Seeing the incredulous look on Jonathan's face the older man nodded, closing his eyes a moment. Then, snapping them open, he stared intently into Jonathan's eyes as he said, "What I am about to tell you, few people have ever heard, and even fewer are still alive who actually witnessed it."

A coughing spasm darkened his face. Clearing his throat, he shook his head and continued in a hushed tone. "I have not spoken of this to anyone for many years."

Jonathan leaned in closer, drawn by the quiet urgency of the older man's words. The surrounding noises faded into the background. Yitzchak sighed, and then began his tale as if he were reliving the events he spoke of.

"I was young then, so very young, and I was already in Israel. Only then, of course, it was called Palestine and the British were in charge. I had been brought out of Hungary almost two years earlier by a religious Zionist organization right after completing a course in agriculture.

I left behind my whole family, at the age of sixteen. Of course, everyone in the village told my mother she was crazy to let me go.

"But off I went, because I was young and very active in my chapter."

Jonathan nodded, mesmerized.

"I don't know if you know this, but at the beginning of the War, the Va'ad Le'umi went to the British and offered to raise a volunteer force of Jewish soldiers. The British, of course, were always worried about offending the Arabs, God forbid, so they decided to make it a joint force. The problem was, none of the Arabs wanted to join. So, the British first took our boys only for medical units. In the first five days, over one hundred thousand Jewish boys signed up. It was a big embarrassment for the British, but what could they do?" he said with a grim smile.

"By forty-two, things weren't going so well for the Allies, so they allowed us to form several Jewish fighting battalions under British command.

"I joined up in the spring of forty-one and saw my first action against the Vichy French in Syria. We fought well and by forty-four the British finally gave us permission to form a larger group. They didn't want to officially recognize us, but after much protesting, they gave in and called us the Jewish Brigade. We were twenty-seven thousand strong, many of us battle-hardened. They shipped me out with my unit under the command of the famous General Montgomery of the British Eighth Army, which by then was in northern Italy."

Yitzchak coughed again. He spit up some phlegm, wiping it away from the corner of his mouth with a white handkerchief that had materialized in his hand. Tucking it away, he cleared his throat again and continued.

"I was so happy. I had two months earlier turned twenty-one. Finally, finally, I was going to get my chance to fight Nazis."

Leaning even closer, Yitzchak sucked in a deep breath and exhaled.

"Everything I have told you so far is common knowledge. What I tell you now, only a handful are still alive to tell, and I am one of them.

"It was early in the spring of forty-four, and as I told you, we were with the Eighth Army in northern Italy. We had been fighting the Germans for months. They were dug in on top of all the mountain passes, and we had suffered many losses in breaking their positions in our drive to Rome. I tell you, the mud was almost as bad as the Germans; it was everywhere. We had to haul most of our equipment up with mules.

"Anyway, one cloudy day in June, the exact date I can never get straight in my head, a British officer came to our command post to speak to our commanding officer. I was sitting nearby on the ground, my back against a tree, writing a letter. I barely looked up as he entered the tent. I could hear them talking but I didn't pay them any attention and went on writing. A minute later, out comes my C.O. with the British officer right behind him.

"So he looks down at me and says, 'Yitzchak, stop writing and get up. Today is your lucky day.'

"Seeing the puzzled look on my face as I jumped up, he starts laughing. Clasping his belly, he claps me on the back and says, 'As of now, I'm placing you on a four day leave to Rome. Go find Shmuli, David, Matis, and Avraham and bring them here. You're to go with Lieutenant Howard here to see a very important person.'

"Then he gives me this strange smile, you know,

like he knows something good but he's not telling. I shrugged, and raced off to tell the others. Rome had fallen to the Allied armies maybe a week before, and we had been stuck guarding one of the main roads that led to Rome. By then I'd been practicing my English for months and I knew how to speak pretty good.

"Later, in the jeep, sitting in front with the young British officer who was driving, I started talking with him, you know, swapping stories.

"Turning to Lieutenant Howard, that was the British officer's name, I yelled, 'Who is this important person we're supposed to meet?'

"Howard yelled back, 'You'll see,' a smile plastered to his face.

"About an hour later, we started to pass through the outskirts of the city. This was our first time to Rome, in fact this was our first leave anywhere since landing in Italy. We were all so excited. The lieutenant took us over a bridge that was still intact. There were many Italians on the sidewalks, but they were outnumbered by all the Allied soldiers we saw everywhere. The Italians were very friendly. They kept stopping to wave to us as we drove by. It was really something," Yitzchak said, a twinkle in his eyes.

"A minute or two later we passed a huge round building with columns. It was the Coliseum. We all craned our necks to get a good look. Howard slowed down just long enough to inform us that the Germans had used it as a supply depot for their parachutists. We went on, to stop suddenly in front of a large church. Next to it was a smaller building. A large number of soldiers in British uniform were going in and out the front.

"We all piled out, grabbing up our packs. Howard turned to us and shouted, 'Get your gear stowed away and make sure you clean up. Your time is your own until 1900 hours. Then I expect to see each and every one of you in dress uniform, at these very steps, buttons shining.'

"He hopped back into the jeep and backed out with a final, 'Good hunting lads,' before he roared off.

"We cleaned up. I took the first hot shower I'd had in months. Twenty minutes later, we were ready to explore the city.

"So, after asking a few directions of some American soldiers, we found ourselves standing on a bridge lined with carved angels. Beneath our feet was the Tiber river. Right in front of us was a large brown castle. It was a great circular fort. We walked in through a large door. After looking around a few minutes, we left it behind, heading off along a broad avenue.

"We came upon a huge open space. On the sides were two long rows of pillars. In the center stood a tall, thin, stone needle and behind that rose this huge building with a big dome on top of it.

"Like school boys, we dashed across the open space to look up at the huge stone needle. It was covered with strange symbols. I remember running my hands over the surface. It was, eh…carved, you know? Anyway, David seemed to know something about it. You see, he was always reading.

"David had to tell us that the obelisk, that's what he called it, was brought to Rome by one of the emperors from Egypt.

"We climbed the steps of the large cathedral in front of us. There were two large statues on either side, and above the entrance was a balcony. David said it was used by the Popes to give blessings to the crowds in the square on holidays. There were two huge bronze doors in the center, but they were closed. They were covered with beautiful carvings of men on horseback, all dressed in armor.

"By the front, two American military guards were posted. Seeing us, they asked us if we wanted to go in. The others said yes, but I realized that my father would kill me if he ever knew I had set foot in a church. Especially such a big one. I was brought up very religious, and at that time I was still much more observant than I am now. So I told the rest of them that they could go in if they wanted. I would wait outside 'til they finished looking around.

"They went in. I was bored, so I walked back down the steps and looked into the small shops lining the square.

"About half an hour later I saw my friends coming out. I waved to get their attention and walked over to meet them. David grabbed me by the arm and started telling me all about what they had seen.

"Avraham cut him off. 'Stop your gaggling. We don't have much time left. You can tell him all about it on the way.'

" 'On the way to where?' I said.

" 'Don't start that again,' he yelled. 'We've looked around and seen the sights, but now it's time to see some other sights if you know what I mean.'

Then he started laughing. The others joined in, and now I was really in trouble. I was dying to go see the famous Vatican museums. I knew that David would come along with me. I also knew that if I tried to get the others to come I would probably have a mutiny on my hands. So I decided to give in.

"I figured that, at best, I could get them all back in time for our deadline with Howard. At the very least I just might be able to keep us all from getting arrested by the military police.

"Well, to make a long story short, we never found the place Avraham was looking for. I was happy, but you can imagine how upset Avraham was. At one point he even accused me of getting us lost on purpose. That almost led to a fight, but the others calmed the two of us down and we finally made it back to our billet with only a few minutes to spare.

"Lieutenant Howard arrived with the jeep right on time. He pulled up and we all climbed in. He yelled, 'Welcome aboard' as he backed out. Opening up the engine, the jeep went into a tight turn around the corner. I had to grab the hand rail to keep from falling out.

"I turned to smile at Howard, and then my eyes went wide as we just missed hitting a lamp post.

"We drove on for a while. There were quite a few angry fists waved in our direction as we narrowly missed hitting several people.

"After a while it started to get dark. Howard switched on the headlights. Alongside the road ran some train tracks. In front of us I could see a large stone wall, stretching off to either side. We passed under the wall through an open gate. The road wound past several gardens and fountains. I could tell, even in the bad light, that we had entered a private area. It seemed too quiet.

"The wind blew through the trees along the road, and above us, the sky was a strange color, like the color of dark blood. The jeep slowed down just before we entered a short tunnel. We came out a moment later into the quiet night air. I remember the smell in the air. It was so fresh, with the hint of some kind of perfume.

"The road ahead began to curve in a gentle arc. At a fork, we turned again to pull up in front of a small stone house."

'All out,' Howard called. Looking at each other and muttering to ourselves, we climbed out. We stood on a gravel path. Small sharp stones crunched beneath our boots. We followed Howard over to a long flight of steps.

"He led us down the steps and we followed slowly. It was very dark by then. Our only guides were the lights from a large building on the next hill that I could just make out through the trees, and the few stars above our heads.

"We followed Howard down to a stone path and came to a small doorway. A tall building rose high above us. In front stood two guards, stationed on either side. But these were not just any guards. They were dressed in the most fantastic uniforms I had ever seen. They wore striped clothing and hose with tall metal helmets strapped to their heads. Thick wooden lances were gripped smartly in their hands. I could just make out that the tips were capped by these wicked looking metal ax blades.

"I remember those guards. They didn't even look at us as we passed, like they were made of stone, you know? Anyway, once inside we all blinked, trying to get used to the sudden bright light. Here we were met by a tall man dressed in a long dark robe; a priest of some kind.

"He nodded to Howard, who answered, 'Your Grace' as he bowed his head.

"David and I looked at each other.

"The priest said in an English with a heavy Italian accent, 'I am Monsignor Dartini. Come with me.'

"Not waiting for an answer, he turned to climb a wide staircase. He led us up a series of steps. By one of the landings, he turned to lead us down a long hallway. The walls here were covered with beautiful paintings. I remember staring up. There were beautiful chandeliers hanging down from the ceiling. They lit up its gold surface, shining down onto the polished marble beneath our feet. To me it was like we were walking on a floor of yellow-white fire.

"The priest led us into a large room hung with huge pictures. He passed quickly through to another room and then another. I barely had time to look at anything as we rushed through room after room.

"At one entrance stood two guards, along with some kind of fancy butler. Here Howard slipped away, leaving us with a jaunty salute. I watched him go. I was sorry to see him leave.

"Our guide ushered us past a long line of paintings of old men dressed in white with tall pointy hats on their heads.

"David whispered one word, 'Popes.'

"I shot him a look. I didn't have much time to look at those faces. We passed through several more rooms, the fancy butler bringing up our rear. At a narrow black wood door we came to a sudden halt. Our guide reached forward to knock softly. I didn't hear an answer, but our guide must have, because he gently eased the door open and went in. We hesitated, but the butler pushed us forward.

"In the room was a huge wooden desk. The walls were lined with bookshelves, neatly packed with old books. They gave off the smell of old leather and dust. Behind the desk sat a man of slight build, dressed all in white. On his nose was a pair of thin round wire-frame glasses. He didn't look up as we came in. Spread out on the desk was a large scroll of some kind. From where I stood I couldn't make out what was written on it.

"He was bent over the scroll. I was surprised to see a thick white skullcap resting on his balding head. Our guide took a few steps across the room and stopped about ten feet away from the desk. He coughed once. The man behind the desk looked up for the first time, as if he had just then taken notice of us. He said to our guide, 'Dartini, has the way been prepared?'

"Our guide answered, 'Yes your Holiness.'

"The man behind the desk looked at us and said, 'We hope your stay in Our beloved city has been pleasant. We have heard that a group of you have been fighting to liberate Our people from the aggressors and We wished to meet you to extend Our sincere thanks.'

"He stopped at this point, and there was an awkward moment of silence. I suddenly realized that he was expecting an answer, and as the designated leader, I realized that I was supposed to give it.

"So I stepped forward. I said, 'We've all been grateful to be a part of the great struggle to destroy the Nazis.'

"'Yes,' he said slowly, as if he wasn't entirely pleased with my words. And then as if changing his mind he spread out his arms and said, 'We welcome you to Our holy city. We wish to hear of your experiences, and of course, some word of the Holy Land.'

"I cleared my throat. It had suddenly become dry. It had dawned on me as he spoke where we were standing, and to whom I was speaking. We five young Jews were standing in the innermost sanctum of the Vatican, and I was speaking to the Pope.

"There was another awkward silence. So I said, 'We haven't been in Palestine in over six months, so I don't think anything we could tell you would be very current.'

"The Pope's thin lips stretched out. He spread his arms out wide on either side and said, 'Tell Us then of your time here.'

"I started to describe to him some of our exploits with the Eighth Army. He seemed genuinely interested. He even stopped me at several points to ask for more details. After a few minutes I started to wind down. The Pope smiled and asked if we had eaten. I tried to decline but he insisted, even adding that all had been prepared kosher. He motioned to Dartini, who led us through a door into a large room. Someone had laid out seven beautiful settings on a long table covered with a rich white cloth. By each setting stood a large goblet.

"At the head of the table was a dark wood chair with a high back. It was carved with beautiful little flowers. The Pope was seated in this chair by one of the many servants who seemed to appear, as if by magic. He motioned for us to sit. The seat directly opposite me was occupied by Dartini. He didn't seem to be too inclined to friendly chatter by the look on his face. The Pope tilted his head and said something in a strange tongue to one of the servants. As soon as he finished speaking, several servants appeared around the table, offering us wine. I shook my head. The others allowed their goblets to be filled. Curious, I lifted up the massive cup in front of me. It was incredibly heavy. Mine was studded with dull dark stones. A servant glided silently around the table, offering plates filled with delicious smelling meats. I saw the others take generous portions. You have to understand. We hadn't eaten meat in months. Of course I didn't take any.

"The Pope turned to speak to Dartini in that same strange tongue. Later, David told me that they spoke Latin, and told me what they were saying.

" 'We believe this would make an interesting picture,' the Pope said.

" 'Do you really think so?' Dartini said.

" 'Do not worry, who would they tell, and who would believe it? I think this would make a fine mural, don't you think? Sadly, there are only seven seated at table and not twelve.'

"Dartini put his head down. At that moment of

course, I had no idea what they were saying. The other boys ate and drank quite a bit. I looked sharply toward David. Our eyes met and he gave me back a strange look. Just then, the servants began clearing the table before disappearing.

"The Pope rose from his seat. 'Come. We wish to show you something.'

"We all got up and followed him, Dartini bringing up our rear. He led us through several passageways which finally opened onto a great open space. We stood on a narrow strip of marble, suspended high in the air. Looking down, I got very dizzy. I grabbed onto the smooth railing. Stretched above our heads was the inner surface of a vast dome. The Pope went ahead. Tearing my eyes away from the dome, I risked a peek over the side. The top of a fancy canopy with statues at the corners, rose up from below. I quickly leaned back and followed the Pope. Going down a series of steps and landings, we finally reached ground level.

"David whispered, 'This is Saint Peter's.'

"The Pope led us straight up to a very large altar framed by four twisted black columns and the canopy I had seen from above. The entire place was deserted. Our footsteps echoed through the great building. I remember thinking how odd it was that no one else seemed to be about, but then it was no stranger than what had been going on up to that point. The Pope climbed up the steps and I got a good look at those strange black pillars. They were striped with gold near the bottom and decorated with gold leaves high up near the top. I heard a slight scraping sound and I looked down.

"The Pope appeared to be sinking into the floor. Running forward, I stared down into a large hole that someone had opened up right in the floor of the altar. I saw a bit of the Pope's white robe at the bottom of some rough wood steps, just before it disappeared. Placing my foot on the first plank, I tested it. It was solid. David nudged my back. I gave him a look, and then I went down. I stopped at the bottom. The floor was covered with a thick layer of dust. The air smelled of wet stone and it was very cold. Behind me, the rest of the boys came down, followed by Dartini. I looked around. There was no sign of the Pope.

"We stood in a large area, sectioned off by stone walls that were crumbling and half fallen down. Some of the walls had been completely knocked down, opening up further sections. Along the walls they had lit torches. Dartini walked past me.

"He headed off without even looking to see if we were following. Of course we followed. I mean, what else could we do?

"He led us past a crumbled section, toward a wall with a dark band running up it from the floor to the ceiling. As I came closer, I could see that what I had thought was a dark band was actually a dark opening. Beyond that was a narrow flight of steps between two walls of rough rock. A small torch burned on a bracket a few steps down. Dartini waited at the top of the steps for the others to catch up.

"Nodding his head, he turned and led us down, taking up the small torch. It was a good thing too. The steps were very shallow and smooth, and even by the light of the torch one could easily have lost his footing and broken his neck.

"The ceiling began to appear as we continued down. At first, the walls were so close I could reach out and touch both sides at the same time. As we walked down, they began to spread apart. The air got even colder. Suddenly, the steps ended.

"Dartini kept walking. Behind us, stretching away in either direction, a long line of torches sat in brackets, high up on the rock walls. We just stood there, staring about in wonder. Spread out all around us was a huge cavern. Its ceiling was lost in the darkness above. I could just barely make out the far end as a tiny smudge off in the distance. Dartini was already a hundred meters ahead of us.

"I called behind me to the rest of the boys, 'Come on. Hurry up.'

"The sound of my voice echoed in that space. As we hurried to catch up, I noticed that the ground had recently been excavated. Looking down, I could see that beneath some scaffolding someone had dug down several levels. All this digging had not been for nothing. They had exposed several large stone tombs of beautiful workmanship. Surrounding them were quite a number of smaller ones, sitting at a higher level.

"Dartini led us along the lip of the excavations, straight towards the largest tomb. The workers had worked hard here. Sticking up almost ten feet high was a huge tomb. By the carvings on its surface I guessed that there might still be many feet buried beneath the dark earth. The priest motioned for us to go down a ladder. We climbed down and walked over to the tomb. We all stared at the carvings that covered the walls. They were of fantastically strange birds.

"Directly in the center of the wall facing us was a doorway that at one time had been sealed off. I could tell that it had recently been broken into. The priest motioned us to enter. Just inside the doorway someone had placed a set of make-shift wooden planks. I went in first and the rest soon joined me. A small torch was set in a holder high up on the far wall.

"The curved ceiling rose up at least twenty meters over our heads. The walls, floor, and ceiling inside were totally smooth. I could just barely make out in the center of the room the vague outlines of a low stone pedestal. By the huge size of a darkened outline on the floor, I guessed that a larger object had once sat there.

"All other thoughts left my head as Dartini stepped in front of me, the torch in his hand held high. In the center, now plain for all of us to see, stood the Pope. But what drew our attention was what was resting on the pedestal right next to him.

"It was a large seven branched candelabra. The flames shone off its shiny surfaces in red and yellow flashes. I couldn't take my eyes off it. It looked to me to be very heavy, especially at its base. We all stood back in shock. The Pope's thin voice broke the silence.

" 'We discovered this cavern five years ago when a wall gave way while We were preparing the last resting place for Our predecessor the holy Peter XI.'

"We just stood there, staring at it.

The Pope seemed to stare directly at me as he said, 'We have always been a friend to your people and have tried mightily to use Our powers to save those We could through these dark, terrible years. Some have objected, saying We were not forceful enough, but We feel We did all We could. This We uncovered but a few months ago, and We wished for you to see it. We want you to know that We will guard it well; have no fear.'

"No one spoke. I could hear my pulse pounding in my ears and a great roaring sound seemed to fill my head. I couldn't think straight.

"The Pope said, 'Now come, the air here gives Us a chill and We would as soon be away from this place as not.'

"We were all too stunned to say anything, so we followed them back up to the surface. My lips were silent, but inside my mind raced with one burning question. What had he shown us?

"Back up again in the bright lights of the cathedral, the Pope stopped for a moment, as if he was about to say something. Then he seemed to change his mind. He was led away by Dartini, leaving us to stare at their receding backs. Two priests in dark robes approached us and motioned for us to follow them. A few moments later we found ourselves outside again, in the cool night air. A jeep stood ten meters away, its engine running. The driver was some British sergeant we'd never seen before.

" 'Hop in lads,' he called to us, so we piled in.

"The next morning new orders arrived. Our leave had suddenly been cut short."

Jonathan, who had been silent all this time, cut in at this moment to say,

"How can you be sure that what he showed you was the Menorah?"

Yitzchak nodded, a sharp gleam in his eyes. "We all asked ourselves the same question. We talked about it for a while among the group, but in the end each and every one of us felt that it had to be the Menorah. I mean, why else would the Pope have bothered to show us some large gold candlestick? Also, the way he spoke of it and the fact that it was so big with seven branches of solid gold convinced us."

"What exactly did it look like?" Jonathan said.

Yitzchak pursed his lips thoughtfully. "Well it was hard to see it clearly in the torch light…but I would say it was somewhat less than two meters tall and the branches were curved on both sides of a central branch, like half circles." Yitzchak emphasized those last words by gesturing with his arms in big semi-circles.

"Tell me," Jonathan said in an excited rush. "Why

do you think the Pope showed it to you? I mean, what reason would he have to do that?"

Yitzchak shrugged, nodding his head. "I've asked myself that same question many times." He paused. Turning his penetrating gaze to stare directly into Jonathan's eyes he spoke with utter conviction. "I have no idea why he showed it to us. But as God is my witness, I swear to you…he did."

# CHAPTER 4

> Take a piece of wood and write on it Judah.
> Take another piece of wood and write on it Joseph.
> Bring them together...and they will
> become one in your hand.
>
> Ezekiel 37:16,17

---

Ian entered the large terminal and crossed over to one of the many monitors high up on the wall. Searching the screen, he found his brother's flight, second from the top. It had arrived on time.

He turned to look around. The place was a zoo. Some of the passengers were trickling down a series of steps, loaded down with their luggage. A large contingent of Hasidim was camped out right in the middle of the floor, awaiting the arrival of one of their sect. He stood there a while, watching reunion after reunion, as the passengers from the flight entered the arrivals hall. He searched for his brother's face. There was no sign of him. The familiar sights and sounds brought back to him his last time at the airport. It had been two years ago. Then too he had been waiting for his brother Jonahan. Their father's condition had become critical again. He'd suffered a massive stroke the day before. Ian had gone in to see his father that day. He remembered leaning his body carefully over all the plastic tubes, to plant a soft kiss on his forehead. The next morning his mother had called him early, waking him.

"He's dead," she sobbed, in shock.

When Jonathan arrived early the next morning, his father was already dead. Ian met him at the El Al cargo terminal. He first saw him standing by the plain pine box as the handlers began to load it into a container for the flight back. His father's wish had been to be buried on one of the hills of Jerusalem. Their parents had gone the summer before to buy plots in a cemetery on a hill overlooking an entrance to the city. Jonathan looked up to stare at him. Ian walked over the cracked black tarmac. They drew close. Jonathan reached out and they embraced.

"I'm sorry you missed saying good-bye to him."

Jonathan nodded. "It was the will of the Rebono Shel Olam. Now he's in Olam Ha-Emes."

"Do you really think there is life after death?" Ian said.

"Of course."

"I hope you're right," Ian said softly.

Someone jostled him, bringing him back to the present. Aware again of his surroundings, Ian gave the man who'd pushed him a dirty look and moved over a few inches. He searched the crowd for his brother, but couldn't spot him among the milling groups of people. Frowning, he turned around to see if his mother had come in and came face to face with his brother, who was grinning at him from ear to ear.

Surprised, Ian let out a sudden laugh. "How long have you been standing there?"

"Just a second," Jonathan said.

"How was the flight?"

"Good, besides losing the circulation in my legs."

"I know what you mean."

"I heard the most remarkable story."

"Really. What was it about?"

"I'll tell you later, when we can sit down and talk in peace," Jonathan said, as someone almost stepped on one of his bags.

"Sure. Come on, let's get out of here."

Shouldering Jonathan's garment bag, he picked up the larger of the two suitcases from the floor and then went to pick up the other one.

"Wait, what are you doing?" Jonathan said. "At least let me carry that one." He grabbed up the remaining small suitcase and hurried to catch up.

They exited through a set of automatic doors and came upon their mother, who had just crossed over from one of the lots. The worried expression on her face quickly dissolved into a warm smile.

"I see you found him. Jonathan, it's so good to see you," she said, a happy lilt in her voice as they came together and hugged.

"How was your flight?" she said.

"It was good."

They all drove back home, their mother commenting the whole trip on how thin and pale Jonathan looked. "You spend the extra money I send on food, don't you?"

"Yes, Mom. I only spend it according to your wishes," he said, grinning. Ian rolled up his eyes in sympathy.

"Mom, just think, now you can put some meat on

those bones," Ian said.

"I only have him for a month, but I'll do the best I can," she said.

That evening, after their mother had retired, the two brothers sat at the dining room table, talking. Ian was giving Jonathan an update on his doctoral thesis.

Ian was studying theodicy, the classic attempt to reconcile an all-knowing, all-powerful, all-merciful God, with the existence of Evil in the world. He gave Jonathan a quick overview of the history and main arguments brought by the major monotheistic religions to explain the problem. Jonathan listened carefully, nodding as Ian went into further detail with one of the explanations. This was the Jewish concept of Hester Panim, the hiding of the Divine Face. Jonathan cut in at this point.

"You know it's funny you should mention that. There was a drought recently in Israel. The water levels in Lake Kineret in the Galilee were very, very low. A group of leading rabbis decided to call the next day for people to fast and say the special prayer for rain. I took part myself with a large group praying at the Western Wall. The amazing thing was, it started raining almost as soon as we began to pray. And it kept raining heavily for three days. Enough so that the levels in the Kineret rose well above the normal water-mark. It was almost as if God was saying, 'I am here. Though I have hidden My Face from you, call Me now and I will answer you as I did in the days of old.' "

"That's very interesting," Ian replied dryly. "But it's not really proof in the classical sense."

"Of course not," Jonathan smiled. "I just thought you might be interested in it. By the way, there's something else I think you might be interested in hearing."

"What's that?"

"Well, you remember I mentioned in the airport that I met an unusual man on the plane. Actually he was sitting right next to me the whole flight. We got to talking, and he told me a remarkable story."

"Right. I remember. What was it?"

"He said his name was Yitzchak Harel. He claimed to have been in a Jewish Brigade unit that fought with the British in Italy against the Nazis. I didn't even know that such a group existed. Anyway, according to him, he and a small group of his friends from his platoon were brought to Rome and…."

Ian went to sleep that night in the old room he had shared with his brother growing up. Tonight, they shared it once again. It reminded him of nights long ago when they would stay up whispering to each other so their parents wouldn't hear them. Ian heard his brother saying the Shema quietly in his bed and waited for him to finish.

"Do you believe that story the man on the plane told you?"

"I don't know," Jonathan said. "But wouldn't it be amazing if it were true? I guess we may never know," he added, stifling a yawn.

"Get some sleep, you must be exhausted."

There was no reply. Jonathan had already drifted off. Ian smiled to himself in the dark. Slipping quietly onto the floor, he did one hundred push-ups on his knuckles, as he did every night.

As a child Ian had become obsessed with learning to defend himself. In third grade, his yeshiva had run a Holocaust Memorial Day program for the students. He had stared at the large black and white posters pasted up on the walls of the auditorium. They were copies of actual photos taken by the Nazis. They depicted their atrocities in graphic detail. He had not slept well after that for a long time.

Every night he would dream that he and his family were hiding somewhere in Nazi-occupied Europe. Always the Gestapo would come searching for them. Sometimes they would be hiding in a shed. Sometimes in a secret room in an apartment. They would remain still, not daring to breathe. But then either Jonathan would start to cry, or he would sneeze, and the SS, with their black leather boots and double-bolt lightning insignias on their collars, would find them. They would all be dragged off to a concentration camp and separated. He would see the Nazi guards beat his father bloody on the other side of a barbed wire fence that separated him from Ian and Jonathan.

Always there was the fear. The fear and the helplessness. He had the feeling that no matter what, eventually they would be sent to the gas chambers. Ian lost weight. He walked around with dark circles under his eyes. His parents asked him what was wrong, but he wouldn't tell them.

Two weeks later, he snuck off to a kung fu movie with his friends. He didn't tell his parents he was going. He knew they would never have given him permission.

That night, he dreamed he was a martial arts expert. This time when the SS came to take away his family, he killed them all, quietly. The next morning he asked his father if he could go to karate classes. His father gave him a strange look and shook his head. He found out where there was a class at a local dojo and how much it cost. He asked his father again the next day, giving him all the details. His father asked him who would pay for the classes. He thought about that for a moment and walked away, silently.

He took a job after school, walking a neighbor's dog. Five weeks later, he went to his father and asked him again if he could take the classes. He told him that he would be responsible for any and all costs. His mother happened to be walking by and heard what was going on.

"Nu, let him go," she said. "Maybe he'll put on some muscle. You know, a healthy body is necessary for a healthy mind."

His father looked up from the religious text he was learning. "Fine, let him go. But if there are any problems I hold you responsible."

He learned well. He learned quickly. He reached black belt at the age of fourteen. He reached third degree black belt at sixteen. He won several tournaments. The dreams faded.

Climbing back into bed, he rearranged the blanket around him, shifted into a comfortable position and was soon fast asleep.

---

The first days of Passover and the sedarim went by uneventfully. He kissed his mother good-bye, and after hugging his brother, made his way back to his apartment on the upper west side. At eight-thirty the following morning, he arrived at the main campus.

Dr. Berluonti's office in the philosophy department was sandwiched in the corner of one of the older buildings on campus, wedged on the second floor between two larger offices. It had two windows on both sides of the building, affording it excellent views of the grassy quadrangle below.

Ian knocked softly, and received a muffled reply. Shrugging his shoulders, he opened the door and walked in. The tiny office was choked with books. Books lined the walls from floor to ceiling. Books were stacked in uneven piles on the floor. In the small space between a large swivel chair and a small desk piled high with even more books stood Dr. Berluonti.

He was a strikingly tall figure, his massive frame at seeming odds with his cramped surroundings. He was staring down at the quadrangle, his broad back to Ian. Dr. Berluonti stood there for a while, gazing down silently at the scene below. Ian leaned patiently against a bookshelf, waiting.

Speaking languidly, as if in mid-thought, Dr. Berluonti commented, his back still towards Ian, "Interesting, isn't it? Spring comes, denying death in such a pleasantly quiet way. Life springs up, in beautiful synchronicity to girls' skirt-lines. How goes it with you?" he remarked as he turned around to plop down into his chair.

Ian cleared his throat. "Pretty well actually," he said. "As we discussed last time, I'm fleshing out the dynamics of my unified formulation. After that, I still have to work on my summation, but that shouldn't take too long."

"I actually have some pretty exciting news for you," Dr. Berluonti uttered in his usually dry, bemused tone. "Now where did I put that?" he muttered to himself as he sifted through the morass of papers on his desk. "Ah, here it is," he said, as he picked up a large envelope with a slightly self-mocking flourish. "I received this a few days ago and I've been thinking about it, off and on, all weekend long. It's been a damn nuisance, but I think I've finally come up with the solution." He stared at Ian, an enigmatic twinkle in his eyes.

"Might you enlighten me as to what you're talking about?"

Dr. Berluonti took a deep breath and then said offhandedly, "Well it seems that I hold here in my hand an all expenses paid invitation for a promising young scholar to spend the next six months in Rome, perusing the archives of the famous Vatican library." He added in mock afterthought, "And the only one I could come up with was, you."

"Really! I didn't know you had a connection with the Vatican."

Dr. Berluonti leaned back further in his chair. "It's not something I talk about often. I have an uncle in the Curia; that's the administrative arm of the Vatican. I think he's pretty high up, his title is Undersecretary for the Sacred Office, whatever that means. I never could get straight the hierarchy of the Church."

Ian interrupted him. "Why me, I mean you know—"

"Know what?" Dr. Berluonti said.

"That I'm Jewish."

Dr. Berluonti laughed. "What difference does that make? Now don't let this go to your head, but you happen to be the most qualified student I have right now. If you don't mind rubbing shoulders with some priests, I guess they'll just have to open their hearts with some Christian brotherly love for you."

"I don't mind at all. In fact, I'd love to get a look at some of those original texts on early Church philosophy as it pertains to my thesis."

Dr. Berluonti grunted. "It's settled then. You leave Thursday. I'd brush up on your Latin by the way. I was led to believe that the program is quite unstructured. You can fax me every so often as to your progress."

"This Thursday?" Ian said, thinking about Jessica for the first time.

"Yes, this Thursday," Dr. Berluonti said. "I know it's short notice, but the tickets are closed and there's no way to change them without incurring a whopping penalty."

"I guess I could do it," Ian muttered. "My passport's

current and I suppose I could dust off my Latin by then."

Professor Berluonti handed Ian the envelope with the invitation and the tickets. "Good luck then. I envy you. Italy is glorious this time of year and the women…well, you'll see for yourself."

Ian blushed, grinning. He thanked the professor, shaking his hand firmly. Turning, he let himself out, shutting the door behind him.

Unbelievable, he thought, standing outside in the empty hallway, the large envelope clutched in his hand.

As he strode down the corridor, he unconsciously carried himself erect. His long muscular legs carried him swiftly to the wide staircase. He galloped down, bursting through the doors as the excitement welled up inside.

He was going to Rome, he thought, as it started to really sink in. He would have unlimited access to one of the greatest libraries in the world. The bright sunlight and the smell of new grass charged him with an almost manic mood. He nearly bounded across the lawn, paying little attention to the steady stream of students who were on their way to classes.

He paused a moment to stare at the fancy gold seal on the large envelope. He ran his fingers briefly over the embossed surface. Opening his knapsack, he dropped the envelope inside. As he was passing through the wrought iron gates at the entrance, he decided to walk back to his apartment.

It was too beautiful a day to take the subway and besides, he thought, I need the exercise to calm myself down. Engrossed in his thoughts, he barely noticed the three youths who were busy handing out flyers on the sidewalk in front of the gate. He passed them by, mentally constructing a list of all the things he would need to bring along for the trip.

A slight commotion behind him snapped him out of his reverie. A young female student had stopped in front of the three young men. They were dressed in leather jackets and dirty ripped jeans. All three were white, their heads shaved, their faces unshaven. The girl, a flyer clutched angrily in one hand, reached out to grab at a large plastic bag stuffed with more of the flyers that the three youths had placed in front of them. One of them grabbed her wrist roughly.

Ian only caught the motion out of the corner of his eye, but the entire scene registered clearly in his mind. His jaws tightened together. Changing direction, he advanced on the balls of his feet. He could feel his whole body key itself up, just as it had been trained to do.

Leaping forward, he caught sight of a shiny silver pin with a jagged double-bolt lightning insignia affixed to the leather collar of one of the youths jackets. He recognized the symbol as a Nazi SS pin.

His movements were swift and economical. Ian's right arm lashed out, gripping the skinhead's wrist, applying pressure to the nerve plexus. The fingers went numb, releasing their grip on the girl's arm. Ian insinuated his body between the skinheads and the girl in a fluid motion.

"What the fuck you doing?" the first one cried out as he shook his wrist, trying to regain some sensation in his hand.

Ian grabbed the bag of flyers and tossed them behind him.

"Hey, who the fuck do you think you are?" the larger one to the right and a little behind the first one yelled as he lurched forward.

Ian extended his right leg forward in a blurred motion, sweeping him off his feet. The larger skinhead landed hard on the cement sidewalk. Ian came back to the attack position quickly.

"I think you should leave now before you get hurt," he said, his voice filled with controlled rage.

The large one got back up slowly. All three moved forward. Ian's rigid right hand lashed out in a crushing blow to the solar plexus of the lead attacker, who fell like a sack of potatoes. The two behind hesitated, fear plainly written on their faces. A campus security guard, alerted by one of the other students finally arrived at the scene, his face red.

"What's going on here?" he managed to sputter out between breaths, unslinging his walkie-talkie.

The two skinheads still standing didn't bother to reply as they picked up their fallen comrade and started to slink away.

"Hey, where do you think you're going?" the overweight guard called out half-heartedly, but he didn't seem inclined to pursue the matter further, pleased that he had missed all the action.

The skinheads shot Ian hate-filled looks as they shuffled away, carrying their friend between them toward their beat up car. Piling in, they peeled away, leaving only the noxious fumes of their exhaust as a lingering reminder of their presence.

"Everything's okay," Ian assured the guard, a broad grin lighting up his handsome features. The guard shot Ian a stern look. Muttering something under his breath, he strolled off. Ian turned to the girl, whom he focused on now for the first time.

"Are you alright?"

"Yes, thank you," she answered, rubbing her wrist.

"Let me look at that," he said as he came closer.

"No, it's okay," she smiled. She moved back a step, letting her hands fall to her sides.

She offered her hand and Ian clumsily shook it as she said with a smile, "Hi, I'm Beth. Thanks for helping me."

She was extremely attractive with a stunning figure for her petite frame. She had on a long blue denim skirt with a long slit down the side, and a fitted white cotton turtleneck sweater. Ian smiled back as the color crept into his face.

"You looked like you were doing fine on your own. I just thought to even the odds a bit since there were three of them and only one of you."

"You can let go of my hand now," she said, blushing.

Ian looked down, realizing that he still held her hand. Turning crimson, he let go of her hand like he was dropping a hot coal. They both laughed. Ian caught sight of the plastic bag filled with flyers. He went over to pick one out. The top line screamed out in bold tabloid style print: "WORLD JEWRY MEETS IN SECRET TO PLAN STRATEGY."

The rest of the page was filled with anti-semitic propaganda on how the Jews controlled the media, Wall Street and world governments. Ian shook his head.

"It's unbelievable how nothing changes," he said. Picking up the bag, he carried it over to a nearby trash-can. Beth came up behind him and opened the lid so he could cram the bag inside. Their eyes met. She lowered hers first.

"You didn't tell me your name," she said.

She looked up again to stare into his eyes and something caught in his throat as he replied, "I'm Ian."

She smiled. "Do you go to Columbia?" she asked.

Ian thought to himself that he had never met such an engaging person. A sweet gentleness seemed to radiate from her face. Realizing that she had asked him a question, he sputtered, "I'm sorry what was that?"

She laughed again. "I asked if you go to Columbia also."

"Yes," Ian said. "I'm finishing my doctorate, in philosophy."

"I didn't know they taught those kind of moves in philosophy."

Ian grinned. "Oh, you mean the karate? No, that I learned somewhere else. You know," he said half-serious, "you should be more careful who you start up with."

"Are you referring to the skinheads or yourself?"

Smiling, he said, "Umm…tell me, were you on your way to class or do you have time to grab something to eat?"

"Actually I'm probably late for my class."

Seeing the obvious disappointment written on his face, she added, "I guess I can always get the notes from a friend." Staring up at him she asked, "There's a small coffee shop three blocks down, do you know it?"

Ian grinned broadly. "It's kosher, right?"

# CHAPTER 5

Rabbi Bun also sat and expounded:
What is the meaning of the verse (Isaiah 45:7),
"He forms light and creates darkness?"
Therefore the term "formation" is used with regard to it. Darkness has no substance, and therefore the term "creation" is used.
Light was actually brought into existence, as it is written (Genesis 1:3),
"And God said, let there be light." Something cannot be brought into existence unless it is made. The term "formation" is therefore used.
In the case of darkness, however, there was no making, only separation and setting aside.
It is for this reason that the term "created" is used.

The Bahir 13.

Letting himself into his apartment two hours later, he dropped his stuff on the floor and headed for the bedroom. On the way he peeled off his shirt, tossing it in the hamper outside the bathroom. He went into the bedroom and stripped the rest of his clothes off onto the bed. Turning on the shower, he put the water on hot and stepped in, pulling the curtain behind him. He closed his eyes, letting the stinging hot spray relax his still tense muscles. His mind went blank.

Beth's warm smiling face swam up before him. With a sudden stab of guilt, he thought about Jessica. What am I doing, he thought. I don't know what I'm going to tell her, he realized, thinking about the scholarship. Then came another thought. What would his father have said about Jessica? He knew the answer.

Wrapping the towel around his waist, he padded into the bedroom and hunted through the drawers for a clean pair of underwear. He couldn't find any and settled for a pair of sweats. Grabbing another towel, he started to dry off his hair. The phone rang. He walked over to the kitchen. Picking up the receiver, he was surprised to hear the voice of his younger brother.

"Hi Ian. How are you doing? Listen, I called to ask you a favor."

"Yeah sure, what can I do for you?" he said, wrapping the damp towel around his neck.

"Well, I was hoping you could check something out for me. I went today to YIZO to look through their archives. I was searching for some corroborative documents to try and verify that weird story I told you. You know."

"Sure, how could I forget?"

"I haven't been able to forget it either. I started looking and interestingly enough I couldn't find much on the Jewish Brigade, and almost nothing about their activities in Italy. I was about ready to give up when I found a strange footnote in a book about the Arch of Titus, you know, the one with the picture of the Menorah carved on it. It made reference to a plot by a group of Jewish soldiers from Palestine who were serving in what they called the British expeditionary forces in Italy in 1944. According to the footnote, the Jewish soldiers had made preparations to blow the arch up, but the plot was uncovered just before they could accomplish their goal. The book said that the whole affair was hushed up by sympathetic British officers, and that was the end of it.

"You know, I think that man on the plane wasn't telling me the whole story. Don't you think it's a little strange that a group of Jewish soldiers, who just happened to be in Rome at that particular time would've gotten so upset that they would risk trying to blow it up?"

Ian thought about that a moment. "Yeah, it's a little weird," he remarked noncommittally. "What was it you needed my help with?"

"Well, I was wondering if you could think of any other libraries that might have more information on this and about the Menorah in general."

Ian grinned. "Actually I have some exciting news to tell you. I haven't told anyone else yet. In fact, I just found out about it this morning."

"What is it?"

Ian took a deep breath. "I'm going to Rome on a scholarship! I'll be doing research for my thesis in the

Vatican library for the next six months."

"What? That's fantastic news. When do you leave?"

"In three days. I haven't had a chance to tell anyone else, including Mom. It's been an interesting day to say the least," Ian said, as he pulled the towel off the back of his neck.

There was silence for a moment on the other end. "So that means you'll be in Rome for the last days of Pesach. Do you have matzo and wine to take with you?"

"Actually, I hadn't thought about that. I guess I can pick some up if I see Mom before I leave."

"You really should try to come. But wait a minute. If you're going to Rome, maybe you could find something on the Menorah and the Jewish Brigade."

Ian shrugged. "I don't see why not. Why is this suddenly so important to you?"

"Can you imagine if we could somehow locate the Menorah and maybe even the other vessels of the Temple? You do realize that without them, the Messiah won't be able to build the third and final Temple in the Last Days."

"Look, don't get me involved in your crazy fantasies."

Jonathan shot back, "What? Don't you believe we are living in the Last Days? It wasn't just a coincidence that I happened to sit next to that fellow on the plane. Nor do I think it's just a coincidence that all of a sudden you just happen to get a scholarship to go do research in the Vatican library, in the very heart of Rome. You know that the Torah believes that behind everything is the hand of God."

"I can't live my life that way," Ian said heatedly. And then in a more subdued voice he added, "I wish I had your faith. Everything would be so much simpler."

"I'm sorry," Jonathan said. "I really didn't mean to push you."

Ian laughed, knowing that his younger brother

only meant well. "Okay, okay. Look, I'll see what I can find for you when I'm over there, alright?"

"Great. I'm going to the 42nd street library to look in their Judaica section and see what else I can turn up. When did you say you were leaving, Thursday?"

"Yeah, Thursday evening. That is, if I can get ready in time."

"Is the flight going to arrive in Rome before shabbos?"

"Oh," Ian said. "Yeah, I think I should have plenty of time. The flight arrives early Friday morning," Ian finished, a little annoyed.

"Good. When do you think you might come over to say good-bye? You know I'd like to see you before you leave."

"I don't know. I have so much to get ready. Tell you what. I'll call Mom and tell her when I'm coming and you can find out from her."

"I'll see you then. Congratulations again on the scholarship."

"Take care."

"I love you," Jonathan said, hanging up.

Ian busied himself the rest of the day writing down a list of all the stuff he wanted to take, and then gathering as many of the items as he could find in a large pile on the bedroom floor. Looking at the pile, he realized that the small overnight bag he had in the apartment would never hold everything.

He ran out to an army-navy store on Broadway to look for a good duffel bag, cheap. He found a used one at a good price, and pleased with himself, strolled back to the apartment and let himself in.

Standing at the far end of the dining room was Jessica. He hesitated before walking straight towards her. As he came closer, he saw that she'd been crying.

A strong feeling of guilt welled up inside him. He was about to speak when she said first, "When were you going to tell me you were leaving? Or was I just going to come here and find you gone?"

He moved forward, wanting to hold her, to comfort her.

"I didn't know I was going anywhere 'til this morning," he said. "I was going to tell you tonight. I just didn't know what to say."

She held her arms in front of her as if to ward him off. "What happened? Where are you going and for how long?"

"I'm going to Italy. Actually to Rome, to stay in the Vatican on a scholarship for…six months."

"The Vatican. Really?"

"That's not all," Ian said, wincing. "I leave this Thursday."

"What? That's only three days from now."

He moved closer, and they embraced. Clumsily, she pulled away.

She looked up and said, "Let's not make each other any promises."

His throat had gone dry. He didn't know what to say, so he just nodded his head.

They made love that night for the last time. Afterward they lay in each others arms, not speaking, each thinking their own separate thoughts. They fell asleep, apart.

Ian fell into a deep sleep, like none he had ever had before. He dreamed.

He stood on a flat landscape. Looking down at his feet, he traced with his eyes the cracks that spread out in all directions. The ground was hard and parched. He looked up. The sky was black, with dark purple shades streaked through it like the folds of a curtain. Off to his right, in the far distance, he could just make out a range of jagged black peaks. Before him, the ground rose up in a slight rise. Beyond its lip, a strange glow emanated from an unknown source. A sudden wind gusted up, ruffling his garments. He looked down at himself. He was dressed in filthy, soiled rags. He stood there for a long moment, not knowing what to do. As abruptly as it had started, the wind died down. The air was still. All around him was silence. Curious, he climbed over the rise. He stood still.

Before him, shining so brightly that it hurt his eyes, rose up a large golden candelabra. Seven dancing flames burnt atop its seven beautifully carved branches. By the light of the flames he could plainly see two large olive trees growing, one to either side.

A voice spoke softly to him and he jumped back in fear. The words seemed to come right out of the air.

The voice intoned, "What do you see?"

Ian looked around. There was no one. Swallowing to moisten his parched throat he answered fearfully into the air, "I see a golden menorah with seven lights burning and two olive trees growing on either side of it."

The voice asked again. "Do you know what these are?"

"No."

The voice spoke again, but this time it seemed to come from deep inside his heart. A tidal wave of emotion crashed through his very being as he heard, "This is the word of God to Zerubavel. Not by might, nor by power, but by My spirit says the Lord of hosts. Who are you, O great mountain, before Zerubavel? You will become a plain; and he will produce the headstone with shouts of, 'Grace, grace, to it.'"

Ian stood frozen, the hairs on the back of his neck

standing on end. Looking down, he saw to his amazement that he was dressed now all in white. He took a shaky step forward. From behind, a flaming hand seized his leg in an iron grip, tearing at his muscle. He twisted his head back, opening his mouth wide to scream.

  He awoke, drenched in sweat, breathing hard. Feeling his calf muscle twitch uncontrollably, he reached down to massage it. Needles of white fire shot through his right leg briefly. He winced, kneading the muscle. The pain slowly subsided. He looked over to where Jessica lay, sleeping soundly. Careful not to cramp his leg, he tried to shift into a more comfortable position. He fell into a restless sleep.

# CHAPTER 6

A star shall come out of Jacob, and a sceptre shall rise out of Israel.
He shall smite the temples of Moab and destroy all the children of Sheth. He shall rule out of Jacob and shall cause the survivors of the city to perish. The enemy shall be his possession and Israel shall accomplish mighty deeds.

Numbers 24:17-19

---

The next morning he awoke, feeling totally drained. Rubbing his eyes, he twisted and stretched his body, trying to wake up. Turning on his side, he saw that the other side of the bed was empty. On the center of the pillow was a note and the set of keys he had given Jessica. He reached over and picked up the note. Rolling onto his stomach, he propped himself up on his elbows and read:

I need a little space to think things over. Love, Jessie.

Ian stared at the words scrawled so neatly on the

torn piece of loose-leaf paper. Pensively, he crumpled it in his hand. It's probably for the best, he thought, shaking his head. He realized now that he had been deluding himself. He had been lonely and it had all been too easy. They had fallen in together, like strangers with no past. Glancing over at the small alarm clock by his bed, he cursed out loud. It was 8:48.

His mother for sure, was already out of the house and on her way to school. He'd planned to call her early and invite himself over that evening to tell her about the trip. Now he'd have to wait until the afternoon to get a hold of her.

Grunting, he lurched upward, having made a decision. Gingerly, he placed his weight down on his right leg. Wisps of memory came back to him. He shook out his right leg, trying at the same time to shake off the remnants of the previous night's dream. He pulled on a pair of jogging shorts and his favorite old tee-shirt. Lacing up his jogging shoes, he reached behind with his hand to feel the back of his right leg. Exploring with his fingers, he felt a small depression the size of a finger joint on the back inner border of his thigh, just where it joined his right hip. He had never noticed it before. As he rubbed his fingers over it, a shiver ran down his spine. I've been listening to my brother too much, he thought.

Grabbing the keys, he locked up behind him and went out to stretch by a No Parking sign near the entrance to the building. He glanced down at his watch. It was 9:07. He figured a good half-hour run would clear his thoughts, and maybe work the cramp out of his leg.

Twisting his neck back and forth, he set out at a nice even pace, crossing Riverside Drive as he headed up toward Grant's Tomb. Once inside the park, he picked up the pace, letting the sensation of freedom and speed propel him forward. His powerful thighs pumped as he did a wind-sprint along the wide cement path by the river's edge. Slowing down, he struck out off the path, wending his way among the trees. It had rained a little the night before, and the ground was wet. He could feel the wet grass give slightly beneath his running shoes. His lungs expanded as he fell into a steady rhythm, his heart pumping oxygenated blood to his limbs. His tensions and worries seemed to fall away. Straight ahead was the massive stone monument, set majestically among a grove of tall trees.

Racing up the wide stone steps he paused, jogging in place, staring straight ahead. Someone had sprayed some new graffiti in bold red paint over some older faded scrawl at the base of the monument. One word, written in huge bold letters stood out clearly at the center. The word was "BABEL."

Something strange snapped inside him. The word seemed to leap off the stone, rushing straight toward him as everything around him spun out of control. And then, an instant later, it just stopped. Ian shook his head, in shock and bewilderment. Troubled, he glanced back to stare at the word for an instant, before running off through the foliage.

Back in the apartment, he took a quick shower. He dressed and grabbed his list along with some cash.

On the street he bought a pair of polarized sunglasses from a street vendor for five dollars. He popped them on, staring at his reflection in the glass of a storefront window. "Who am I?" he said, looking at the unfamiliar face staring back at him. Then with a wolfish grin, he turned away, continuing his stroll down the block.

"I'm not going to let some weird dream or my overactive imagination get the better of me," he said aloud. He shopped for a couple of hours, picking up most of the remaining items on his list.

Returning to the apartment, he dropped the bags in the living room, glanced at his watch, and headed for the phone. Dialing his mother's number, he was greeted by the sound of his brother's voice.

"Hi. Is Mom home yet?"

"No, she isn't back. She should be home soon though. Is there anything you want me to tell her?"

"Yeah, umm…just tell her that I'd like to come over tonight for dinner if she doesn't mind such short notice."

"Are you kidding?" Jonathan laughed. "She'll be in seventh heaven."

"Okay. Look, I've got to run out again to pick something up for the trip. You haven't said anything to her yet, right?"

"Of course not. I would never tell her without your permission."

"Sorry," Ian said. "I'm just nervous about telling her. "Tell me ahh…who or what is bav…no, zerubavel?"

"I think he was a historical figure. Let me see… I believe he brought the Jews back from the Babylonian Exile. No wait, there's something else about that name that I can't remember. Tell you what. I'll look it up in the Concordance. I'll see what I can find and tell you tonight. What time should I tell Mom that you'll be here?"

"Probably around six," Ian said, as he looked at his watch. "See you then, bye."

He arrived late. There was a signaling problem with the F train and he'd sat in the Queens Plaza station for over twenty minutes. Irritated, he leapt up the stoop at the front of the house and knocked loudly. The doorbell was busted, and his mother had still not gotten around to getting it fixed. His mother answered the door.

"Is everything alright?" she asked. "I was starting to get worried."

"I'm fine," he said, stepping in. "The train was messed up. Sorry I'm late," he said as he gave her a hug.

"I just finished getting supper ready. I got home late from school myself. One of the kids stole my school keys."

"Unbelievable," Ian said, shaking his head. "I guess they're preparing for their future careers, right? I worry about you sometimes, Mom."

"Don't worry. There's a security guard I can always call in, and he's really big. Now come in and wash so you can eat while everything's still hot."

Ian trailed his mother inside. Seated at the kitchen table was his younger brother, a religious text in hand. Jonathan got up to greet him, a big grin on his face.

"Shalom aleichem," he said, extending his hand.

"Aleichem shalom," Ian gave the traditional response, grasping the hand in a firm, warm handshake.

"I looked up that thing you asked me about," Jonathan said.

"Good."

"Come, go wash first," their mother cut in, shooing them over to the sink.

They washed their hands and recited the blessing over the bread. Since it was one of the intermediate days of Passover, they still ate only the unleavened bread called matzo. Ian always loved eating his mother's food. After he finished his plate he cleared his throat.

"Mom, there's something important I have to tell you."

"I don't like the sound of that," she said with a nervous little laugh.

"It's nothing bad. In fact, it's really good news. I've been offered a full scholarship to go to Rome for the next six months. It's going to make my thesis even better than I could've imagined."

"How's that?" she said, puzzled.

"Well, actually the scholarship in not just in Rome. It's in a particular part of Rome: the Vatican."

"What? Are you sure it's safe for you to go there?"

"Mom, don't worry. Remember, this isn't the Middle Ages."

"Sure, sure."

Ian sighed. "Anyway, I've decided to go. The big problem is, I have to leave on short notice."

"How short?"

"This Thursday."

"What? I can't believe it. That means you won't even be here for the second days," she said.

"Well, at least you'll still have Jonathan."

"Sure, until he goes back to yeshiva next week."

"Don't worry I'll write you."

"You just be careful over there and come home safe and sound."

Ian got up to hug his mother. "Thanks for understanding."

They said the Grace, and helped their mother clear off the table. Ian offered to do the dishes but his mother pushed them out of the kitchen.

"Don't worry. I can still wash the dishes. Now go into the living room. You don't get to see Jonathan very often. I'll be right in as soon as I finish up."

Ian and Jonathan sat down in the heavy recliners on either side of the couch. They stared at each other. Jonathan was the first to speak.

"I told you I looked up that thing you asked me about."

Ian perked up, leaning forward. "What did you find?"

"The name Zerubabel turns up several times in the Prophets. I found it mentioned first in Zechariah. In the second chapter he speaks about Joshua the High Priest, and the leader of Israel at that time, a man named Zerubavel, who was of the seed of the House of David. The name means, 'the flourishing one of Babel' or in the Hebrew, Bavel. As you know, the letter 'b' and the letter 'v' are interchangeable in Hebrew. I guess the Babel refers to the Babylonian Exile that the Jews had just returned from. Here, let me get the text and read it to you."

Jonathan pulled a small thick book from one of the many shelves of the bookcases that lined the room. Flipping through the pages, he located the spot he wanted.

He quoted, "The angel who spoke with me returned and woke me, as a man is awakened from his sleep. He said to me, 'What do you see?'

I said, 'I see and behold! — there is a Menorah made entirely of gold with its bowl on top, and its seven lamps are upon it and there are seven tubes to each of the lamps that are on its top. And two olive trees are near it, one to the right of the bowl and one to its left. And I spoke up and said to the angel that was speaking to me, saying, 'What are these, my lord?' The angel who was speaking to me spoke up and said to me, 'Do you not know what they are?' I said, 'No, my lord.'

He spoke up to me, saying, 'This is the word of God to Zerubavel, Saying, 'Not through armies and not through might, but through My spirit,' says the Lord of Hosts. 'Who are you O great mountain, before Zerubavel you shall become a plain! He shall bring forth the main stone to shouts of, 'Grace, grace to it!' "

Jonathan looked up from the small printed page to stare in shock at his brother. Ian's face had turned ashen, like the color of pale stone. His arms gripped the chair convulsively, his eyes bulging outward. He appeared to have stopped breathing. Jonathan jumped out of his chair, rushing to his brother's side.

Grabbing him by the shoulders, he shook him repeatedly as he said, "Are you okay?"

Ian roused himself, as someone reviving themselves after an accident. Some color returned to his face as he croaked in a small voice, "Yeah…I'm alright."

Jonathan relaxed. "God, you gave me a scare. Do you want something, some water, maybe?"

Ian sat up straighter and cleared his throat.

"No, it's okay, I'm alright," he said, the strength returning to his voice. He waved Jonathan away.

"What happened? One minute I was reading to you and the next I look up and you look like you're about to expire right on the spot, God forbid."

Ian laughed shakily. "Don't worry, I'm not going to die just yet."

Jonathan sighed as he sank back into his recliner. They could hear their mother still washing up in the kitchen.

"Tell me what's wrong."

Ian shrugged his broad shoulders. "To tell you the truth I don't know. Some strange things have been happening to me the past few days, and I don't know what to make of them."

He paused a moment, ruminating over the last few days' events.

"Go on," Jonathan prodded.

"I don't know. It's just that all of a sudden I get this scholarship to Rome, right after you tell me that weird story about the Menorah, and then, oh, forget it."

Jonathan had slid forward to the edge of his seat.

"Forget what? You've got to tell me."

Ian slumped back into the cushions. He spoke quietly, his eyes staring fixedly into space as the words spilled forth.

"I had a weird dream last night. I stood in this strange landscape. I was dressed in filthy rags. Over a rise, I could see a glow from some kind of light. Curious, I walked toward it. In front of me stood this large golden menorah. There were seven flames burning on it. Beside the menorah grew two large olive trees, and oil flowed from the trees, feeding the flames.

"Suddenly, a voice spoke to me out of the thin air. I looked around but there was no one. It asked me what I saw, and I told it that I saw a menorah. I looked down at myself for some reason, and now I was dressed in beautifully flowing white garments. The voice spoke again, but this time it seemed to be coming from inside me. And it said the exact words you just read. And then a burning hand grabbed me from behind on the back of my leg and I felt this unbelievable pain. I opened my mouth to scream and then I woke up," he finished, rubbing the back of his right leg absentmindedly.

Jonathan jumped up. Grabbing Ian's leg, he hiked up the pant leg, bunching the material around the thick muscle. Pulling the yellow light from the lamp on the side table closer, he turned Ian's leg to the side to stare at a mark on the inside of Ian's thigh.

Letting go he said, "Amazing. Is that where the hand grabbed you?"

"Yeah," he said in a husky voice.

"It's right above the nerve."

"So what?"

"That's the exact spot on the body where the patriarch Jacob was wounded when he struggled with the angel of Esau. That was to illustrate the historic struggle throughout the ages between the children of Jacob and the children of Esau for the fate of the world."

Ian remained silent as Jonathan continued.

"You know that the Torah considered Rome the heir of Esau and his grandson Amalek. When I go back I'm going to try to speak to Reb Yossl Bereditch. He lives in Mea Shearim and I heard him give a Torah class once. He is a Gadol and is known to be a kabbalist and a very pious and holy man." He shrugged. "It looks like your destiny lies in Rome."

CHAPTER 7

No nation scorns Israel, openly spitting at
them, as Edom.
They tell Israel that Jews are all impure.
And they boast, "We are the children of the
Living God, in us will His Name be honored.
We rule the world for we are great...
But Israel is the most inconsequential of all...

　　　　　　　　　　　　Zohar Ki-Sisah188b

---

　　Undersecretary Alberto Maglione was a man who strove to leave nothing to chance. Stacked exactly equidistant from each other on the massive wood desk in front of him were three neat piles of papers. Relaxing his body into the soft contours of the thickly padded leather chair, he stared intently at the slip of telex paper he held before his eyes. His eyes narrowed to slits. He peered at the bold type imprinted on the translucent sheet between his manicured fingers.

It read: Sending student. Stop. Arrives as per your schedule. Stop. Name is Ian Charosh. Stop. Warmest regards. Stop. Signed, J. Berluonti. Ph.D. Stop.

Placing the sheet down neatly on top of the nearest pile, he mused aloud, "Charosh. A strange name." Well, he thought, pleased with himself, except for one last detail I've pretty much taken care of this annoyance. He pressed a small intercom button and spoke into the air.

"Send him in."

There was a slight pause. The heavy door opened with a soft click. Into the dimly-lit office stepped a young priest, dressed in the simple robes of the Dominican order. The coarse weave hung on him in folds and but for the rope belt around his narrow middle, it would have held no shape at all.

Undersecretary Maglione's deep set eyes glittered with intelligence. They seemed to bore right into the delicate features of the young priest as he stopped a few feet away, to stand stiffly before him. A slight smile creased Maglione's bloodless lips.

The Undersecretary enunciated in a crisp, passionless voice. "The annual doctoral student is coming this year from America, Brother Michel. He will be assigned to your room. I expect you to report to me personally each week on his activities."

Brother Michel's frail body started slightly. The Undersecretary's keen eyes took note of the subtle involuntary motion. He snapped, "Is there something you wish to say?" his eyes suddenly flashing wide.

"No. No, your Eminence," was the high pitched reply.

"Good. Speak to my assistant outside. He will provide you with further details."

Ian couldn't sleep. He knew he should try to get some rest. He hadn't slept the night before, gathering together all his research papers, footnotes, and source material references. He'd said good-bye to Jessica at her dorm room the day before. It had been difficult. He felt torn. A part of him had wanted to crush her to his chest, to tell her everything was going to be alright. But another part of him knew that it was better to end it. He hadn't meant to hurt her. He could see now that it had been a terrible mistake. Yes, he thought, something has definitely changed inside me. The time has come to get out from under the shadow of my father. I can't live my life like it was some chess game. It's time to stop fooling around, in more ways than one.

He began to do some breathing exercises as he sought to shut out his immediate surroundings. He concentrated instead on breathing in and out as he emptied his mind. He closed his eyes.

A minute later, someone passing in the narrow aisle jostled his shoulder and banged his knee. Passing by Ian's aisle seat he muttered a quick, "Sorry," on his way to the lavatory.

Ian opened his eyes and sighed. The flight was packed with tourists and businessmen. He was flying coach, and all the seats were filled. Pulling out a small sheet of paper and a disposable pen from the breast pocket of his shirt, he started to compose a list. He'd made five entries and was about to slip the small piece of paper back in his pocket, when suddenly he reconsidered. Grasping the pen thoughtfully, he placed at the bottom and somewhat to the side, a sixth entry.

It was the single word, "Menorah." He stared at

the list for a few moments, his eyes lingering at the bottom of the page. Then folding it once, he tucked it and the pen back into his shirt pocket.

About half an hour later the stewardesses began to serve the meals. Staring at the tin foil cover with a mixture of surprise and fascination, he thought, I don't remember ordering kosher food. Opening the rather unappetizing foil cover, he wasn't surprised to find that the meal inside was even less appealing than the outer packaging.

He stared somewhat longingly at the more sumptuous meal that the seasoned businessman in the seat next to him was devouring. He smiled at him and then resignedly started to eat his own meal. It's really not so bad, he thought, as he polished off the barely warm brisket drenched in an unidentifiable sauce.

After several hours, the pilot announced that they were getting ready to make their final descent into the Leonardo da Vinci airport, better known by the name of its location, Fiumicino. After what seemed an interminable period, the plane actually touched down. They had arrived.

People started getting up and began taking out their overhead carry-ons, ignoring the stewardess's entreaties over the intercom to remain seated until the plane had come to a complete and final stop.

Ian grinned. Getting up himself, he thought, when in Rome, do as the Romans do.

He grabbed his knapsack and wind-breaker from the overhead compartment and waited for the plane to finish taxiing up to the terminal. Ian waited his turn and made his way down the steps onto the hot black tarmac. They'd left the previous evening and it was now around ten thirty in the morning, Rome time. The sun beat down, creating a strong glare.

Squinting, he followed the rest of the passengers to the arrivals hall. It took him over an hour to locate his large green duffel bag.

Slinging the heavy bag over his shoulder, he made his way through customs without any problems. He was traveling on a student visa that was good for a full year. Exiting the hall, he stepped outside into a scene of frenetic activity.

People were busy loading or unloading their cars, saying good-bye to relatives or greeting them with huge hugs and kisses. The air was filled with the smell of gasoline fumes. Stepping to the side, Ian noticed a faded blue bus parked at a bus stop off to the right, with the name ACOTRAL, written in bold type on its front. Thirty yards beyond, in the bright sunlight was a taxi stand. A long line of yellow cabs were queued up beside it.

Pulling out his sunglasses, he put them on as he looked out over the busy airport parking lot. He hesitated, not sure what he should do. In his pocket was an address but he had no idea how to get there. Stepping off the curb, he was assaulted by an unsavory looking fellow, his shirt unbuttoned almost down to his navel, revealing a hairy chest and a potbelly. An idiotic grin was affixed to his unshaven face. He grabbed Ian's arm, motioning to his dented Gypsy cab, parked not ten feet away.

He jovially said, "Come, I take you," over and over again.

With a subtle movement, Ian extricated himself from the cab driver's grasp and waved him off. With a not so subtle expletive and an accompanying hand gesture, the cabby departed, only to latch on to another tourist immediately. Ignoring the commotion around him, Ian looked around, finally seeing a young man carrying a small white placard in front of him with the name "Carosh" written on it in block letters. Ian stopped. Changing course, he hesitantly approached the man with the sign.

"Hello, I know this may sound a bit strange but are you looking for Ian Charosh?"

The young man stared at him a minute. Then, looking down at his sign for a second, he looked back up and smiled. Extending his arm forward, he grasped Ian's hand in an exuberant handshake.

"Scusi, my spelling is not too good. But then neither is my English," he said, still pumping Ian's hand.

"Nice to meet you," Ian said, releasing his grip.

"Piacere! My name is Marcus. I have been sent to take you to your, eh, accommodationes. Please to follow me."

Ian nodded and gestured for Marcus to lead the way. Threading his way through the crowds, he led him over to a large Fiat van parked on the side. Opening the hatchback, he gestured for Ian to put his duffel in the back. The van sagged a bit from the bag's weight.

"Sorry, it's a little heavy."

Marcus grinned as he hopped into the driver's seat and motioned Ian into the front passenger seat.

"I was lucky I found you," Ian called out loudly above the whine of the motor kicking on.

"The Monsignor only said to go pick up young American at airport, but I had no idea, what you look like. Tell me, where are you from?" he yelled while careening narrowly past two cars on the highway.

"I'm from New York," Ian yelled back, gripping the dash for dear life as horns blared and voices hurled insults.

Ian rolled down his window to catch the breeze on his sweat-stained face. His shirt was plastered to his back and he reached behind to peel it away.

Sticking his head out the window, he missed catching

what Marcus was shouting to him. Bringing his head back inside he turned to say, "Sorry, what was that?"

Marcus yelled, "I ask you if you ever been to Roma?"

Ian shouted back, "No, never."

"Oh, it is multo belissima. You will love it. I was born here. My familia has been here for many, many, generations. My papa and his papa all have worked for el Vaticano, and so I too."

The van swerved off the highway onto the Via Aurelia. Ian got his first glimpse of the imposing walls that surround the Citta Del Vaticano. Making a sharp left, the van sped onto an elevated road alongside some train-tracks. It passed under a high stone wall to a gate. On the other side stood two men, dark maroon berets affixed jauntily to their heads. They were dressed in nondescript dark khaki military uniforms, automatic weapons slung over their shoulders. Marcus grinned and waved to them in the brilliant sunlight. They nodded sourly, leisurely swinging open the gates to let them pass through.

Driving at a more sedate speed, they passed a large building on their right.

"That is the railway station," Marcus said, pointing to it. "Over there on top, is the Governor's Palazzo, and way over there, you see? The big basilica there," he pointed again, driving with one hand.

"Yeah, I see it."

"That is San Pietro."

The road curved away to the left and they pulled up in front of another large edifice. Marcus jumped out and Ian followed him to the back of the van. Marcus lifted open the back and Ian grabbed the duffel and slung it over his shoulder.

"Let me take the little one," Marcus said.

"No, don't worry, I'm fine, really," he reassured him.

Marcus shrugged. Turning around, he led Ian inside. The great stone hall was filled with tall columns that divided the huge space. It was distinctly cooler. The light was dim, giving a somewhat gloomy ambiance to the place.

"This is the Collegia Ethiopia," Marcus said in a hushed voice.

Ian stared around, turning from side to side to catch sight of several young priests in black flowing robes passing silently by, intent upon their tasks. Marcus led Ian up wide stone steps to a landing and then up a shorter flight to the next floor. Passing several more priests, Marcus took him down a long corridor and into another stairwell. They trudged up another flight and through another door leading to a very long corridor with a low ceiling. This was punctuated at intervals by many doors on either side. Ian immediately recognized where he was. I guess all dorms look the same, he thought.

Marcus led him to one of the doors. He opened it, ushering Ian in. It was a tiny room, barely able to hold the two narrow cots set against each wall. It also held a small desk, crammed tightly up against the far wall by a tiny slit of a window. Right behind the door, was a small stained porcelain sink and towel rack.

There were several books lining a small shelf above one of the cots, as well as some toiletry items and a towel by the sink. The beds, though, were so neatly done up that one couldn't tell if anyone had slept on them recently. Ian sighed as he dropped the heavy bag down on the floor.

"I think that one is yours." Marcus pointed to one of the cots. "Under is a trunk to put your things," Marcus added, staring at his watch. "Escusa. I must to be going. Here is your pass." He placed a large card on the bed.

"Carry it with you at all times. Maybe I see you again soon. Arrivaderchi."

He scooted out before Ian had a chance to ask any questions. Rushing to the door, Ian stared down the now empty corridor.

Entering the room again, he shrugged and said aloud to the bare stone walls, "Oh well. I guess I'll knock around a bit."

Stowing away his bag in the large storage chest under his cot, he headed for the door. He paused at the sink to drink some cold water from the faucet, splashing some on his face. Feeling much refreshed, he noticed there was no lock on the door. I guess they don't have a theft problem, he thought, a smile creasing his face.

Heading down the hall, Ian retraced their footsteps. Emerging into the dazzling sunlight, he popped on his sunglasses. He headed for the great dome shimmering above the buildings and trees in front of him. He strode down a curved walkway, passing the Government House off to the side, and entered a formal garden. Admiring the lush plants along the path, he came upon an ancient church. The air here was fresh and scented with lilacs. Going around the church, he spotted, over a low wall, an enormous twenty foot long stone bath filled with water. Continuing on, he came upon the imposing structure that is Saint Peter's. Staring up at the magnificent edifice and the dome high above it in the bright glare, he didn't even notice the guard until he felt someone grab him by the arm. Ian looked down at the hand that was grasping his arm and controlled the urge to break the grip.

Staring directly into the Swiss soldier's eyes he said calmly, "What seems to be the problem?"

The guard, decked out in formal attire with the

traditional plumed helmet replied, "How did you get here? Do you have any papers, identification?"

Ian slowly reached with his free hand for his breast pocket and then realized that he had left the pass Marcus had given him back at the dorm. He grinned sheepishly.

"Look, I just got in. I'm a student from the States and I was invited here on a scholarship. I left my pass in my room. If you let go of my hand I can get out my wallet and show you some ID."

"Alright," the guard snapped, letting go of his arm. The guard watched him intently. Ian slowly pulled out his wallet. Fishing out his Columbia University student I.D. card, he handed it to the guard. The guard stared at the photo on the laminated card and then back at Ian. He seemed to be satisfied by the grunt he let out.

"Come with me."

Ian followed the guard through a side entrance, and down a short flight of steps.

They came to a door and the guard knocked twice before opening it. Ushering Ian in first, they stepped into a small office. An officer sat behind a small desk. On the ceiling an ancient fan turned slowly, producing no perceptible effect. The first guard saluted.

"I have here a tourist who I found coming from the gardens without a pass. He says he's an invited guest on a scholarship and that he just arrived and forgot his pass in his room, sir."

He handed Ian's card to the seated officer who examined both sides minutely, staring at the photo.

He looked up at Ian.

"We can't have people roaming around the grounds without a pass. I'm going to call for someone to take you back to your room and locate your pass. If you cannot produce your pass my young friend, I can assure you that we can find you suitable accommodations in our jail."

Ian smiled back. Picking up the phone, the officer spoke quietly in what sounded to Ian like German. Placing the receiver back on its cradle, he glanced sharply up at him.

"Please have a seat."

Turning to the guard, he motioned for him to leave. The guard saluted and spun around, letting himself out. The officer turned his attention back to his papers, ignoring Ian. Ian sat down. He leaned back in the plain heavy wood chair against the wall and surveyed the office. Several schedules and notices were tacked up on a bulletin board on the opposite wall. Ian removed his sunglasses and placed them in his breast pocket.

I'm not here ten minutes and already I'm in trouble with the local law, he thought, chagrined.

The room was somewhat stuffy. Time seemed to slow to a crawl. Ian stared up at the fan. He glanced down at his watch. Finally there was another knock on the door. A new guard entered. He saluted the officer. The officer looked up from his papers.

Turning to Ian he said, "You will show the sergeant to your room."

He buried his head back into his papers, no longer interested. The sergeant hustled Ian out of the officer's presence none too gently. Ian decided to ignore his rudeness. Once outside again, the guard gestured to Ian.

"Where?"

"This way."

Ian led the guard back the way he had come. Several priests passing by glanced back curiously to watch them. Ian unerringly took him back to his room. He had always had an exceptional sense of direction. Back in the room, Ian was relieved to find the pass sitting right where he had left it on the bed. He handed it to the guard who accepted it silently. The guard took him back by a slightly more direct route in total silence. Back in the office he saluted the officer and handed him the pass. The officer looked at it a moment. Picking up the phone, he put a few terse questions to the person on the other end. Satisfied, he hung up the phone. He looked up at Ian.

In an impersonal monotone he said, "It seems all is in order. In the future, please carry your pass with you at all times. You are free to go. By the way, my name is Captain Meier." With that, he handed the pass and Ian's student I. D. card back to him.

Ian laughed. "Thanks. Sorry for the trouble. I'll make sure to keep this on me from now on."

At the door he nodded to the two men. With a slight smile he said, "Gentlemen, good day."

"Good day," Captain Meier responded, his face a blank.

# CHAPTER 8

When I see Your heavens, the work of your fingers, the moon and the stars...what is Man that you mind him.

Psalms 8:4

---

Outside once again, he paused a brief moment to smile at the original guard who had stopped him. Flashing his pass, he proceeded by him without a word. The guard stared wordlessly after him.

Ian entered St. Peter's by a side door. Inside, he stopped immediately to take in the vast scope surrounding him. Definitely impressive, he thought, but not exactly his taste.

In high spirits, he strode over to where a group of tourists were being led about on a tour. The guide was speaking Italian of which he knew very little. The guide appeared to be describing the altar before them. He caught the name Bernini, whom he surmised was the artist responsible for its design. Tagging along, he followed them as the guide stopped in front of a statue of what looked like one of the Popes, flanked by two recumbent female figures in flowing gowns. He heard the guide mention the name Michael Angelo. Skirting the periphery, the guide stopped at several more monuments.

Becoming restless, Ian took the opportunity to break away from the group. He was fascinated by the massive altar in the center. He stared upward at the canopy cover suspended high above by four enormous spiral columns at each of its corners. He went over to examine more closely the details of the columns. For some reason he couldn't identify, they disturbed him. They were deeply grooved, of alternating yellow bronze and black. He traced their twisted convoluted shape upward with his eyes. They struck him as resembling the horns of some great evil beast.

A few feet away, Ian noticed another group of tourists exiting some stairs around the corner of the nearest pillar. Intrigued, he waited for them to ascend and file out before going over to investigate. There in the floor to the right of another statue was a narrow flight of steps, leading underground. They were dimly lit and appeared to be deserted.

Ian looked around. No one seemed to be paying him the slightest attention. Carefully watching his step, he went down. Flanking the entrance were two old statues, as if standing guard to the crypt. As he descended, a sudden realization came to him. This must be the same crypt Jonathan had mentioned in that story.

Shaking his head in wonder, he paused to look around. The dim overhead lights cast a yellow gloom, but what struck Ian was the abrupt drop in temperature. Two long halls with low ceilings stretched out before him. At intervals stood large sarcophagi and massive headstones. All around him was silence. Suddenly, another group of tourists popped around a corner. This one had a guide who spoke English. Making himself inconspicuous against the wall, Ian listened to the guide's descriptions for a while. The sound of the guide's voice faded as the group moved off to the left. He was alone again.

Curious, he began to explore. The wall off to the right seemed somewhat different than the rest and Ian went over to take a closer look. He felt the texture of the stone blocks with his hand. This part of the wall was very old and he surmised that it must have been part of an earlier structure.

Further to the right, he was surprised to come upon another opening. From where he had been standing earlier he hadn't noticed it. Someone had placed a small stand on the floor in front of it. In several languages were printed in bold characters the words, "No Admittance." A thick twisted rope set in dark metal hooks on either side further barred the way. Ian considered the sign a moment. He hesitated. Just then a figure appeared, seeming to materialize out of the gloomy cold.

It was an old man, dressed in severe dull-black voluminous robes, his face creased and lined with age. He sidled forward like a lean gray rat, making agitated motions with his pale hands. He muttered something unintelligible, repeating it over and over as he advanced. Ian retreated, feeling a palpable resentment emanating from the old man. He felt a little like a schoolboy who had been caught by the principal performing a rash act. Extending his open hands outward in a sign of peace, he hastily departed back the way he had come. Before the first flight of steps he glanced backward. There was no sign of the old man. Thinking for a moment about going back, he thought better of it. Instead, he climbed the stairs back up into the light. I don't need to get in trouble a second time today, he thought.

Stepping off the massive marble altar, he glanced at his watch. It was almost 6:00 p.m. He was surprised how much time had passed. Shaking his head, he lengthened his stride. He figured he had enough time to check out the library and find his way back to his room before sunset and the onset of the Sabbath.

Slightly amused at his re-discovered need for observance, he headed for the exit. He stopped to ask directions from a Swiss guard standing at a gate in the Piazza del Forno who directed him, after checking out his pass.

Passing through the gate, he headed to the left, striding under a covered gallery that led to a spacious garden: the Cortile del Belvedere. A lovely statue stood in the center of the rectangular space, and Ian paused in midstride to take in the exquisite beauty spread out before him. Then, remembering his mission, he hastily crossed the space to one of the many openings in the three-tiered building directly in front of him.

He entered through a large set of heavily embossed doors. He stood in a long corridor, a high vaulted ceiling soaring overhead. The hallway was deserted. Along one wall sat a large array of little iron cupboards. Ian went over to take a closer look. Each cupboard had a door with a lock. Curious, he tested one of the doors. It was securely locked.

Wasting no more time, he went over to a door with a beveled glass insert and tried it. It was locked. Peering through the thick glass, he could just make out another long hall punctuated by columns. Sensing some kind of motion within, he tried to call attention to himself by rapping on the glass. No one seemed to respond, so he rapped harder.

A dark shadow appeared on the other side and Ian shouted, "Please, let me in."

There was a long pause and then the door opened outward. He stepped smartly back.

Facing him was a young man dressed in the simple robes of a brother of the Dominican order. He wore wire rimmed spectacles reminiscent of an earlier time above his gaunt sallow cheeks. He seemed somewhat annoyed, but a pleasant smile won out on his thin pale lips as he addressed Ian.

"The library and museum are closed. Please come back tomorrow morning."

"I'm sorry to trouble you," Ian said. "My name is Ian Charosh and I'm a graduate student on a visiting scholarship sponsored by the Vatican." He extended his hand.

The young priest blinked in surprise. Then grasping Ian's hand in a weak handshake he gestured for him to enter.

"Ahh, come in. I am Brother Michel."

Ian entered a large room. They don't believe in empty wall space, he thought, looking in all directions. The walls, pillars and groined ceiling around them were entirely covered with painted figures and scenes. They stood on a rich marble floor made of alternating gray and off-white polished squares set in a checkerboard pattern. Glass-encased dark wood tables were arranged in rows, each containing a display of manuscripts. Ian walked over to one of the desks to stare down in fascination at the documents laid out under the thick glass. Before him lay an illuminated Latin manuscript of a Bible from the eighth century. Ian shook his head in wonder.

Turning to Brother Michel he said, "I'm sorry to be a nuisance but would you mind very much directing me to the library?"

"I was just on my way there when I heard you knocking," Brother Michel said, a sweet smile lighting up his features. "Come, I'll show you around. I work in the archives evaluating documents and manuscripts."

"Evaluating them for what?" Ian said, as he followed the young priest down a long high-ceilinged corridor.

"To see if they are damaged and require repair or restoration."

They continued down the empty corridor in awkward silence.

Brother Michel broke it by saying, "Where are you from?"

Ian smiled. "I'm from New York, Columbia University. I've come to gather some more material for my thesis."

"What is the topic of your thesis?"

"It's a discussion on theodicy, reconciling God and Evil."

Brother Michel nodded knowingly as they entered a vast room. Stretched out before them stood long rows of shelves crammed neatly with books, row after row encompassing a great space. Rolling ladders allowed access to the books on the top shelves. Stairs led up to a second floor lined with more bookshelves. Ian craned his neck to take in the magnificent frescoed ceiling high above. Letting out a long breath, he shook his head in amazement. What a collection, he thought.

"How many books are there?"

"There are over sixty-thousand manuscripts and half a million books in the library," Brother Michel said reverently.

Leading Ian over to a desk, Brother Michel seated himself in front of a large monitor and keyboard. Switching it on, he waited for it to warm up.

Over his shoulder he remarked, "There are several terminals located throughout the library. I'll show you how to gain access and conduct searches."

Ian stood right behind him. They waited a few moments. At first, nothing happened. Finally the screen flickered, the machine giving off a slight whirring sound.

"It's a little slow," Brother Michel said.

As words began to appear on the screen, Ian observed over Brother Michel's shoulder that they were in Latin.

"Are there any programs in English?" Ian said.

"No, it was decided several years back to have everything in Latin. When I first came, it took me a while to get used to it. Now it's almost second nature."

"Where are you from originally?"

"I am from France. But it has been many years since I have been back to my birthplace."

Over the next hour he showed Ian how to use the computer. Together they located several call numbers of texts that he was interested in seeing. Without Brother Michel's help, he could never have referenced them himself. Looking at the reference numbers, he asked the young priest how to locate them.

"Oh, you can't take them out now. The librarian is gone for the day and you need to have a stamp made up before you can take anything from the shelves. Tomorrow morning after ten, apply at that counter over there."

He pointed to a long high counter by one of the walls.

"I must be going now," he said.

Ian, feeling a little guilty, looked at his watch.

"I'm so sorry to have taken up so much of your time. Thank you. I really appreciate all your help." Another thought crossed his mind.

"By the way, do you happen to know what time sunset is here?"

Brother Michel frowned, considering. "I think about eight this evening. Why?"

Ian glanced down again at his watch. It was almost seven-thirty. He'd been so caught up this afternoon, he had completely forgotten to make any preparations for the Sabbath. Besides being the Sabbath, the next two days were also the last days of the Passover holiday. He knew he had some food he had brought with him in his luggage. I guess I'll have to make do with what I've got for the next two days, he thought.

Looking up, he asked in a rush of words, "Could you just point me in the direction of the exit?"

"I will show you myself," Brother Michel said.

Once back outside, Ian bid the priest a hasty goodbye. Brother Michel waved as Ian sprinted away, leaving the young priest to stare in astonishment at his behavior.

Startling several other priests strolling the grounds, he barely noticed them as he flashed by. The sun was already beginning to set and Ian wanted to set up the candles his mother had given him and light them before it was too late. He located the Ethiopian College without difficulty. After sprinting up the many steps two at a time, he arrived at his room, barely breathing hard.

Frantically, he rummaged through his luggage. He stopped a moment, pausing in his search. He couldn't be sure, but it seemed to him that someone had been looking through his bag while he had been out. More slowly, he went through his things again. Nothing seemed to be missing, just slightly rearranged. Whoever had gone through them had tried to put things back in the way he had packed them, but Ian noticed some slight changes. His small tefilin bag for one, had been near the top. Now it was stuffed right at the bottom. Pulling it out, he opened the zipper and removed his siddur. Placing it on his bed, he rummaged some more, locating two small candlesticks and candles. He fished out a bottle of Kedem Royal 18 wine and a small silver cup. Carefully, he pulled out the box of matzos his brother had given him before leaving. Breaking the plastic seal, he opened the box. He was delighted to find that only one of the thin wafers had broken in transit. Pulling the storage chest out from under his cot, he set up the candlesticks and candles on it. Glancing up, he heard the door open. Into the tiny room stepped Brother Michel.

Ian sat back on the lumpy cot, in total surprise. Brother Michel stood uncomfortably by the door. Ian let out a surprised chortle as he shook his head in disbelief. Looking down at his preparations, he felt uncomfortable and slightly embarrassed.

Chiding himself, he quickly recovered his composure and said, "You really surprised me. What are you doing here?"

Brother Michel's face had turned crimson. He managed to stutter out, "This is my room."

Ian smiled as he waved his hand. "Well then, come in. I guess we're going to be roommates."

The young priest tentatively stepped further in, seating himself on the narrow cot opposite, to stare across in fascination at Ian's preparations.

Ian glanced down at the candles, the wine and silver kiddush cup, and the matzos. Raising his eyebrows he said with a smile, "I'm Jewish. The Sabbath is about to start. I hope you don't mind if I light these."

Brother Michel's color had returned back to normal. In a friendly tone he replied, "No, of course not. Please, go right ahead." He paused and then added, "I only hope I am not disturbing you."

"Not at all," Ian quickly reassured him.

Brother Michel smiled, bobbing his head with his thin neck.

Ian dove his hands back into the large green duffel bag and withdrew a small box of matches. Carefully removing one of the slim wooden sticks, he struck the head with force on the side of the box. The small flame flared up. Cupping it carefully, Ian lit first one candle and then the other. Extinguishing the flame just before it touched his fingers, he closed his eyes and recited the blessing in a soft murmur. Opening his eyes, he smiled at Brother Michel who, despite himself, was surreptitiously staring at Ian in total fascination. Ian pursed his lips and nodded silently in the young priest's direction. Brother Michel nodded his head in return, smiling.

Picking up his siddur, Ian flipped to the proper page. Holding his place, he looked at Brother Michel. "I was just going to start my, ah, prayers...."

Brother Michel's face flushed slightly as he said, "Of course, of course. I just stopped by to pick up a book."

Not waiting for reply, he hurriedly rose up from his cot, and turning, lifted a book from a small shelf on the wall. Turning around, his face still somewhat flushed, he added, "I'll leave you to your prayers."

Nodding politely, he hastily retreated from the room, shutting the door silently behind him.

Orienting himself, Ian recited the Shmoneh Esre, the silent prayer. All Jews, since time immemorial, prayed facing in the direction of Jerusalem and the Temple mount. He began the evening prayer of Kabalat Shabbat, ushering in the Sabbath. He sang the stanzas with a melody that had been his father's favorite. He closed his eyes, a sudden wave of emotion sweeping over him. He had not felt so connected to his father in many years.

"What am I feeling?" he asked himself in a state of confusion.

Troubled, he rose up to finish the last stanza, tears forming at the corners of his eyes. There was a bitter-sweet taste in his mouth. He heard soft footsteps in the hallway, receding. He looked up for a moment. They did not repeat themselves.

Opening the wine, he filled the silver cup and recited the special kiddush for the Sabbath and the Passover holiday. He drank the sweet wine slowly. He hadn't realized how hungry he was. Stepping over to the sink, he used the now empty silver cup to wash his hands. Going back to the locker, he recited the blessing over the bread and broke one of the matzos. He munched on the dry flat bread for a while, working his jaw muscles. He washed it all down with some more of the wine. He could feel a warm glow as the alcohol entered his bloodstream. In the outer pouch of his knapsack he located the map of Rome he had purchased in New York, along with a guide book. Spreading the map out on the narrow cot, he flipped to the guidebook's index.

Gazing down the listings under the letter "J", he found the entry he was seeking. Turning to the appropriate page, he read a short paragraph on the Jewish ghetto and synagogue. He used the small map on the opposite page to trace a path on the larger map spread out on the bed. He sat up for a while, memorizing the street names and turns. The overhead light was on but Ian resisted the impulse to turn it off. When did I become so religious?, he thought.

The candles had dripped down until they went out. Clearing off the locker, he slid it back under the cot. He lay down on the coarse wool blanket, the lumpy pillow propped up behind his head.

He didn't remember drifting off. He was startled awake by the strong feeling of a presence near him. Snapping open his eyes, he stared directly into the wan visage of Brother Michel looming over his bed. The young priest's face quickly darted away.

A moment later, the room was plunged into darkness. Ian heard the rustling of cloth as Brother Michel prepared himself for bed. He heard him slip under the covers and the unmistakable creaking sound of the ancient narrow cot as the priest shifted his weight on it.

He decided he was too tired to get out of his clothes. Kicking off his shoes and socks, he pulled away the stiff covers and the blanket. It was warm in the room but he didn't bother to get up and open the small window. Tossing about, he shut his eyes and almost instantly drifted off to sleep.

# CHAPTER 9

Bare your holy arm, and hasten the End
for salvation—
Avenge Your servant's blood from the
wicked nation.
For the salvation is long delayed for us,
And there is no end to the days of evil,
Repel the Red One in the nethermost shadow...

Siddur

---

He awoke, glancing blearily at his watch. It was almost 7:20. The sun shone through the small narrow window with startling intensity. Rolling over, Ian toppled off the side of the narrow cot onto the hard bare floor. He landed with a heavy thud. Groaning, he painfully lifted himself back into a sitting position on the cot, ruefully rubbing his shoulder.

He hadn't slept well. The cot left much to be desired. Besides being so narrow, it was several inches too short for his tall frame. The mattress was lumpy and sat right on the battered wooden frame of the cot. I guess they never heard of a box spring, he thought as he arched his stiff back and twisted his hips from side to side. There was no sign of Brother Michel. His bed was neatly made up as if no one had ever slept on it.

He still hadn't unpacked. It took him some time to locate his khaki colored dress pants and one of his white long-sleeve dress shirts.

Going over to the small porcelain sink by the door, he splashed some cold water on his face and rubbed some on the back of his neck with his hand. He twisted his thick corded neck around to loosen the stiff muscles. Walking back to the cot, water dripped from his face. Squinting, he located his hand towel and dried himself off.

Dressing quickly, he rolled up his shirtsleeves as he spread the map out again and went over his route one last time.

From his tefilin bag he fished out his knitted yarmulke and tucked it inside his front pant pocket. He found his pass and tucked that in as well. On his way out, he cupped his hands together and took a quick drink of water. The water didn't taste too good this morning. Wiping his mouth, he shut the door behind him without a backwards glance.

Once outside, he realized he'd forgotten his sunglasses but decided not to go back for them. Squinting from the already strong glare of the sun, he made his way out of the Vatican without incident. In the impressive square in front, he strode quickly over to the massive obelisk. He paused to stare up at it, shading his eyes from the bright sunlight.

Looking down again, he peered closely at the

words inscribed on the granite base. He read: "Ecce Crux Domini; fugite parets adversae; vincit leo tribu Juda." It took him a few minutes to puzzle it out. As far as he could make out it translated roughly as, "Behold the Cross of the Lord; fly away all enemies; the Lion of Judah has Conquered."

He shook his head in wonder. Leaving the massive monument behind, he passed onto the Via della Conciliazione. He could feel his spirits lift. Fishing out the knit yarmulke, he affixed it to his head with the bobby pin that was attached to its center. He stretched out his legs for some serious walking.

Not too far beyond, the way opened and he soon found himself on the banks of a broad river. Off to the left loomed the massive round bulk of a brown castle. To the north, a bridge spanned the river further upstream. Going to the water's edge, he peered down at the dull-yellow muddy torrent surging by. Looking downstream, he saw several bridges spanning the water at intervals, until a bend in the river obscured his view.

Setting off to the right, he headed downstream on a broad avenue paralleling the river. Ian stopped to watch several people busily hustling about their own affairs. Several fashionable restaurants lined the avenue, with small open air cafes facing the river. They appeared to cater as much to the local denizens as to the tourists. Ian glanced down at his watch. It was almost 8:30 a.m. He had no idea when they began the morning services but he figured it had to be sometime between eight and nine.

Spurred on by that thought, he lengthened his stride. Passing a bend in the river, he looked further downstream. Squinting in the bright sunlight, he was just able to make out an island off in the hazy distance. That must be it, he thought confidently.

Starting into a slow jog, he passed by two more bridges on his left. Two young Italian men standing by a cafe whistled at him as he jogged by, and he paused to glance back, puzzled. They laughed and whistled again and then realization dawned on him.

He was wearing a yarmulke. They were jeering at him. Smiling to himself, he controlled his anger and gave them the middle finger. Not bothering to wait for a reply, he jogged off, ignoring the louder whistles that accompanied him out of earshot.

He left behind another bridge and now the island bulked out clearly before him. A large building dominated the island. Reaching the bridge, Ian quickly crossed over. Immediately he was struck by the quiet atmosphere that surrounded him. The large building seemed to be some kind of hospital and nearby stood a smaller structure, the ever present church.

Traversing the breadth of the narrow island in a few minutes, he crossed the bridge that led to the opposite bank. Here he noticed that the narrowness of the streets and the heights of the buildings seemed to produce an almost claustrophobic effect.

This must be the old Jewish ghetto, he thought sardonically. He turned to the right and felt a strange vertigo overcome him. Looking around, he thought, yes, that must be the way.

He shook his head in amazement. It was as if he had been here before. He seemed to recognize the buildings and the distinctive way the light struck the cobblestones beneath his feet. The sense of deja vu was almost overpowering. How can this be, he thought, I've never been here before. Bewildered but excited, he made his way to the big synagogue with the bronze roof.

He walked through the grounds to the impressive entrance and climbed the massive steps. He was sweating, but his breathing was even and normal. Opening one of the doors, he stepped into a two-storied vestibule. The ceiling rose high above. Crossing the polished marble floor, he passed under an open portico that led directly into the main sanctuary. Galleries lined the walls around the large prayer hall. Down the center, a long carpeted aisle led straight to the front. Two adjacent platforms stood there. One was a podium, the other, a soaring ark.

The service was already in progress. Scattered sparsely among the pews were the congregants, prayer shawls wrapped over their shoulders, singing a hymn. Ian smiled.

Here he was, thousands of miles from home, in the capitol of the Holy Roman Empire, and even here he could immediately recognize a song he had known since his youth. He noted that despite the large size of the edifice, or, maybe because of its great size, the assembled worshipers appeared to be very few.

He slipped between two rows of pews and took a seat in the back. Locating a siddur on a shelf built into the back of the pew in front of him, he found the correct page.

Following along, he recited the Hallel, or prayer of thanksgiving, as today was the first of the last two days of Passover. He watched as the cantor and another congregant removed a Torah scroll from the massive ark. Near the ark stood a short man with a gray beard, a large ornate chair behind him. Ian assumed he was the rabbi.

The cantor carried the Torah in a procession around the sanctuary, the rabbi and the other worshiper trailing behind him. The rest of the congregation lined the aisles, kissing the Torah's ornate brocade cover with the fringes of their prayer shawls as the procession passed by.

Atop the Torah scroll was one of the most magnificent silver crowns Ian had ever seen. All three men gave Ian a curious look as they swept past on their way up to the podium. He had noticed several other congregants glancing in his direction and then speaking amongst themselves.

He was a little amused by all the surreptitious attention he seemed to be getting. A large middle-aged man wrapped in a prayer shawl approached him, a broad smile on his face.

"Buon shabbat," he said.

"Good shabbos," Ian replied hesitantly, smiling back.

Recognition lit the fellow's face. Switching to English he said, "Welcome. You are an American, yes?"

"Yes, I am."

"Are you a Cohen or Levi?"

"No."

"Here," he said, handing Ian a small white card.

He took it. In Hebrew letters were spelled out a single word, "Shishi." Ian looked up, but the man was already on his way back to the podium where the cantor had already begun to read the portion of the week.

Of course Ian understood what the card meant. He was being given the honor of being called up for the sixth section of that week's reading.

He looked around for a Bible to follow along, but didn't see any near him. Keeping a mental count of the others who were called up before him, he knew when it was his turn. The man who had handed him the card gestured for him to come forward.

Ian rose up out of his pew and approached the ornate podium, acutely aware of the curious stares being cast in his direction. He mounted the steps to stand in front of the table on which the Torah scroll lay. The man handed him a prayer-shawl and Ian wrapped it round his shoulders. The man held out his hand and Ian tendered him the card.

"What is your name in Hebrew?" the man said.

"Yosef ben Yisrael," he said softly.

In a loud, booming voice the man called out in Hebrew, "Arise, Yosef ben Yisrael, the sixth portion."

The scroll was opened and the cantor pointed with a silver "hand" to the correct spot. Ian kissed the line on the parchment with the fringe of his prayer-shawl and in a clear strong voice he recited the blessing in flawless Hebrew. The cantor answered, "Amen" in a loud voice and began to read the next section. At the end of the section Ian kissed the Torah again, reciting the closing blessing.

It had been several years since he had been called up to the Torah. He was relieved that he had remembered the blessings so well.

The next person was called up and Ian slid over next to the large heavy-set man who had called him up. The man congratulated him with a warm handshake.

When it was time for Ian to step down, the man leaned forward and said, "Are you here alone?" a ready smile on his face.

"Yes," Ian said.

"Good, then you must come to my house for lunch."

Ian didn't know what to say. He stepped off the podium as the cantor began to read again. On his way back to his seat, several men rose up to shake his hand. Gratefully, he sank back into his seat in the back pew. The reading ended a few minutes later. The Torah was lifted and rolled back up in the traditional manner as everyone stood to honor it. They all responded in unison, "This is the

Torah that Moses placed before the Children of Israel, by the mouth of God, in the hand of Moses."

The Torah was covered and the crown placed on it as another reader stood up on the podium to recite the weekly reading from the Books of the Prophets. Ian leaned back in his seat. For the first time he noticed a Bible on the shelf in front of him. Someone must have left it for me, he thought. Glancing around, he noticed several men involved in a conversation, while others appeared to be following along with the reader. Picking it up, he leafed to the back section where the readings from the Prophets were to be found. The words the reader sang were from the book of Samuel.

They were the words of David, king of Israel. "And the earth quaked and roared, the foundations of the heaven shook; they trembled when His wrath flared. Smoke rose up in His nostrils, a devouring fire from His mouth, flaming coals burst forth from Him. He bent down the heavens and descended, with thick darkness beneath His feet."

Ian looked up a moment. By the time he looked back down, the reader was nearing the end. He followed along the final words. "You bring me forth from my enemies, and raise me above my adversaries, from a man of violence You rescue me. Therefore, I will thank You, God, among the nations, and sing to Your Name. He is a tower of salvation to His king, and does kindness to His anointed one, to David and to his descendants forever."

Ian sat staring at the text. Looking back up, his eyes were drawn forward, towards the massive ark. His gaze rose upward, where a replica of the two Tablets of the Law sat at its apex.

Light, streaming through the stained glass windows far above, struck two large replicas of the Menorah that stood atop two flanking columns. Higher up on the walls stood two more large replicas of the Menorah.

A shiver ran down his spine. He stared fixedly at them. Heaving a great sigh, he looked back down at the open text on the shelf before him. Closing the Bible, he picked up the siddur.

He watched the procession wend its way back to the ark, placing the holy scroll back in its resting place. The congregation recited the special holiday prayers and the rabbi rose up to speak. He spoke in Italian, and Ian was hard pressed to make sense of what he heard. The rabbi's voice echoed through the nearly empty prayer hall.

A young boy got up to finish the service, and the sparse crowd joined in weakly. The final stanza wound down and everyone got up to wish each other a good Sabbath and holiday, as the men began folding and putting away their prayer shawls.

Ian felt like slinking off. Getting up to leave, he caught sight of the man who had called him up to the Torah striding in his direction. Resisting the impulse to flee, he waited uncomfortably by his pew.

He wondered why he was so nervous. At the very least I'll get to eat something, he thought. He realized how hungry he was and how meager his own supplies back at his room were. The man came up to him, trailing a boy who looked to be fifteen or so. Stretching out his hand, he grasped Ian's hand, wringing it enthusiastically.

"Buon Shabbat, Buon Yom Tov," he cried. "My name is Baruch Fragnini. This," he said, tilting his head to the lad beside him, "is my son Eli."

"Nice to meet you," replied Ian. "My name is Ian Charosh. I'm a student. I'm here on a scholarship to complete my thesis for my doctorate."

Don Fragnini nodded politely as if this was the most natural thing in the world. "When did you arrive?"

"Just yesterday."

"Ah, good. Where are you staying?"

"Actually I'm doing my studies at the Vatican. They've been kind enough to provide me with a room."

Don Fragnini's eyebrows rose slightly. Ian noticed the subtle gesture. Don Fragnini recovered smoothly.

"Come then, you must be starving. We live close by and my wife loves to have company. I hope you have a good appetite," he boomed cheerily, clapping Ian solidly on the back.

Ian coughed from the blow. "I'll do my best."

"Good, then it's settled." Turning to his son he said quickly, "Eli, go run ahead and tell your mother to set another place at the table."

"Si, Papa," the boy said, hurrying off.

"Come," Don Fragnini said with a hearty laugh. "We go to make kiddush."

# CHAPTER 10

If not for my covenant day and night,
I would not have appointed the laws of
heaven and earth.

Jeremiah 33:25

---

He led Ian outside and through the narrow cobblestone streets. The way opened onto a small courtyard. On the far side, somewhat apart from the cramped houses surrounding it, was an imposing structure. The entrance had a pleasing semi-circular stoop. A profusion of pots and urns overflowing with green plants and colorful flowers were artfully arranged to either side. The building had several floors, the upper ones with balconies. These were covered by charming green and white striped canvas awnings. The doorway was inset, with a small cupola above to protect those beneath it from the elements. On the doorpost was affixed a large solid gold mezuzah in the shape of a roaring lion. A slight figure watched them from the shadows of an overhang across the square.

Ian was ushered inside. He smelled a delicious medley of aromas wafting through the house. Ian's mouth watered involuntarily as he swallowed into an empty stomach.

Following Don Fragnini through a wide hallway, they passed by a sweeping spiral staircase that led up to a balcony. Wide archways opened into adjacent chambers. Entering a large salon, Ian noted the tastefully decorated furnishings done up in a light neo-classical style. Everything had about it a feel of opulence coupled with impeccable taste and style. It was clear that the Fragninis lived in circumstances of elegance and comfort.

They glided through, into a high ceilinged room with two marble pillars at the opposite end. A great chandelier hung suspended in the center, directly over a plain stone slab set on ornately carved stone legs and feet. Ian guessed that it must weigh several tons. Over the table was spread a white lace cloth. The chairs were plushly upholstered in a stone-colored fabric to complement the table. At the head of the table, a large silver plate held several silver cups and a crystal and silver decanter formed in the shape of a swan.

Don Fragnini deep voice boomed out, "Come in for kiddush."

Into the room loped Eli.

"Where is your mother and sister?" Don Fragnini said.

"Mama is in the kitchen, with Marta. I don't know where Arianna is," Eli responded, ending with a shrug of his slender shoulders.

"Go get your mother and ask her where your sister is hiding too," Don Fragnini yelled with emphasis.

As Eli hurried out, he yelled to his retreating back, "Hurry, I'm starving, and tell your mother we have a hungry guest here also."

Don Fragnini smiled at Ian as he began pouring some dark red wine from the swan-shaped decanter into a large silver cup. Just then his wife, an extremely attractive woman in her early forties, entered the dining room, a small white apron tied neatly in front of her stylishly short dress. The dress was made of a cool off-white linen. Behind her stood a thickset girl in her late twenties, dressed in an earth-colored frock, a large heavy white apron covering her ample front. Eli slid by to stand next to his father.

"Where is Arianna?" Don Fragnini asked his wife.

"She's coming, she's coming," she replied.

"Hmm," grunted Don Fragnini. Turning to Ian, he said, "This is my lovely wife Gabrielle, and that is Marta who helps around the house, and of course you already met my son Eli. This," he said waving his hand, "is Ian. Scusi, what was your family name again?"

"Charosh."

Gabrielle Fragnini smiled gracefully as she said, "It's a pleasure to have you here as our guest."

"Thank you."

There was a moment of silence. Don Fragnini broke it with, "Well, as soon as our daughter decides to grace us with her presence, we'll make kiddush. I'm telling you Gabrielle, if she's not here in the next two minutes I'm starting without her."

As if on cue, a tall slender girl in her early twenties appeared through the open columns behind Ian.

She said, "Don't worry, Papa, I'm here. I was just out in the garden."

Ian turned to see who was speaking. He caught sight of her as she went round the table to stand by the seat directly opposite him. He stared at her and she returned his gaze as she tilted her head slightly, raising her delicate eyebrows in mild surprise.

He could see that she had gotten her looks from her mother. Silky honey-blonde hair flowed smooth as water to her jawline. Her arch features were regular and evenly spaced. Her glowing tan and sparkling blue eyes seemed to radiate with an almost palpable vibrancy. She wore a fitted pale gold linen pants suit that showed off her slim tanned figure to advantage.

Don Fragnini paused, apparently noticing the look that passed between them.

Chuckling, he addressed Ian. "Yes, this is my daughter Arianna. Be cautious. She has a very peculiar sense of humor and she hates to lose."

"Oh, Papa. What a terrible thing to say." She laughed, pouting her lower lip in mock displeasure.

Gabrielle spoke. "I thought you were in a hurry to eat! Make kiddush before all the food dries out."

Don Fragnini waved his hands in the air, picking up the silver cup filled with wine. In a deep baritone he recited the Sabbath kiddush with a sephardic pronunciation. He drank from the cup and then poured out some of the wine into the other cups on the tray. These were passed out, and as Ian downed his, he could actually feel the cool liquid travel down his parched throat to rest as a warm glow in the pit of his stomach.

"Come," Don Fragnini said, waving his arms about. "Let's go wash."

Don Fragnini herded Ian along with the rest of the family into the kitchen. Ian waited his turn in line. Turning to hand the silver laver to the person behind him, his hand brushed across Arianna's fingers. Ian felt his face flush. She lowered her eyes and then raised them quickly, a faint smile quivering on her full lips.

"Thank you," she said softly.

"You're welcome," he mumbled, not making eye contact as he retreated back to the dining room.

Ian sat down in the seat that had been set for him to the right of Don Fragnini. Arianna took hers directly opposite him. Sitting down, she smiled at him and he found himself unable to avoid smiling back.

Don Fragnini recited the blessing over the matzos and broke them in several pieces onto a large silver platter. He dashed some coarse salt on them and then passed the platter to Ian first. Ian bit into his piece and thought he had never tasted anything better. As he munched, Marta filled the table with some of the most delicious smelling dishes Ian had ever smelled. He waited as the heavy silver serving trays were passed around, placing healthy portions from each one onto his own plate.

Don Fragnini cried, "Eat, eat," as he dug in himself.

Ian tried to pace himself, but five minutes later he found to his chagrin an empty china plate staring up at him. Looking up, he caught Arianna looking his way. She quickly stared down in mock concentration at her plate, a ghost of a smile playing across her lips. Ian grinned as Marta handed him another dish.

Don Fragnini turned to him. "So tell me. What are you doing in el Vaticano?"

"Well, actually not too much so far," he answered as he hastily swallowed another mouthful. "I just arrived. I plan to use the Vatican library to help me complete my thesis."

"Ahh, so you are here for how long?"

"The scholarship is for six months. I hope to finish my work by then, but who knows?" he finished with a shrug of his shoulders.

Don Fragnini waved his hands in the air as he addressed Ian.

"A church is not a place for a Jewish boy to spend shabbat. And definitely not the place to be on Passover. I insist that you spend the rest of the holiday here with us."

Ian tried to decline, but he was cut off by Don Fragnini's wife, Gabrielle.

"No, really, you must stay. We have plenty of room and Marta always has a guest room ready. It's no bother at all and we would all be sad if you were to say no."

Ian was at a loss for words. He stammered out, "It's really very kind of you. Thank you."

"Good. Then it's settled," Don Fragnini huffed contentedly.

Lifting a bottle of wine from the table, he poured a generous amount into Ian's glass.

Raising his own he boomed, "L'Chayim," and drank deeply.

Everyone at the table echoed his words and Ian tilted his glass up, feeling the sweet liquid glide down his throat. He leaned back to rest a moment, his stomach full, his head spinning slightly from the wine.

Don Fragnini said, "So where in America are you from?"

"New York."

"Wonderful. I don't remember if you told me what it is you are studying."

Ian tried to control his spinning head as he replied, "Actually I don't think I did. I'm doing my doctoral thesis in philosophy. To be more specific, my thesis is on theodicy: reconciling God and the existence of Evil."

Don Fragnini was visibly impressed. "I studied philosophia when I was younger also at the University. Of course I ended up in my father's business, but I remember those days well. Yes, those were good times." Pausing, he looked towards his beautiful wife and said, "Remember, Gabrielle?"

Gabrielle smiled back gently as she said, "How could I forget?"

"Papa, may I leave the table?" Eli whined, cutting in on the conversation as he squirmed uncomfortably in his chair.

Don Fragnini turned to face his son, a disapproving look on his broad features. "Where do you think you are going? We have a guest at the table and you have not recited the Grace after the Meal yet. And by the way, I haven't even heard you sing a single song."

"Okay. So let's finish. I promised my friends I would meet them at Rami's house," Eli said.

"It's not polite to talk so in front of our guest. Now sit quietly and listen. Don't worry. Your friends will still be there when we finish."

Eli slumped back into his seat. Gabrielle shot Eli a reproving look and then turned to Ian.

"Have you seen any of our city since you arrived?"

Ian's head had finally begun to quiet down. "Not too much. I was picked up at the airport and taken straight to the Vatican City. But I did see some beautiful buildings on my way to the synagogue this morning."

Gabrielle turned to Arianna who was playing with the food on her plate.

"Why don't you show our guest around this afternoon?"

Arianna looked up. Her lips curled at the corners of her mouth into an impish grin as she said, "Sure, why not? I will take him on a grand tour, or at least until our feet get tired."

Gabrielle turned to Ian. "Arianna is studying

architecture at the University. She is probably the best guide you could ask for."

"And the most beautiful, I'm sure," Ian replied.

"Well put," cried Don Fragnini, downing another glass of wine. Gabrielle acknowledged his compliment with a slight nod of her head. Arianna's eyes flashed as Eli let out a raucous laugh.

"What is so funny?" she snapped at him in Italian.

"Nothing, nothing," he chortled back.

"Please, it's not nice to speak in Italian when our guest doesn't understand," Don Fragnini scolded. "Maybe you two could help Ian to learn our language. That would be something nice, instead of your Mama and I having to hear the two of you constantly bickering."

"Yes, Papa," they answered.

"Good, now Eli, start a song for us."

Eli began to sing a popular Hebrew song. Ian recognized the words, but the tune was new to him. He listened carefully and joined in tentatively, along with Don Fragnini who was already booming away in a deep baritone. The chorus came around again and Ian raised his voice more confidently. Don Fragnini banged the table in syncopation to the beat. The song ended on a high note.

Don Fragnini said, "I see you have an ear for music. Do you play an instrument?"

"No," said Ian. "I always wanted to, but I never seemed to have the time. In my early years I spent a great deal of my spare time studying the martial arts and so I neglected other areas that I might have gone into."

Eli perked up, leaning forward excitedly. "Do you mean you're a karate man? Can you show me how to, you know," he said, raising his right hand in a karate chop, his eyes shining brightly.

Ian laughed easily. "No, that's only in the movies. The control and discipline are what's important, not the fighting. I'd be happy to teach you some of the basics, if you're interested."

Eli turned to his father. "Papa, please. Can I?"

Don Fragnini smiled. "I'm sure our guest is just being polite. He has much work to do, and he can't be spending his time coming here to teach you."

Turning to Ian he said, "Thank you for offering to teach the boy, but it's not necessary."

Ian hesitated. Then shrugging he replied, "Actually I wouldn't mind at all. I don't have any set schedule, and I'd enjoy getting out every so often."

Don Fragnini turned to his wife. "Well what do you think?"

Gabrielle smiled. "I don't see why not. But you," shaking her finger at Eli, "better not let your studies suffer."

"Yes, Mama. Don't worry. I am doing well in all my classes. It won't be a problem at all. I promise."

"Fine. Then it's settled," Don Fragnini said, clapping his thick hands together. "You have a new student, Ian. If he gives you any trouble, you tell me."

Ian laughed again. "I'm sure he'll be no trouble at all."

Don Fragnini honored Ian by having him lead the Grace after the Meal. Afterwards, as Marta was clearing the table, the family drifted away from the dining room. Eli, with a sly wink to Ian, ran out to his friend's house. Don Fragnini let out a great yawn and then tried to cover it up after catching a look from Gabrielle.

"You must excuse me," he said. "This is my nap time, and so I must leave you in the capable hands of my wife and daughter."

"Thank you. Enjoy your rest."

"Chag Sameyach," Don Fragnini called down from where he was ascending the wide marble steps to the second floor bedrooms.

Gabrielle turned to Arianna. "I'm going into the garden to read. Why don't you take Ian over to the Piazza Mattei?"

"What do you say?" Arianna said.

"Sounds good to me," he grinned back, trying to sound relaxed. The truth was, his heart was beating like a trip hammer and he felt a little too giddy to blame it on the wine he had consumed throughout the lavish meal.

Arianna slipped her arm in an easy manner around his and led him to the front entrance. Turning back, she called over her shoulder, "Good-bye, Mama," as she led him out the door.

"Just make sure you're back before the evening services," her mother called, but they were already out the door before she finished.

Arianna led him at a brisk pace on the shady side of the winding narrow streets of the Jewish ghetto. The other side of the street was bathed in dazzling sunlight, and the sharp contrast was painful to Ian's eyes. Most of his attention though, was focused on the delightful young woman walking beside him, arm in arm. He could feel her soft skin pressing against his flesh and he felt both uncomfortable and excited by the close proximity. Somehow divining some of his feelings, Arianna slowed her pace and then stopped, letting go of his arm.

"You don't have to hold my arm if you don't want to," she said, smiling coyly.

"No, I don't mind at all," he said.

"Good," she said, slipping her hand into his. "It's just that it's faster to take you like this."

They resumed their pace. She led him around several quick turns, and Ian realized that should she leave him, he would be totally lost. A moment later the narrow way led out onto a fair-sized open space, the Piazza Mattei. A beautiful fountain stood a little bit off its center, and it was there that Arianna led him.

"Isn't it lovely?" she said, sitting down on a low bench in front of the fountain.

"Yes, it is," he replied, sitting down next to her.

"This is called the Fontana delle Tartarughe. In English that means, the Fountain of the Turtles, and you can see why," she said, pointing to the turtle statues. Several turtle statues "drank" the water sprayed forth from the mouth's of four bronze dolphins held by four bronze youths.

"This is my favorite fountain in all of Rome," she said, as a slight breeze wafted a cool spray across their faces. She leaned her vibrant body close to his and sighed. "Since I was a child I've always enjoyed coming here. It's almost as if a certain magic hangs over this place, drawing me to it," she murmured as she stared at the falling water.

They sat there for a while, lulled by the musical sound of the water splashing into the marble shells of the fountain. Then, prompted by some impulse, Arianna clasped Ian's hand in hers and leaping from the bench, she broke the spell.

"Come. I want to show you something else," she said, excitement rippling through her words.

She led him across the piazza and down several steps to a narrow lane. By a doorway, she stopped. Stepping through, they entered a far older courtyard. This was filled with all manner of sculptures both large and small. Arianna led him around, giving him short descriptions of each piece.

"I see you've been here before," he said with a grin, in the middle of one of her longer explanations.

"Yes, many times," she called back, playfully darting behind a large statue.

"Am I boring you?" she said, her head popping momentarily into view.

"No. Not at all," he answered, entranced by her antics.

They played a game of hide and seek, alone amongst the forest of stone. She was remarkably quick and twice he thought he had her, only to have her slip from his grasp at the last instant. Both felt the challenge as the game subtly changed its nature, becoming something else.

He lunged at her again, but she managed to elude him. He sighted a bit of bare sun-tanned shoulder and golden hair peeking out from behind a large stone block.

Creeping up silently, he inched his way around the other side. Leaping forward, he caught her in his powerful arms. They laughed, her silky golden hair spilling forward across her face. He instinctively reached down to brush it away as she lifted her head up. For a moment their faces came together.

He hesitated, but then she reached up with her hand to brush his cheek and he couldn't resist any longer. Bending his head down, he kissed her warm full lips. Flustered, Arianna pushed him away. Her chest heaved. Straightening her sleeveless blouse where it had slipped down, she tossed back her head and took a deep breath. A little laugh bubbled past her lips.

She said brightly, "Come, there's more I want to show you."

Ian was confused, but as she pressed her hand against his, he allowed her to lead him back out onto the narrow street.

As they strolled, he turned to say, "I didn't mean to, you know…"

She smiled, nodding silently.

He stopped and said, "I can't tell you how nice it is to come to a strange place where I know absolutely no one, and have your family take me in like I was some long-lost relative. Anyway, what I'm trying to say is," looking into her fresh young face, "that I really like you and I hope I didn't offend you, you know, by what happened back there."

Arianna smiled gently, and then arched her eyebrows.

"Don't worry," she said. "I didn't mind at all. Now enough about that. You are slowing us down," she said in mock seriousness. "It's a long way to where I want to take you and I'm supposed to have you back before evening services. So let's go!"

"Okay," he laughed, shaking his head. They picked up the pace. Along the way she pointed out different sights and told him their names.

"Where are you taking us?"

"You'll see," she said.

After traversing a bit more of the city they turned a corner to stand in front of a wide open area. It was dominated by a large number of imposing ruins set among some greenery.

"This is the Palatine," she said. "What do you think?"

"It's beautiful," Ian murmured, drinking it all in.

They spent the next few hours roaming with the other visitors around the extensive ruins. Ian marveled at the massive columns and statues. They followed the Via Sacra past the many temples and the great arched vaults of the Basilica of Maxentius. Beyond its ruins, on a small spur, stood a large arch. Ian was drawn inexorably to it. Slowly, they walked up to it.

Here it was far quieter, away from the crowds. Deep inside, he knew what it was even before he saw the deeply carved relief on its side. They walked right up to the massive triumphal arch. The late afternoon sunlight, glancing off the ancient stone, highlighted the surface of the deeply cut figures that were shaded by the overhang above. Ian and Arianna stood there, staring up at the scene before them.

She said softly, "This is the Arch of Titus."

Words came up from his throat, strained and husky. "Yes, I know."

Arianna moved close to him, putting her arm around his waist. She leaned against him.

"Come," she said softly, tugging at his arm. He allowed her to lead him away. They stood at the edge of the spur, looking down at the spectacular view spread out below. Ian could make out the massive Coliseum far away.

He was so quiet that Arianna said, "Are you alright?"

He stared down silently for a long while. Finally he said, "Yeah, I'm fine. I just wasn't expecting to see it."

"Why does it bother you so much?" she said, pressing her warm body against him.

"I don't know."

# CHAPTER 11

...and behold, a great and awesome darkness
fell upon him. And He said to Avram: Know
clearly that your seed shall be a stranger in a land
not their own...

Genesis 15: 12-13

Fell upon him... this is the exile of Babylon,
great... this is the exile of Persia,
darkness... this is the exile of Greece,
awesome... this is the exile of Rome.

Genesis Rabbah 44:17

---

"What do you have to report?"

Brother Michel cleared his throat. "Your Eminence, the scholarship student is Jewish. He is collecting material for his thesis. It is on the subject of theodicy."

The Undersecretary's head snapped up. A Jew, he thought. Aloud he said, "Have you noticed any unusual activities?"

"Yes, your Eminence."

"Well spit it out."

Swallowing hard, Brother Michel stuttered, "He practices certain religious rituals which I have never seen before."

"Such as?"

"He performed sacramental rituals of some kind on Friday evening and also I saw him wrap leather straps with strange black boxes on his arm and head one morning before reciting his prayers in Hebrew."

"I see…"the Undersecretary replied, losing interest.

Brother Michel stood uncomfortably in front of the massive desk, studiously looking down at the strip of marble at his feet.

Undersecretary Maglione shuffled some papers, carefully transferring a set of papers from one neat pile to the next. Picking up a sheet from a third pile he asked, "Well?"

Brother Michel snapped up his head. "There was one more thing."

"What?"

"This past Saturday morning I observed him leaving el Vaticano in a great hurry and he did not return for two whole days."

Undersecretary Maglione's eyes narrowed as the sheet he'd been looking at dropped haphazardly to the desk top. Brother Michel now had his full attention.

"Do you know where he went?"

"Yes. I started to follow him but I lost him in the crowds in the square. I didn't know what to do so I went back to my room. Luckily he had left a guide book open to the page that described the Jewish ghetto, and the Jewish synagogue. I studied a map he had left behind and walked to the synagogue."

Undersecretary Maglione let out a grunt of approval. He uttered one word. "Continue."

"I waited behind a tree near the entrance for nearly two hours. Finally the worshippers began to come out. He came out near the end, but he was not alone. I almost missed him."

Undersecretary Maglione snapped, "Just give your report. Truly, if you were not my sister's son I would have sent you long ago to some missionary in the jungle."

Brother Michel visibly cringed. Summoning what remaining courage he had left, he replied in a quavering voice, "Yes, Uncle."

Undersecretary Maglione scowled, waving his hand for him to continue.

"He came out with a heavy-set man and a young boy. I followed behind, at a safe distance. They led me through the old ghetto. At the end of a small open court was a large house. The big man led him up the stairs and inside. I waited a long time, but no one came out. I didn't know what to do. I decided to take a chance, so I ran across to get a closer look. I don't believe anyone saw me. I stopped by the bottom of the steps. I noticed that on the right doorpost hung a large gold lion. I decided to leave before someone should notice me. He came back two days later and continues his research in the library. That is all."

Undersecretary Maglione sat back, his eyes near slits. Startled, he thought, a gold lion. Could it really be them, after all these years?

Aloud he said, "Fine. Watch him carefully. Report to me as usual."

Brother Michel turned to leave. He was brought up short as the Undersecretary barked, "Oh, and never call me Uncle again, do you understand?"

Brother Michel turned back, inclining his head to the ground. "Yes, your Eminence."

Gratefully, he closed the heavy door behind him. He nodded politely to the older priest seated by a small desk situated a few feet from the door. The older priest nodded back silently, continuing to watch Brother Michel's retreating back until it disappeared down a bend of the long corridor.

Back in his office, the Undersecretary sat in his chair, fingers laced together in front of him, tapping absent-mindedly on his upper lip. Could it be, he wondered, pursing his lips. After all these years. Shaking his head, his thoughts wandered back to an earlier time.

He had been only twenty at the time. Life then had seemed so filled with endless possibilities. He smiled bitterly, remembering.

He'd been attending the University of Rome only a few weeks when he'd finally gotten up the courage to go over and talk to her. He'd noticed her the very first day of classes. She'd been sitting right in the first row. Coming in late, he apologized to the professor, passing right by her seat. He'd found an empty seat three chairs away where he could easily look at her from the side.

I had no idea what the professor discussed that first lecture, he thought, the bile rising in his stomach. He'd been too busy stealing glances every few seconds at her. That same day he found out her name by asking one of the other students. He repeated it now to himself.

"Gabrielle."

He sighed, remembering bitterly the magic that name had once held for him. He sneered at himself, surprised by the poignancy of his longing even now. The memories flooded back even stronger.

What an utter fool I was, he thought. He'd gone over to her a week later. He hadn't been able to stop himself. She'd been sitting, not twenty feet away, beneath the shade of an apple tree. Building up his courage, he'd walked straight up to her and blurted, "Hello. What did you think of the lecture?" his face flushing a bright red.

She'd laughed sweetly and he remembered how he thought he'd never heard such musical sounds. Smiling up at him she replied, "I found it quite interesting."

Nodding, he had introduced himself.

"I am Alberto Maglione."

She acknowledged the introduction with a slight nod of her head. "My name is Gabrielle Levi."

He remembered his initial surprise. Of course, he thought with pride, he had not let her see it.

Everyone knew of the famous Levi family. They were a rich and powerful merchant family of Jews who had lived in Rome for centuries. Several centuries back, they had even been advisors to some Popes. During the Second World War they had been vacationing in the Swiss Alps when Hitler had signed his infamous treaty with Il Duce. Remaining in Switzerland for the duration of the war, they had still managed to maintain their far-flung business holdings through trusted intermediaries. Rumor had it that they were now more wealthy than ever.

He could not pretend to be other than what he was: second son to a moderately successful pastry baker on a side street of Rome.

Still, he had asked her if he could sit down. To his absolute amazement, she had said yes. What followed, was the most enchanted afternoon of his life. They had discussed many things: politics, the theater, even religion. By the time she had excused herself, she was late for a class, he was floating in another realm. As he watched her leave, her shining hair glistening in the early autumn air, he realized in amazement that he had fallen hopelessly in love.

There was a knock at the door. Blinking, Maglione said, "Enter."

# CHAPTER 12

When Jacob saw the power of Esau (to come) he became fearful, saying "Who can stand up against all of this?"

To what may this be compared? To camels coming [towards a smithy] loaded down with flax. The smith saw them coming and said, "Where will all this flax fit?" A clever fellow was standing there and said, "Why worry? One spark from your hammer will get rid of it all!"

Here too—Jacob saw Esau and all his power and was frightened, and the Holy One said to him, "Your spark will burn it all up—and that spark is Joseph."

Tanchuma Vayeshev 1

There was a tap on Ian's shoulder. Startled, he twisted around to stare up at the pale face of the young priest.

Brother Michel smiled as he said, "I hope I didn't disturb you?"

"No, not at all," Ian said, with a laugh. Brother Michel darted his head around nervously to see if anyone had noticed Ian's outburst.

Realizing that he had been a bit loud, Ian whispered, "Sorry. You surprised me."

Brother Michel bobbed his head several times, smiling broadly.

He hesitated, and then slowly choosing his words he uttered softly, "I was wondering if you needed any help?"

Smiling back, Ian responded, "For the moment, no. I'm doing pretty well on my own since I picked up this dictionary," he said, lifting one of the thick books in front of him.

Brother Michel seemed visibly disappointed.

Ian hurriedly remarked, "Don't worry. I'm sure I'll be pestering you soon enough. In fact you'll probably want to get rid of me before long," he whispered.

Brother Michel, a shocked look on his face, replied, "Why would I want to do that?"

Ian realized that Brother Michel had totally misunderstood him. Grinning he said, "I was joking. I would be happy to have your assistance."

Brother Michel took a seat. "How is your thesis work coming along?"

"Quite well…"

Almost an hour later they were still discussing Ian's work. Brother Michel looked up a moment. Staring at them, not ten feet away, stood the librarian.

Jumping out of the chair, Brother Michel said, "I'm sorry, but I must be getting back to my duties. If you do need any help, look for me in the Archives department."

Ian rose out of his chair and shook the soft hand of the priest.

"Sure," he responded. "Thanks so much. I really enjoyed our talk. I'm sure I'll be taking you up soon on your kind offer. I'll see you later, right?" he finished with a friendly smile.

Brother Michel nodded again, politely turning away. He headed past the librarian, his eyes to the floor, and moved out of Ian's view. The coarse fabric of his simple robes made a distinctive rustling sound which quickly faded. The librarian moved on, disappearing between two tall bookshelves. Ian shrugged, sitting back down at the table. In front of him were laid out all his papers.

He had been making good progress toward completing a difficult segment of his thesis. He sat for a moment, staring vacantly at the work spread out on the table. Then he realized, I forgot to ask him where the archive department is.

On a sudden impulse he stood up, stretching his long frame. Looking down, he shrugged, deciding to leave his stuff right where it was. He headed eagerly past several aisles of tall bookshelves. He came to the far wall.

There, behind a high desk, sat a tall thin priest dressed in severe black, perched on an equally narrow stool. This was the librarian. Ian suppressed a rueful grin as he came up to the desk. He'd been having some difficulty with the librarian from the very first moment they'd met.

The librarian was a man of indeterminate age, though the deep lines on his face and the narrow neck that rose above his stiff collar spoke of advanced years. He wore the same dour expression Ian had come to expect, as if the librarian thought he was about to insult him in some egregious fashion.

Wincing, Ian asked in a politely hushed voice, "Bon giorno. Vorrei lo so dov`e` umm… archives ?"

He waited, hoping that he hadn't totally mutilated what he'd wanted to say. The librarian's eyes bore into him like a dentist's drill.

"Che cosa?" he uttered in a monotone.

Then, divining Ian's question, he answered in a tone that Ian suspected might hold a note of grim satisfaction, "No permiso."

Shifting his body ever so subtly, the librarian looked away. In his mind Ian had ceased to exist.

Ian stood there, staring at him. The librarian paid him no heed, now seemingly engrossed with some papers in front of him. Ian considered for a moment trying to get the librarian's attention again.

What's the use, he thought. From the moment he had presented his pass and haltingly explained what he was doing in the library, the librarian had been a constant thorn in his side. He'd refused to help him, and at times even seemed to delight in finding ways to impede his work. Just two days ago, he had refused to let Ian use the only Xerox machine in the library. It was located in a small room directly behind the librarian's desk. Ian had offered to pay, but the librarian had insisted that the machine was for staff use only. Because of the strict rule that none of the books or manuscripts could be taken outside the library, Ian had been reduced to copying by hand any pertinent source material. His fingers were constantly stiff from all the copying he'd been forced to do.

Throwing his hands up in an uncharacteristic display of frustration, Ian stalked away, rolling the foreign words around in his mind. He'd been trying to pick up as much Italian as he could these past few weeks. He'd seen Arianna twice more and she had been coaching him a little. She had an apartment that she shared with another girl near the university, and he'd met her both times at trendy restaurants in the heart of the city.

"No permiso," he muttered under his breath, repeating the librarian's words.

Restless and irritated, Ian wandered aimlessly down one of the halls leading from the library. He was too upset to go right back to his work.

Passing a young priest coming the other way, on a whim he asked in broken Italian, "Per favore, dove` il eh…archives?"

The young priest stopped. "Archeota?" he said, puzzled.

"Si," Ian said eagerly, a bright smile lighting his face.

Pointing behind him the priest answered, "Avanti dritto, a sinistra."

"Grazie," Ian said.

The priest continued on.

"I think he said, straight ahead and then a left," he muttered to himself. Following the directions, Ian continued on, turning left at the first tall archway he came upon. This led down an extremely long flight of steps to a long low corridor. At several doors along the way he paused to test the handles. All the doors were locked. Looking around, he got the unmistakable feeling that this was an area that was not much used.

Discouraged, and about to head back, he stopped in his tracks as a door much further down opened up, and out popped Brother Michel. Not noticing Ian, he headed off down the hall in the opposite direction, immediately disappearing behind another door.

Caught by surprise, Ian didn't even have a chance to call out to him. Grinning to himself, he strode down the long dimly lit corridor to stop in front of the door Brother Michel had just entered. He raised his hand to knock. He hesitated.

Letting his hand fall to his side, he turned around, retracing his footsteps. He stopped, to stand in front of a plain wood door. This was the door he'd seen Brother Michel exit. Staring straight ahead, he mouthed the word, "Archeota." The small letters had been painted at eye level in aged gold leaf on the plain surface of the door. He hesitated, and then chiding himself, he lifted his hand and knocked, waiting.

There was no response. He reached forward and knocked a bit louder. Glancing down the empty hallway in both directions, he tried the large brass handle. To his surprise, it turned easily. Tentatively, he opened the door and stepped inside. Letting go, it shut quickly behind him with a heavy whoosh, followed by a strange sucking sound. Had he not stepped forward quickly, it would surely have whacked him in the back.

He stood in a dimly lit room with a very low ceiling. Its dimensions were difficult for him to gauge. A low humming sound vibrated through the air. He surmised that the sound might be coming from vents hidden somewhere in the huge room, though where they were located he hadn't a clue. It appeared that he was in a controlled environment. In long rows stood immaculate stainless-steel shelves, spaced apart at regular intervals. They stretched from floor to ceiling. They were neatly packed with a great variety of contents, each one individually enclosed in some kind of clear plastic pouch. The rows stretched away as far as the eye could see.

Ian stood there, staring about in amazement. A wild pulse of excitement quickened his heart as he thought, My God, look at all the stuff they're hoarding here.

In a small alcove off to the side, Ian noticed several polished steel tables and chairs. On a separate small stainless steel desk rested the familiar sight of a large computer terminal. He looked around. It appeared that he was alone.

In a loud voice he called out, "Hello. Anybody here?" and waited for a response. The only sound that greeted his ears was the steady low throb of the vents.

He sauntered over to the computer terminal. Glancing down at the screen, he was delighted to see that it was already on.

Staring down at the terminal, he cursed under his breath. The words on the screen were in Latin and he'd left his Latin/English dictionary in the library. Well, he thought, it's too late to go back for it now.

Locating the search button, he tapped a key. He waited impatiently for the machine to stop whirring and then typed in slowly the word, "Menorah."

"Now why did I type that," he said aloud to himself.

On the top of the screen the Latin words for "no response" popped up. Ian furrowed his brow. His palms were clammy. He realized that it would be very awkward if someone were to return and find him messing with the archives computer.

He was about to press the return button, when, on a sudden impulse, he typed in the word, "candelabrum."

He stared at the word on the screen. Shaking his head in a self-mocking manner, he was about to press the delete key when the computer started to whir and onto the screen popped several entries.

Surprised, he frantically patted down his pockets for a pen or pencil. Coming up empty-handed, he searched the desk-top. There, in a metal tray, lay several thin black pens. Each had the gold-colored crest of the Vatican imprinted on it. Grabbing one, he scribbled the three reference numbers on the screen onto the palm of his left hand. Reaching down, he quickly tapped the delete button. The original screen popped back up.

Staring at the numbers scrawled in black ink on the palm of his hand, he considered. Two of the long number sequences were nearly identical, and he reasoned, they must be quite near each other. The third had a totally different sequence. He glanced down at his watch. How long have I been here, he wondered. Taking note of the time, he mentally gave himself five more minutes.

Making a snap decision, he headed toward the nearest row of shelves. Raking his eyes across the bold black number sequences on the plaque affixed to the front of the first aisle, he made a right and looked at the numbers on the front of the next aisle.

He was heading the wrong way. Pivoting, he reversed direction and four aisles down found the one he was looking for. Rushing down it, his eyes quickly scanned the number sequences printed on small white labels attached to the front of each pouch. He slowed as he came up close to the first number.

Tracing the labels on this shelf carefully, he came upon the first sequence. He glanced down for an instant at his sweating palm to make sure, and then tremulously reached for the clear vinyl pouch sitting on the shelf directly in front of him. His fingers closed around the clear plastic, and for a brief moment he stopped to consider what he was doing.

I'll just look at it and put it right back, he rationalized. He started to zip it open, when his ears, alert to any change, picked up a soft whooshing sound. Someone had opened the door.

He froze.

"Damn."

He reached over silently to place the pouch back in its spot on the shelf. Somehow, he couldn't bring himself to do it. He had to see what was in that pouch.

Tucking it gently inside his shirt, he rose up on the balls of his feet and crept forward. Utilizing every shadow, he floated forward like a wraith. Peering around the corner of the aisle, he saw a priest standing by the computer terminal, his back to Ian. Ian recognized him immediately. It was Brother Michel.

I don't think this is the right time to ask him for help, he thought, a smile forming at the corners of his mouth. He flattened his body to present the smallest profile, and mentally set his mind and body to wait.

Brother Michel sat down at the terminal and, after a brief pause, began to type. He stopped to drink from a tall cup he had brought back with him before placing it down on the desk. The screen was tilted away from Ian's direct line of sight and, besides, it was too far away for him to make out the tiny characters written on it. Brother Michel leaned back against the steel chair. Straightening up, he resumed his typing.

Half an hour later, he was still hard at it. Ian glanced at his watch. The librarian might be getting suspicious by now, he realized. He'd never left his papers unattended in the library for such a long period of time.

Maybe the librarian would put two and two together and come looking for him in the archive department, he thought, anxiety beginning to gnaw at his belly. Peering back to where Brother Michel sat by the small desk busily typing away, Ian watched him finish off his drink.

Does this guy ever go to the bathroom, he wondered. Ten long minutes passed. Ian willed himself to remain calm, shifting his body ever so slightly to prevent his muscles from cramping.

Brother Michel sighed, getting up from the small desk. Glancing back at the screen for a moment he hesitated, almost sitting back down again. Ian groaned inside. Obviously satisfied with his progress, Brother Michel turned away and walked to the door. The door opened and closed with a double whoosh, followed by that same strange sucking sound.

To Ian, it was the most wonderful sound he had ever heard. Cat-like, he loped forward and a few seconds later stood by the door. Carefully easing it open, he slipped out, praying that no one was about. Snapping his head both ways, he was relieved to find the hall empty. He quickly headed back the way he'd come.

He retraced his way back to the main library without incident. Shifting the pouch further down inside his shirt, he strolled casually towards the table where all his papers lay. Pleased to find that they had not been disturbed, he gathered up his things and the books he had taken out that day. He stacked the texts he had been studying into a neat pile and carried them around to the librarian's desk.

The space behind it was empty. Placing the books down gently, he craned his neck. Out from the back room glided the librarian, like some tall black heron whose feathers had been ruffled.

He stared intently at Ian, a dour expression on his face. He asked, "Dov`e` un francobollo?"

Ian fished out of his front jeans pocket a small crumpled slip of paper. Smiling apologetically, he smoothed it out before placing it down on the high countertop. The librarian handled it fastidiously, as if it might harbor some horribly infectious disease. He stamped it and turning to the side, gingerly placed it in a small cubbyhole behind him. Ian had not waited. He walked away slowly, feeling the librarian's eyes boring into his shoulder blades.

At each step he expected to hear the librarian yell out, "Stop."

Nothing happened. Exiting through a set of doors, he crossed the street, strolling casually through a garden area behind the library. His heart hammering in his ribcage, he paused for a moment to breath in the fragrant air of the garden. He sighed, basking in the warmth of the brilliant sunlight. Coming from the musty air of the library, his lungs expanded as his heart rate slowly returned to normal. Setting off at a brisk pace, he headed for his favorite spot.

He'd found it the very first week while exploring the extensive grounds that comprised the Vatican City. Of course, he realized, he still hadn't seen a tenth of all there was here to see. Wending his way through the foliage that surrounded the building which housed the Pontifical Academy of Sciences, he passed by two delightful fountains that were situated by its front face. Today he was far too busy to stop and admire them. He hung a right before the large Fountain of the Aquilone, and set off into a wooded area intersected by many paths.

Passing another smaller fountain, he trod down a

path shaded by trees on either side. He felt a sudden hunger pang in his stomach but ignored it.

He came upon a series of shallow steps laid out next to a fountain. It had been built to flow in a delightful series of small waterfalls. He'd come here several times already to sit on the wide sun-drenched steps. He would close his eyes and listen peacefully to the sound of the water as it cascaded down the little falls.

Today he was more alert. Scanning the area in all directions, he saw only the lush green foliage that surrounded him. No one else seemed to be about. He'd come here instead of going back to his room. He'd decided not to let Brother Michel know what he had done. He seemed like such a nice fellow, but back in the vast archive room he'd already made up his mind, at least for the present, to tell no one.

Seating himself down on one of the sun-warmed steps, he twisted around one last time to make sure no one was coming. Slipping his hand under his shirt, he pulled out the clear vinyl pouch. It was quite thick. He turned it on either side, gazing intently at the contents.

Faded black ink characters were neatly scribed on both sides of a mottled brown parchment. To his eye it appeared that it might contain only a single document. It looked to be very ancient. Also of interest was a small paper note affixed to one side of the parchment. Unzipping the pouch, he gently teased the stiff parchment out. It was folded, just as he had suspected. Delicately unfolding it, he laid it out carefully on the step. Now it was obvious that the writing was only on one side of the parchment. He groaned inside, recognizing several of the words.

It was written in Latin. Shifting his attention, he scrutinized the small note affixed to the back. It was written in French and initialed at the bottom, O.S. Luckily, he actually knew a little French. Puzzling out the words, he translated the note first.

It read: Remove to heretical section with Temple scroll.

Carefully folding the parchment back along the original creases, he tucked it along with the note back into the pouch. Zipping it up, he slipped it back under his shirt. He picked up his knapsack and sprinted up the broad stone steps.

Past the large Fountain of Aquilone, he hung a sharp right, passing a huge statue of St. Peter on his left. He jogged along a road that led past the rear of the Ethiopian College. Opening one of the rear doors, he quickly traced the now familiar route to his room.

He opened the door. The room was empty. That doesn't mean Brother Michel won't be dropping by at any moment, he warned himself. Gingerly placing his knapsack down, he swiftly undid the tie and pulled out his dictionary. Grabbing a pad and pen, he carefully extracted the parchment from its pouch and began copying the text as fast as he could. Ten minutes later he sat back, surveying his work. Satisfied, he refolded the parchment, inserting it back into the pouch.

Staring at the shiny plastic, he thought, where can I hide this till I can get it back to the archives? The sound of leather sandals slapping on worn stone echoed in the hall. He stuffed the pouch into his knapsack along with the copy he'd just made and kicked it under the narrow bed, simultaneously pulling out a large plastic shopping bag. Rummaging through it, he lifted his head. The footsteps continued on down the hall. He felt his empty stomach growl. Looking back down, he continued sifting through the contents. As he searched for something to eat, a recent encounter he'd had with Brother Michel popped into his head.

He'd gotten up early to go for his usual run. It reminded him of his usual routine, and he'd found it to be a fun way to explore the extensive grounds. He was amazed at all the things he'd come across so far. There were tennis and basketball courts, a heli-pad, radio station, railway station, and even an observatory. Coming in quietly, so as not to disturb Brother Michel, he'd grabbed a towel to dry his face before going over to the small shelf that hung over his bed.

Reaching over, he'd pulled down his tefilin bag. Its front was colorfully embroidered with Hebrew letters. The letters spelled out his name. His father had given him the bag along with the tefilin a month before his thirteenth birthday. He'd brought them along with him even though he'd used them only on rare occasions in the past few years. Of course that had all changed since his strange dream back in New York. He'd begun to put them on now almost every morning. Pulling out of the bag the two boxes that housed the phylacteries, he'd wound the black leather straps of the first phylactery around his left arm and recited the blessing silently. Then he'd placed on his head the second phylactery and recited the blessing over it. Finally, he'd rewound the leather strap on his left hand to spell out in Hebrew the word, "Shaddai", one of the Hebrew names of God.

He'd removed his small siddur from the bag, and facing in the direction of Jerusalem, he'd recited the morning prayers. Fifteen minutes later he was finished. Unwinding the phylacteries, he had rewrapped the straps around their protective boxes. Brother Michel had been staring curiously at him from his cot for the last few minutes.

Swinging himself into a sitting position, Brother Michel coughed, and cleared his throat.

"I want to ask you something."

Turning around, he'd sat down opposite him on his own cot.

"What is it?"

"I was wondering," Brother Michel said. "Do you really believe you are special?"

"What do you mean?"

"I have been reading some books lately. You call yourselves the Chosen People. I knew this for a long time. It is mentioned many times in the Bible. I just never really thought much about it before."

"I guess each person has to choose his own path to God," he'd replied.

"And what is your path?" Brother Michel said.

"I don't know yet."

---

Ian pulled out a can of sardines from the plastic bag, again concentrating on his hunger. Signora Fragnini insisted on giving him a large care package each week to take back with him. He'd actually acquired a taste for sardines over the past few weeks. He'd found opening them to be a delicate affair. If he placed too much pressure, the key snapped the thin metal lid too soon. Concentrating, he didn't hear the young priest enter the room.

He felt Brother Michel's intent gaze upon him. Looking up he said, "Hi."

"Hello," the young priest responded, a peculiar look on his face.

Ian was prompted to ask, "What's the matter?"

"Nothing," Brother Michel said. "I've been thinking about our talk in the library earlier. I have also been thinking about some of our other discussions lately. And I have been reading more."

"Okay," Ian said in as nonchalant a voice as he could manage, not knowing what to expect.

Brother Michel continued. "I was reading from the Gospel of Mark. Are you familiar with it?"

"Sort of. I haven't read it in a long time."

"I was going over where Mark describes Our Lord's feelings for his mother and brothers. Mark negates Christ's relationship with them, calling instead his disciples his true family. Then later, Mark disparages these same disciples, especially Saint Peter. This of course directly contradicts Matthew, where Peter is described as the Rock on which Our Lord would build the Holy Church. Our Lord even gives Peter the keys over the kingdom of heaven. What do you think about that?"

"Hmm," Ian responded, placing the uneaten sardines down. "To be honest with you, I'd have to look the texts over again." Then thinking about what Brother Michel had said he asked curiously, "You just mentioned that Jesus had brothers. I thought he had only one brother, umm, James, wasn't it?"

"No, Matthew tells of four brothers. James, Joseph, Judas, and Simeon."

"Really, I didn't know that." Reflecting on that, Ian said, "Who was the oldest, you know, of the brothers?"

"It must be Our Lord. He was the first born of the Virgin Mary."

Ian smiled politely. He glanced at his watch. It was almost one p.m. Brother Michel should be going to eat lunch in the dining room with the other priests.

Looking back up at Brother Michel he said, "Oh, I see," with as much conviction as he could muster.

Brother Michel walked over to the small porcelain

sink and removing his glasses, splashed some cold water on his face. Wiping himself dry, he perched his glasses on his nose and turned, another question on the tip of his tongue. He hesitated.

Stepping to the door, he paused to mumble over his shoulder, "See you later," before heading down the hallway.

Ian sat on his cot, listening. The soft tread of the leather sandals and the unmistakable rustle of Brother Michel's robes faded out of earshot. Silently, Ian rose up and tip-toed over to the doorway, sticking his head out. The hallway was empty. Swiftly striding back to his cot, he pulled out the knapsack and removed the plastic pouch. Tucking it back under his shirt, he adjusted it snugly against his body and shut the door behind him. He quietly slipped out the back, turning to be sure no one was following him.

He set off at a brisk pace, skirting a formal garden. He passed a building along the way that he'd only recently found out housed the Vatican's radio station. Following the road behind it, he walked past a group of gardeners busy working by a tall stone wall hard up against the tower of St. John. This was a massive round tower in the Medieval style that dominated this entire section of the grounds. Anyone standing on its ramparts would have a commanding view of the area below.

Ian waved to them. One of the younger ones waved back. Ian couldn't remember his name, but he had met him several times on his early morning runs.

Following the retaining wall of the tower, he eventually reached its end. Now he was cut off from the view of the gardeners. He climbed four wide steps. Directly to the west rose St. John's tower, now fully exposed on the other side of the retaining wall. On his right, another garden stretched away to end by the outer wall that encircled the Vatican City. In the center of the serene garden stood a statue of one of the Popes. Beyond it rose a huge structure: the Vatican radio tower. Crossing over, Ian walked around the heavy metal girders at its base, carefully scanning about in all directions. He squinted up at the top window turrets of St. John's tower. It was impossible to tell if anyone was up there, looking down on him. Maybe I should have waited 'til dark, he thought.

Beyond the radio tower was a paved semi-circular area. Arranged around its perimeter stood eight neatly pruned trees, their leaves and branches trimmed in the shape of perfectly round balls. In front of them grew a thick low hedge. The trees were right up against a section of the outer wall. Ian hopped over the hedge and walked over to stand by the fifth tree. Five had always been his favorite number.

Stepping behind the trunk, he was hidden from all but the most careful scrutiny. He got down on his hands and knees and began to dig a small hole with his bare hands in the soft earth. Removing the thick pouch from his shirt, he checked to make sure the zipper was fully closed. It should be waterproof, he mused. He gently placed the pouch into the hole and covered it up. Tamping down the rich brown dirt, he took care to remove any signs that he had been there.

Back in the room he had decided to hide the parchment for now. Eventually he would return it to the archives, but for now he couldn't keep it in his room. He still suspected that someone had searched through his bags that first day. Who could it have been, he wondered for the hundredth time.

Getting up, he peered around the tree-trunk. His heart skipped a beat. Not ten feet away, two aged priests were strolling by, one dressed all in white. A large ruby ring shone dully on the left hand of the other one. A third priest walked behind them, at a discreet distance. But they were not the only cause for Ian's alarm. Thirty feet behind them strolled two security guards. These were dressed in the same drab khaki uniforms Ian had seen on the guards at the gate the first day he'd arrived. They carried the same snub automatic weapons slung over their shoulders, and Ian thought as they passed by, they look like they mean business.

He quickly ducked his head back. They passed by. Off to the west a strange whining sound began to fill the air, growing in intensity. Ian immediately recognized it, though he'd never heard it before in real life. It was the unmistakable whine of a helicopter's rotors revving up. The sound increased further. Ian risked a quick peek. The gravel path in front of him was empty. Overhead, a large helicopter flew off, the beat of its large blades pulsating in the warm air. The sound diminished off into the distance. The air around him was suddenly still. He heard several birds chirping nearby. He dared not move.

His patience was rewarded. Moments later, the same two guards came into view, conversing to each other in Italian. One stopped on the path directly opposite his tree, to pull out a cigarette. Ian held his breath. Lighting it, the guard puffed a few times. Looking ahead, he quickened his stride to catch up to his companion. Reaching him, the guard with the cigarette snapped out something in Italian. The other guard slapped him on the back and they both laughed as they continued on down the path and out of sight. Ian waited a full five minutes before emerging from his hiding place. Slipping quietly away, he stole past the radio tower and back across the grounds.

Standing in the narrow hallway, he hesitated before

opening the door to his room. It was empty. Gratefully, he peeled off his sweat-soaked shirt and reached under his bed. He pulled out of his knapsack the copy he'd made earlier of the original manuscript. Plopping down on the rickety cot, he opened his dictionary and began translating the text.

CHAPTER 13

How can the scribes say that the Christ is the son of David?

Mark 12:35

---

Several hours later he was finished. He sat back, re-reading his translation. It was time to ask someone for help. But who could he trust?

Brother Michel's earnest face popped into his mind. Maybe I can slip by a few casual questions into our next conversation, he mused. Putting on a new shirt, he tucked the copy with his translation in the breast pocket.

Back at the library, it didn't take him long to locate the known copy of the manuscript. It lay on the table, spread out before him. By this time he knew that it was a work by a second century Christian scholar named Hegesippus. Looking about, he slipped out the copy and translation that he'd made in his dorm room of the original manuscript he'd taken from the archives. He compared it to the text in front of him line by line. Five minutes later he sat back, smiling.

He heard the slight rustle of coarse cloth. With a subtle movement, he swept his own copy underneath the text on the table. Looking up, he saw Brother Michel approaching his table, a smile on his lips.

Ian waved to him and Brother Michel nodded as he stopped, to stand a few feet away.

"Sit down, sit down," Ian said, waving his hand in a friendly manner.

"Thank you," Brother Michel replied, sinking gratefully down next to Ian.

"What is this that you are studying?" the thin priest asked, curiously scanning the document spread out on the table.

"It's a copy of a manuscript by a Christian historian."

"Do you mind if I look at it?" Brother Michel said.

"No, please do."

Brother Michel poured silently over the text.

"This is very interesting, but I don't see how it relates to your thesis," he asked several minutes later.

"Actually, it does in a way," Ian said. Then he asked, "Tell me, what do you make of this line here, where he says that James drank no wine nor shaved his head and wore linen not wool."

"I don't know," Brother Michel shrugged. "Why, what do you make of it?"

Ian puffed out his cheeks. "I'm not sure. It sounds like James took on the vows of a Nazirite. What the linen versus wool is all about I haven't a clue."

Brother Michel sat thinking. He leaned over again to stare at the text.

"There's a term here I don't recognize."

"What's that?"

"This one right here."

Ian leaned forward. "Oh, that's not Latin. It's a Hebrew term. It says that James was called the Moreh Zadok, or Moreh Zedek. That would translate as the 'Teacher of Righteousness.' " He paused to mutter to himself, "Now where have I heard that before?"

Brother Michel sat staring down at the text. Getting up, he said, "Well, good luck. Let me know how things are going. I wish I could stay longer but I have to be getting back to my work."

"Thanks again," Ian called softly to Brother Michel as he walked away, robes swishing.

Ian felt a little guilty. Trying to reassure himself, he thought, no, I'm right not to involve him, just in case I get caught. Cutting short his speculations, he realized that he had to hide the copy of the real manuscript as well. But where? He still wanted to have access to it to study it further. He slipped the copy out from under the manuscript and stuffed it back into his knapsack.

Ten minutes later he was back in his room. Brother Michel was nowhere to be seen. He pulled out the copy, studying it again.

He sat back, thinking. It was starting to become obvious what some censor might have done many centuries ago, and he was even beginning to think he knew why.

Folding up the copy of the true text, his eyes alighted on his tefilin bag. Folding the page many times, he opened the embroidered bag, unwrapping the long black leather straps. Now he opened one of the square covers, placing the small folded slip on its top inner surface. Rewrapping the straps, he tucked it back in the bag.

Just then, he felt his stomach growl. It was late in

the day, and he'd forgotten about lunch in all the excitement. He leaned over to snag the still uneaten sardines. His eyes happened to fall upon a small napkin that lay directly beneath the tin. He slipped out the napkin, staring at the words scrawled on its side.

Hitting his forehead with the palm of his hand he cursed out loud, "Damn, I forgot."

He was supposed to meet Arianna that evening. Flexing the cramped fingers of his right hand, he checked the time. It was 6:20. He shook his head, exasperated. They had made up to meet at seven. She'd jotted down the directions on the little napkin at the end of their last date. Dropping onto the cot, he quickly stripped down. He glanced at his wristwatch. He'd never make it in time if he took a shower. Leaping over to the sink, he turned the spigot. He cupped his hands, about to stick them under the stream of cold water. Then he saw them.

Three long number sequences stared up at him, plainly marked in black ink on the palm of his left hand. Jerking his hands away, he grabbed a pen from the cot and jotted the numbers down on the napkin.

Back at the sink, he splashed cold water over his face and neck, making sure to rub the small ink numbers off his left palm. After drying himself off, he quickly dressed in a pair of jeans and his last clean shirt. He laced up his hiking boots and was already on the back stairs before he realized he'd forgotten the napkin on the bed. Running back, he snatched it up. He bolted out again, careening past three startled priests on the landing. Yelling an apology over his shoulder, he burst out the back doors, and set off at a canter across the grounds.

The restaurant was called Le' Vivre. With the help of Arianna's directions, he could find his own way around.

This particular eatery was located in that section of the city known as Old Rome, on the opposite side of the Tiber.

Fifteen minutes later he was at the foot of the Vittorio Emanuelle II Bridge which spanned the sullen yellow-gray waters. Jogging across, he leaned over the side to gaze down at the surging flow.

For a brief moment he lost himself, mesmerized by the sight and sound of the torrent rushing beneath his feet. A sudden powerful urge to dive in, to become lost in them, swept over him. Behind him, the blare of a taxi horn cut through the air.

Standing erect, like a warrior of some by-gone era, he strode wearily across the bridge, the setting sun bathing his close-cropped hair in a golden halo. Veering to the left, he followed the Via dei Coronari. This was a wide avenue that led directly into the heart of the old city.

As he walked on, he came back to himself. He checked the time. It was almost seven. He was sweating and starved. He debated for a moment whether to try and grab a taxi. Mentally, he calculated how much money he had on him. Most of it was still in traveler's checks but he had converted some into liras.

Am I crazy?, he thought. I have to watch my spending, if I expect to be here for six months. He'd shelled out quite a bit of cash on their last two dates. The time had definitely come to reign in his expenses. Besides, he thought, who knows how expensive this restaurant's going to be?

It was a little past seven thirty before he finally found it. The entrance was so inconspicuous that he'd actually passed it by twice before realizing where it was.

He hated being late. Scanning the interior, his eyes rested on her precious form almost immediately. She was standing by a wall off to the side. Their eyes met. She smiled, coming forward.

"Are you alright?" she said.

"Yes," he answered, flashing her a quick smile. "I'm sorry I'm late. I got caught up in my work and then I had a little trouble finding the place."

"That's okay."

Seeing the sweat on his face, she said, "You look like you could use a drink. Come, I had them set aside a table for us."

Taking his hand, she led him to a table. On the way over, he forgot how tired he was. Arianna signaled a tall waiter standing nearby. She requested something in an Italian that was far too fast for Ian to follow. The waiter nodded and returned a moment later, carrying in his hand a pitcher of ice-cold mineral water. Ian didn't notice the unusually strong hands of the waiter as he poured water into Ian's glass. Lifting the glass, Ian drained it immediately. Much refreshed, he leaned forward to stare at Arianna's beautiful face. A smile spread across her lovely features. She was prompted to ask, "What?" in an arch tone.

Ian laughed. Seeing her eyebrows furrow, he quickly explained. "I was just thinking how sweet you are."

Seeing the still puzzled expression on her face he continued. "It's just that I know how I hate it when someone's late for me, and you were so nice when I came in, worrying about me."

Arianna smiled mischievously, her luminous eyes flashing brightly. "Actually, I have to confess. I was really angry at you until just five minutes ago. But then I started worrying that something might have happened, and when I saw you come in, I was so glad to see you that I forgot to be mad."

The waiter appeared again, handing them menus.

He swiftly departed. Prompted by his strange robes, Ian said, "I see the help here has some very interesting uniforms. What type of food do they serve?"

"It's mainly French cuisine, but they also have many fine local dishes."

Another waiter passed by to serve a group of four seated at a nearby table. He was dressed in the traditional clothes of a Chilean steppe-dweller.

"Then what's with the outfits?"

"Oh that," Arianna said. "The restaurant is run by Catholic missionary workers from all over the world."

"Really," Ian said as he ran his eyes over the menu. It was in Italian.

Giving up, he put it down. Smiling at her, he said, "What do you suggest?"

"Don't worry," she replied with a soft laugh. "Tonight everything is on me."

Ian tried to protest, but she cut him off. "No, no," she said. "It's only fair. I feel so bad that you have been paying all the time. You must let me pay tonight."

"Okay, but just tonight," he agreed.

Arianna signaled the waiter, who set down a basket filled with steaming rounds of bread.

"These are crostoni. They're fried in olive oil. Try one. They're delicious," she said.

Ian picked up one of the warm pieces, gingerly breaking it open. The warm aroma wafted upward. Not waiting, he tore into it with a gusto. Arianna ordered for them.

Ian finished his second roll. Reaching over, he rested his hand where hers lay on the soft white tablecloth. He tentatively stroked the back of her hand as he stared deep into her eyes.

"What?" she said. She shifted uncomfortably

under his gaze.

"Nothing," he said. "I was just thinking how lucky I am to have found you."

Her chest heaved slightly. She spoke softly, her eyes looking down at her empty plate. "I was thinking about you too. Today I could barely concentrate on my studies, waiting to see you tonight."

The waiter returned with their appetizers. They were two small plates of Vol-au-vents, or filled pastry shells. Ian devoured his almost instantly. Grinning, he apologized.

"I'm sorry. It's just that I haven't eaten anything since early this morning and it's been quite an exciting day."

"Really? Tell me about it," she said, leaning forward.

Ian looked around. No one seemed to be paying them any attention, and their waiter had yet to emerge from the kitchen.

"Actually, it was quite bizarre," he began. "I don't know where to start, but I probably should give you a little background first. You remember that I told you about my younger brother Jonathan who is a rabbinical student in Israel…" Ten minutes later he concluded with, "…so you see if James, the brother of Jesus, was of the priestly line, and they both, at the very least, had the same father, then Jesus also was of the priestly line, because the priesthood is passed on by patrilineal descent. And," he finished in an intense whisper of triumph, "…you can't be of the priestly line and also be a descendant of the House of David. It's impossible."

Arianna sat back, playing with her fork. "I don't understand. Why is that so important?"

Ian leaned forward. "Because the early Christians also believed that the true Messiah mentioned in the Prophets must be of the seed of David. And since they believe that Jesus was and is the true Messiah, he must be of the royal House of David in order to fulfill biblical prophecy. I still haven't fit all the pieces together. I remember reading something unusual about that time period a few years back when the whole controversy over the Dead Sea Scrolls exploded in the media. I know there's some kind of a connection, but I haven't been able to put my finger on it."

Just then the waiter arrived with their main dishes and Ian abruptly cut off what he was about to say. The waiter placed them silently down before heading off to another table.

Ian stared down at his plate, his mouth watering. "What is this?"

"It's Melanza alla parmigiani with gnocchi alla romana," she said.

"It's delicious," Ian managed to get out after a minute, his mouth full.

Arianna laughed, nodding her head as she picked up her fork.

After a delightful dinner, they strolled leisurely down the ancient streets, arriving at the Piazza della Rotonda. Here they stopped by one of the many shops selling giolliti. Arianna bought them two cones topped high with the rich, soft ice cream. Hand in hand, they strolled the square, trying to lick the melting confection before it dripped down onto their fingers. Arianna leaned against him. She snuggled her soft hair against his chest. He instinctively wrapped his arm around her shoulder.

By a small fountain they stopped, to gaze at the water. They embraced, Ian stroking her silky hair. Arianna lifted her lips to his ear.

"Be careful," she whispered.

He bent down and kissed her upturned lips. She

pulled away, continuing.

"You don't know who might be watching you. I don't think you should trust the priest, what was his name?"

He bent down, brushing his lips gently against hers. "Brother Michel," he whispered softly in her ear. They kissed again, more passionately. She struggled to pull away, breathing heavily.

"Please don't go back for the other pouches; you might get caught," she pleaded.

"Don't worry," he whispered.

He kissed her neck, her mouth. They didn't speak for a while, lost in each others arms. Behind them, not twenty yards away, a tall man stood in the shadows of an overhang, watching their every move. A muscle twitched in his cheek.

Walking hand in hand, Arianna turned to Ian and said, "Come back with me tonight."

Ian could not believe his ears. "Are you sure?" he asked.

"Yes."

They looked for a taxi. Out of the corner of his eye, a strange movement caught Ian's attention. Twisting around, he saw several other couples strolling by. A day laborer hurried past, rushing to be back with his family. Shrugging his shoulders, he caught up to Arianna. She had run forward to snag a cab. He opened the back door and they jumped in, speeding off into the night.

---

Arianna unlocked the door to her apartment. Taking his hand in hers, she led him inside, towards her bedroom. Ian held back.

"What about your roommate?" he asked.

"Don't worry. She's at her parent's house in Brussels.

She won't be back 'til next semester."

Tugging him by the hand, she led him into the bedroom. They stood an inch apart, by the side of the bed. Ian caressed her bare tan shoulders. She began unbuttoning his shirt, kissing his bare chest with her moist, warm lips. They sank down onto the bed.

---

In the morning, Arianna leaned down and kissed him while he lay drowsing. She was already dressed in a short pleated skirt and fitted blouse with matching flats.

"Look, I have an early class this morning. I don't want to leave, but I have a project to present," she said.

"Really, what's the project?" he said, still half asleep.

"I'll tell you about it this weekend. I've decided to go home, so I can spend it with you. You were planning on being there, right?"

"I wouldn't want to disappoint your brother. He attacks me as soon as I go through the door," he chuckled, waking up some more.

"Well, do you think you could take away a little time from your busy schedule for me?"

"I guess I could spare a few minutes," he said, making a grab for her.

"Oh, very funny," she yelled, hastily backing away. Grabbing a pillow from the foot of the bed, she threw it at his head. His arm snapped out reflexively, catching it an inch from his face.

Leaving, she called out behind her, "Help yourself, there's food in the kitchen. Just close the door when you leave, it locks by itself."

He rolled over to catch a little more sleep, not yet ready to get out of bed. He heard her tip-toe back into the room. Feigning sleep, he waited. Then, he twisted up, grabbing her around the waist. Pulling her on top of him, she let out a surprised squeal. She struggled as he kissed her, finally melting in his arms. Reluctantly, she lifted herself up a few minutes later.

"I'll see you this weekend," she said, straightening out her outfit.

She blew him a kiss as she grabbed the large portfolio case she had mistakenly left by the side of the bed. Ian heard the front door slam shut. He lay back, luxuriating in the softness. Compared to the hard, narrow cot in his dorm room, this was heaven itself. Groaning, he pulled himself out of bed.

# CHAPTER 14

This shall be the assembly of the men of renown called...when the Priest-Messiah shall summon them: He shall come at the head of the whole congregation of Israel with all his brethren, the sons of Aaron, the Priests...

Dead Sea Scrolls

---

He sat on the cot, surrounded by his books. In front of him lay a copy of the Old Testament. It was opened to the book of Genesis. He'd been sitting there most of the day. Walking back from Arianna's apartment that morning, he had mulled things over.

Yes, he thought, looking down at the text—it begins here. Here, where Jacob gives the blessings at his death-bed to his twelve sons. Here, where he gives each one his own special blessing that was to apply to the tribe that bore that son's name for all time. In essence, it was a prophetic blessing, given through the power of divine inspiration.

According to the text, Jacob gave to Judah the exclusive right to kingship over all of the tribes, "until the coming of Shiloh" whatever that means, he mused. Then much later, in the book of Samuel, David is anointed king over all Israel. Flipping through the thick tome, he turned to the book of Kings. Carefully he scanned the text.

His finger stopped at a verse in chapter two. Here it is, he thought with satisfaction. Here David relates to Solomon on his death-bed the eternal promise made to him by God. God has promised him, David tells his son, that his line shall never die; that all future kings of Israel shall be of his direct seed, including the final king, the Messiah, who will bring down the kingdom of Heaven to Earth in the Last Days. Another connected thought came to him.

Wasn't the prophet Elijah supposed to herald in the Messiah and anoint him? He remembered a legend he had learned as a child. According to it, Elijah was reputed to be a reincarnation of Phineas of the Bible. And Phineas was the original priest-warrior who had been "zealous for God" in the time of Moses. He flipped to the spot in Numbers.

"Right," he muttered aloud, staring at the text. Phineas was the original Zealot on whom all subsequent Jewish Zealots had patterned themselves.

Things were becoming clearer. He stared upward, his eyes unfocused. Suddenly, the tantalizing bit of information that he had been searching his mind for since he had stumbled upon the secret manuscript the day before finally snapped into focus.

I know where I saw the term the Teacher of Righteousness, he exulted, jumping off the cot. That was the title used by the Zealot sect that wrote the Dead Sea

Scrolls to denote their leader! Pacing back and forth, he recalled the circumstances of the scandal.

Several years back, under mounting pressure from other scholars, the Israeli antiquities department had been forced to fire the head of the group of scholars who were supposed to be translating the scrolls.

According to one of the articles, up until that time, only this small group of scholars were allowed access to the scrolls that had been found decades before at a place called Qumran, near the shores of the Dead Sea. The scrolls had remained hidden in some caves nearby for almost two thousand years.

By a quirk of fate, a Bedouin youth had accidentally come across them right around the time of the founding of the State of Israel in 1948. These scrolls, and several others found by a further expedition in the surrounding caves, had been transferred to a building funded by the American Rockefeller Institute.

This was located in a sector of Jerusalem that was then under Jordanian control. The original group of scholars kept tight control over the scrolls, which remained shrouded in mystery. Only a tiny portion of their contents were dribbled out over the years. In 1967, during the Six-Day-War, the Israeli Defense Forces captured this section of the city and the scrolls suddenly became the property of the State of Israel. Still, nothing was done to change the secretive monopoly over the scroll material, now under the control of the hand-picked students of the original group of scholars.

Each original scholar had bequeathed his scroll material to his chosen protégé. The scandal had finally come to a head when the leader of the current team of scholars had been quoted in a magazine interview making anti-semitic remarks. He had been sacked by the Israeli

Antiquities department and in the aftermath surrounding the scandal, the monopoly over the scrolls had been broken. A startling thought came to him.

Wasn't the original group of scholars who had been in charge of the scrolls a bunch of priests? Tantalizing new possibilities presented themselves. He racked his brain, trying to remember anything more. Giving up for the moment, a conviction crystallized in his mind. He must go back to take a look at those other pouches.

He was about to head straight back to the library, but thought better of it. Sitting back down on his cot, he composed a quick letter to his brother. Fifteen minutes later he was finished. Sealing it, he grabbed his knapsack and headed for the post office. He checked his neck to make sure he was wearing his pass. It was almost second nature by now. Ever since the incident with the Swiss guards that first day, he had placed it securely on a chain that he wore around his neck.

To get to the Vatican post office required going through a building that contained the new wing of the Chiaramonti Museum. From there, it was necessary to traverse the famous Inscription Gallery. Ian barely noticed the priceless works of art as he passed swiftly through the magnificent marble-lined corridors. Exiting through a tall set of doors, he strode past a small garden to the square building that housed the post office.

Entering its cool interior, he followed the signs to one of several identical glass windows with ornate metal gates in front. Behind each gate sat a priest, dressed in plain black robes. Ian bought several stamps. Affixing them to the envelope, he handed the letter over to the priest seated behind the gate. He watched carefully as the priest dropped the letter into a large canvas mail bag behind him. Maybe I should have mailed it outside, he worried to himself. Oh well, he thought, it's done.

Leaving the post office, he headed back to the library. Lost in thought, he strode down the soaring marble halls, debating with himself if he should risk going back to the archives. He had just decided to call it off when, passing by a display case in the Gallery, something caught his eye.

Doubling back, he stepped over to have a closer look. He peered through the thick glass. Inside on a stand sat a large ancient clay jar, its lid set neatly beside it. A small bronze plaque lay right below. Ian pressed his face up close, trying to make out the tiny letters. Squinting, he read out the word: Qumran.

Circling around to the side, he discovered a larger bronze plaque mounted on the side of the case. It was neatly inscribed with the words: donazione- Ecole` Bibliot. Startled, he stood on his tip-toes. Carefully balancing himself, he strained as he stared down through the top of the case.

Behind him a large group of tourists passed by on a guided tour of the museum. Ian didn't notice. He stood in his own world, oblivious to his surroundings. In it was only himself and the empty black mouth of the jar, staring back at him, mocking. A strange pressure built up inside him as he gazed down into that dark pit. A wild feeling bubbled up from deep within. He felt like shouting at the top of his lungs. Someone jostled him, and he came back to his senses. Looking about to see if anyone had noticed him, he adjusted his knapsack squarely on his shoulder and continued on, his jaws firmly set, fire glinting in his eyes.

Back in the library he purposely laid out his books and papers at his favorite table. Sitting down, he pretended to work. Nothing would deter him. Staring down unseeingly at the papers in front of him, his mind worked with an icy clarity he had never before known. It was all so very clear to him now.

Half an hour later he got up and casually strolled off. He wandered about, perusing some of the books on the shelves. He kept one eye alert to see if anyone was watching him. To a casual observer it would seem only pure chance that brought him within view of the librarian's desk.

Darting a glance in that direction, he was surprised to find it empty. Maybe he's skulking in the back room, he thought. He dared not risk taking a closer look. Walking past several more shelves, he located the long hallway that led to the archive room. Not looking back, Ian quietly descended the flight of steps to the now familiar long corridor. He walked purposefully up to the door with the faded word "Archeota" painted on it. He realized that he was now in a vulnerable position. Should someone challenge him, he would have to say he was lost. Another disturbing thought came to him. What if Brother Michel happened by, or even worse, was inside? Coolly, he looked both ways down the hall. It was deserted.

He pictured the empty black mouth of the clay jar staring up at him. He turned the heavy brass handle. It opened smoothly. Stepping quickly inside, the massive door closed behind him. He craned his neck, checking the small alcove that contained the computer terminal. It was empty. Striding swiftly over to the terminal, he glanced down at the screen. It was filled with Latin words.

The room held the unmistakable feel of recent occupation. He pulled out a tiny slip of paper from his front jeans pocket. On it were neatly written two long number sequences. With swift economical movements, he located the first sequence. It was on the same aisle as the manuscript he'd already taken. Carefully taking it down from its shelf, he stared at it in fascination. Inside the clear plastic was a thick rolled up scroll of great age. He stared at it for but an instant before slipping it under his shirt, hooking it under the belt he had worn especially for that purpose. The pouch made a distinct bulge under his shirt. Sweat beaded his forehead. Should he risk going for the second one? Might as well, he grinned, tightening his jaw muscles.

He found the second pouch several minutes later. Racing to the door, he stuffed it down beside the first. The door opened with the now familiar whoosh of air. He stepped out into the long empty corridor. Turning swiftly, he took only a few steps when he heard a voice behind him call out. He pretended not to hear and kept walking.

He distinctly heard the sound of running sandals, and a voice that he now recognized shout, "Ian."

Ian spun around, deftly avoiding a collision with Brother Michel.

Smiling ingenuously, he greeted the young priest. "Hi. I was actually looking for you, and I was just about to give up."

Brother Michel smiled back, catching his breath. "Didn't you hear me? Well, no matter. What can I do to help you?"

Ian racked his brain and covered with, "I was wondering if I might look for any material in the archives on early Christian theology."

Brother Michel considered the request. His face took on a serious cast as he said, "You may not know this, but you need special permission to do research in the archive department."

"Oh, really?" Ian said. "Who's permission would I need?"

"Why, the librarian's, of course."

Ian nodded. "Okay, well, I won't trouble you any further then. I'll go see the librarian right away."

"I'm sorry," Brother Michel replied.

"Don't be," Ian reassured him. "I can't thank you enough for all you've done."

"Arrivederci," Brother Michel called out.

"Arrivederci," Ian called back over his shoulder as he strolled away.

Looking down at his shirt he noticed the distinct bulge at his waistline. He wondered if Brother Michel had noticed it too. One thought burned through his mind. I've got to get out of this place. If he were caught with the pouches on him he didn't know what they would do with him. He grinned wolfishly. I don't think they still have the power to burn people at the stake, he mused, not even a Jew.

He entered the main library, walking over to the table where he had left his things. He couldn't help but sneak a glance over to the desk where the librarian stood, staring right at him. Shit, he cursed mentally.

Paying him no heed, he gathered his things and packed them into his knapsack. Slinging its heavy weight over his shoulder, he adjusted the weight better on his back and started to walk out.

"Alt," he heard a voice call out loudly behind him.

He froze in his tracks. Turning around slowly, he looked around. The librarian was waving his arm in an agitated manner in his direction.

Pointing innocently to himself, he saw the librarian nod his head. Ian walked back to the tall desk.

"Che cos`e`?" Ian said politely.

"Dov`e` un francobollo?" the librarian shot back.

"Oh," Ian replied, pulling out a slip of paper from his knapsack. He had forgotten to return the receipt for the text he had taken out the day before.

The librarian grimaced. "Dov`e` si chiama?" he asked, peering at the slip.

"Mi spiace," Ian replied swiftly. Shifting his knapsack around, he reached inside and pulled out the first pen he could find. He signed his name and placed the slip back on the desktop.

"Dov`e` chiuso?" the librarian said, looking at Ian's pen.

Ian stared at his hand. His heart went cold. He was holding the same slim black pen he had taken from the archive room the day before.

"Dare lo di mi," the librarian croaked, his voice filling with rage.

Ian dropped the pen on the counter like a hot coal. It rolled to a stop, the gold seal of the Vatican staring up at them.

"Where did you get that?" the librarian repeated in Italian, staring down at the seal, his voice creaking to a high-pitched scream.

Several priests, perusing the shelves nearby, turned around to stare in surprise.

Ian stood there, flustered. He was about to say that he'd found it, when he saw the librarian's sharp eyes dart down to the bulge at his waistline. Ian watched in detached fascination as the librarian's eyes widened, his face turning a reddish-purple. An inarticulate scream bubbled forth from his lips.

He gained enough control to wail out in Italian, "Get him!"

The priests nearby were staring in their direction, puzzled expressions on their faces.

"Get him, he's a thief," the librarian screamed.

The priests moved forward, hesitantly. The librarian, exasperated, lunged forward to try and grasp Ian with his long bony fingers.

Ian had been standing there, in shock. He lurched back, barely avoiding the hooked talons of the librarian. He swiveled. Leaping to the right, he soared past the startled group of priests who had been slowly converging on him. Several giant bounds brought him to the doors. As the doors closed behind him, the shrill sound of the librarian's screams were mercifully cut off.

Leaping down the wide steps, he sprinted across the road behind the library, the late afternoon light splashing on his head. Behind him, he could hear a loud commotion. Twisting his neck, he looked back. There, outside the door, stood the librarian, gesticulating wildly with his arms to the group of younger priests that surrounded him. The librarian looked across the way with the all-seeing glare of a wrathful god. Catching sight of Ian, his malevolence concentrated itself.

Stabbing his outstretched finger accusingly in his direction, he screamed at the priests milling around him. Ian sprinted in the opposite direction, coming to an abrupt stop after just a few feet. Two Swiss guards were strolling towards him from the gardens.

Abruptly altering course, he darted to the left, passing beneath the shadow of a massive stone archway. Past a small fountain he slowed down, strolling innocently by a Swiss guard stationed in front of a side entrance to St. Peter's. A vague plan had begun to form in his mind.

Entering the cool interior of the cathedral, he strode over to one of the many tour groups and attached himself to them. This particular one consisted of a group of tall Danes. He followed them as the tour guide led them about, stopping frequently to drone on about one of the many points of interest. Ian scanned the wide open expanse in all directions. At first he saw nothing to excite his interest. Then, in the midst of twisting around a second time, he caught sight of something near the far entrance that nearly sent him flying.

It was the librarian, surrounded by several Swiss guards. They stood a few hundred feet away, scanning the crowds. Controlling the urge to flee, Ian slipped in amongst another group which had by this time made its way to the massive central altar. The tour guide began to descend the steps leading down into the catacombs. Bending down, Ian shuffled along with them, tensely keeping one eye on the librarian and the guards. The guards had by now fanned out, making it nearly impossible for him to track their locations. It came his turn to descend. Gratefully, he stepped down, close behind a middle-aged woman. At the bottom he moved to the side to let those behind him go ahead. He hung back, quietly slipping into the shadows.

He headed off to the right, moving slowly in the cold gloom. Suddenly, his fingers closed around a thick twisted rope. He ran his hand over the rough weave of the hemp fibers. In the faint light he could just barely make out the sign he had seen that very first day. Peering closer, he read again, "No Admittance." Ignoring it, he ducked under the rope.

# CHAPTER 15

Blessed is He Who distinguishes between the
Holy and the profane,
between light and darkness,
between Israel and the nations...

> Blessing at the close of the Sabbath.

---

Ian looked down. After the first few steps, a solid wall of darkness rose up. For all he knew, he could be stepping into an abyss. He shrugged. There was only one way out now.

Tentatively placing one foot forward at a time he began to descend into the black void. A clammy breeze wafted past him.

The uneven surfaces of the stone steps were pitted with age. He was forced to use both hands as he felt his way down slowly, guided only by the rough stone walls on either side and the feel of the stone beneath his feet. As he descended, the darkness seemed to reach out and envelop him.

Calming himself, he took several cleansing breaths before proceeding. After what seemed an eternity, the steps finally came to an end. Near the end, the wall on his left had widened away, forcing him to use only one hand against the right wall as a guide. He moved slowly forward on the flat floor, reluctant to break contact with the last remaining wall. He advanced, counting his steps mentally. At each step came the brittle crunching sound of some kind of hard particles beneath his hiking shoes. That, and the heavy sound of his own breathing, were his only companions.

After what seemed like several minutes of walking through what must be an enormous chamber, off to his left he was able to make out what appeared to be a faint flickering glow. Turning hopefully in that direction, he continued on.

It was unmistakable. The light had intensified to the point where he could now make out his surroundings. He looked around in awe. He was treading the floor of some vast underground cavern, its ceiling lost in the darkness above. In front of him, maybe a hundred yards off, he could make out the vague outlines of several large rectangular shapes. The wavering light appeared to emanate from them. He strode forward more confidently, the light increasing exponentially each step he took. He stopped thirty feet from the first structure to stare at it in amazement.

It was a simple rectangle, built from massive stone blocks. Each block was at least six feet across and four feet in height. He had no idea how thick they were, but he guessed that they each must weigh at least a ton. They rose up to a height of well over twenty feet. Stepping up to it, he ran his fingers over the fantastic carvings etched deeply into its face. In the dim light, he could just barely make out the shapes of strange mythical beasts intertwined in a bizarre mosaic. He had never seen their like before.

Coming around the corner of the building, he saw a long line of several more rectangles of about the same size as the one he stood by, surrounded by many smaller ones stretching away into the distance. A thick layer of dust covered everything. Entranced and burning with curiosity, he moved forward.

These must be the crypts that man on the plane told Jonathan about, he marveled. His attention was diverted off to the side. There, an even larger crypt stood at a lower level. It had been excavated with great effort from the dark rock floor of the cavern. It appeared to be the oldest of all the structures he'd seen.

Here was the source of the light. Shifting his knapsack, he stealthily picked his way down. As he came closer, he saw that the now bright light was coming from a doorway on the far side. Walking around, he took note of the ornate carvings covering the walls of this crypt. These were the most fantastic ones he had yet seen. Staring back at him were the repeated images of some wildly exotic bird, their hooked beaks and wicked eyes staring balefully at him. A slight shiver ran down his spine as he stared at those cold eyes.

Standing in the entranceway, he peered inside the crypt. In brackets high on the crypt's inner walls, two large torches burned, a thin black smoke curling up from the flames. To his nostrils came a faintly acrid smell.

Ian stood frozen in the doorway. There in the center of the crypt sat a plain stone pedestal. And upon it rested a large golden object. The flickering flames shone on its shiny surfaces and intricate carvings, reflecting glints of brilliant light. The light was so bright that it hurt his eyes to look directly at it. Shading his eyes, he stepped across the threshold and walked straight up to the pedestal, like one walking in his sleep. Standing a few feet away, he squinted, staring at it in total disbelief. It was just as he had dreamed it. He reached out to touch the surface of the Menorah.

Out of the corner of his eye came a blurred image, but Ian couldn't be sure it wasn't just a flicker of the torch light. He turned partway around when he was struck with great force. His powerful frame rocked with the blow, his knapsack flying off to land a few feet away on the dusty floor of the crypt.

Heaving convulsively, he broke the vise-like grip of the powerful hands that had clamped themselves around his knees. Bouncing away, a black form lunged forward with frightening speed, gripping him again, this time round his ankle. Fighting to retain his balance, Ian felt long sharp fingernails, like an iron comb, tear into the large muscle on the back of his right thigh. Screaming in pain, he lashed out with his other foot. He could feel bone and tissue crush beneath his shoe. The dark figure let go of his leg, falling in a limp pile at his feet. He stumbled away to stare in mute horror at the collapsed form that lay before him. His attacker had not uttered a single sound.

Ian limped forward, sweating profusely. Cautiously, he turned the huddled form over. Leaning down, he lost his balance. Falling, he barely avoided landing atop the black heap. He righted himself, wincing in pain. Reaching out with a trembling hand, he pulled away the hood, exposing the face of his attacker. Ian leaned back in shock.

Staring up at him with dull, lifeless eyes, was a hideously ugly face. The flames played across its harsh features. It was chalk-white, drained of all color. It was the face of the old priest who had scared him that first day in the catacombs. Bending over the body, he desperately felt for a pulse. There was none.

Hot tears sprang up at the corners of his eyes. He

hadn't meant to kill him. Replaying what had happened in his mind, he shook his head in disbelief, marveling at the speed and strength with which the old priest had attacked him.

Why, he asked himself. Why did he attack me like that? Struggling to his feet, he tried to feel the back of his leg. There was no blood, but some muscle tissue and possibly the ligament were torn. He tested the leg, placing some pressure on it. Pain lanced up the right side of his body like a knife. He stared down at the lifeless body. Placing his palm on his forehead, he ran his fingers through his hair.

There was nothing more he could do for the old priest, he realized. If he turned himself in along with the stolen pouches, he had no illusions about what would happen to him. There's no way they're going to believe me, he thought. I don't even know if they have the death penalty in Italy. Actually, he corrected himself, I'm on the soil of the Vatican which technically is its own state. I wonder what the punishment for killing a priest is here?

He limped back over to the stone pedestal. Shading his eyes, he paused to stare at the massive golden object before him. It seemed to pulse with its own light, as if it were almost alive. He reached out, but hesitated, afraid to touch it. It was too beautiful.

Instead, he stooped down to pick up his knapsack. At the doorway he stopped one last time to steal a glance at the seven-branched candelabrum. His gaze shifted to the floor. There, the black shrouded body of the old priest lay in a heap. It's best, he thought, if I put some distance between the two of us, and as soon as possible.

Shuffling into a broken gait, and ignoring the stabbing pains that shot up along his right flank, he headed away in the opposite direction. The light around him began to fade the farther from the crypt he went. Not too long after he was forced to slow down, unsure of his footing.

He cursed himself. In his haste to get away, he hadn't thought to take one of the torches from the crypt. Picking his way forward carefully, he followed the floor of the great cavern for what seemed an eternity. In a state of near exhaustion, he reached the far end. Directly in front of him yawned the dark mouth of a large tunnel.

He hesitated but an instant, plunging headlong into its dark depths. Almost immediately, he was forced to slow down even further. The floor, which had begun to slant downward, was choked with debris. The walls were slick with a thick coating of condensed moisture. He heard a sharp scratching, and the sound of scurrying feet. Rats, he thought. Feeling his way ahead, he negotiated the tunnel, inch by inch.

Somewhere along the way, his numb mind realized by the change in the pitch of the floor, that he was starting to ascend. With renewed hope, he urged himself on. The pain in his leg had by now changed to a powerful throbbing. It pounded in his head like a huge gong.

Forcing himself to pick up the pace, he willed his body up the now sharply inclined floor. The darkness surrounding him became less claustrophobic. Another hundred feet later, he felt a slight breeze waft against his face. Fatigue weighed heavily upon him. Steeling himself, he climbed on.

He came to an abrupt halt, crouching down low by a four foot high opening. His breathing came in sharp gasps. The pain in his leg had become almost unbearable. In front of him, a thick iron grate barred the way. He rested a moment, trying to catch his breath. Running his hands over the iron bars, he tested it. It didn't budge. Through the bars he could just barely make out what looked like some gardening implements. Through a veil of pain, he shook his head in surprise. Focusing his immediate attention on the grate, he stuck a hand through the bars, tracing with his fingers where it was bolted on the outside.

He counted six bolts. Leaning back to rest, he shifted the pressure off his bad leg.

He felt along the edges of the bolts with his fingers, grimacing with satisfaction. Whoever had put in the grate had done a poor job. Instead of drilling directly into the rock on the other side, they'd stuck some cement onto the rock-face and then bolted into the cement. Feeling around again, he finally found what he was looking for. Around the bottom left corner bolt, the cement had begun to crumble. Dropping his knapsack, he lay down on his back on the floor of the tunnel.

Due to the incline, his head was now below his feet. He could feel the blood rush to his head. Thankfully, the pain in his leg subsided a bit. Taking several deep breaths, he focused his flagging energies upon the few inches of bar on the bottom left corner. He felt something tug his hair sharply. Thrashing his head wildly, he heard a large rat scurry away. Taking a deep breath, he tried to calm himself. Bracing his arms against the sides of the tunnel, he lashed out with his left leg and felt the hard impact rattle his teeth as the heel of his hiking shoe smashed against the iron bar. The pain in his right leg flared up again, forcing an involuntary sob from his tautly drawn lips.

Setting himself again, he kicked out a second time. He was rewarded as he felt the bar give with a loud grinding sound. Scrambling painfully around on his hands and knees, he grasped the bars and strained forward with his powerful upper torso. The muscles on his neck stood out with the effort. The bars bent slowly outward. Panting heavily, he leaned against them, using his entire body weight. Sweat dripped down his face. The grate bent slowly outward. He lay there a moment, exhausted.

Lifting himself up, he grabbed his knapsack, pushing it through the gap. It fell a few feet beyond the lip, to land on the floor below. Flipping onto his stomach, he tried to squeeze himself through, feet first. He got his legs through, resting them for a minute on the floor. Twisting his shoulders, he managed to slip half his body through, but not before his left shoulder became caught, stuck on a small projection of metal. He twisted, trying to pull himself free. It was no use. He was stuck. Great, he thought, nearly hysterical. Then he heard them. His face was now level with the floor of the tunnel. They were running towards him, their sharp nails clicking on the stone floor.

Gritting his teeth, he slid his body down, tearing a long gash in his left shoulder. He screamed, collapsing to the ground. He lay there for a long time, unable to get up.

# CHAPTER 16

"Glory" is the thigh about which it says of Jacob, "And he was limping on his thigh."

> Zohar Breishis 26b

---

The fire burned dully in Ian's eyes. Remembering the rats, a small measure of strength returned. He rose up shakily, using the rock wall for support. Swaying onto his feet, he surveyed his surroundings. The light was poor, but it was enough to see by.

He seemed to be in some kind of tool shed. There were large bags of what looked like fertilizer or maybe dirt stacked in neat piles near the center. Along the walls on racks hung several hoes, rakes and other gardening tools. A large wheelbarrow rested on the floor near a door.

Leaning wearily against the rock wall, he felt with his right hand along the gash on his shoulder. His fingers came away, sticky with half-dried blood.

The bleeding appeared to be stopping. He straightened

up, feeling the strength return more fully to his aching body. Wiping the sticky blood on his pants, he stepped back to the grate. He shuddered once, but there was no sign of the rats. Grasping the grate, he grunted as he pushed it back in place. He tottered back. Unless anyone came really close to inspect it, it should pass unnoticed, he thought.

Satisfied, he bent down clumsily and hoisted his knapsack back over his right shoulder. Limping to the door, he turned the knob. To his relief it opened easily.

Easing it open, he peered out. Tall rows of corn stood high over his head. At his feet, a narrow gravel path wound between the corn stalks, to end by the shadow of a wall. Limping outside, he made sure to close the door behind him. He stopped to look up, not recognizing where he was. It was nearing the end of the month and the moon was but a sliver in the night sky, casting a cold, feeble light. The stars above were numerous, like brilliant gems. Ian felt exposed, alone on the star-lit path. Hurrying forward as best he could, he made it to the shadow of the wall.

There, set deeply in it, was an arched doorway. A heavy iron gate covered the opening, barring his way. A large chain had been twisted through the bars, a thick lock securely attached to its ends. He shook the chain.

He leaned his body against the gate, in disgust. What is their problem, he thought. Are they afraid someone's going to steal the corn? He moved back to assess the wall. In good shape, it would have been no problem at all. In his present condition he had grave doubts whether he could climb over.

He realized he didn't have a choice. Slipping the other shoulder strap of his knapsack on, he tightened the straps snugly. He winced, feeling the left strap rub against the deep gash on his shoulder. He could feel it start to bleed again.

Ignoring the pain, he traced out with his bleary eyes his hand-holds and foot-holds. The wall, he guessed, was about twenty feet high. Psyching himself, he reached for his first hand-hold.

"Admit it," he muttered aloud, grunting, "You're afraid of heights." He started to laugh giddily from the pain but then controlled himself. Taking deep breaths, he pulled himself up by his dirt-grimed fingers, grasping at the small corner projections of the stone blocks.

Twice he almost fell, nearly giving up from sheer exhaustion. Staring straight ahead, he tried to ignore how high up he was as he approached the top. Straddling the wall, he flattened himself as best he could. He looked down. Below was an empty narrow triangular shaped courtyard, flanked on two sides by tall buildings, and on the third side by another high wall. Twisting his head, he noticed a gap in the wall. He couldn't climb down. His right leg would never support his weight.

He slid over the lip, hanging for a moment by his fingers. He exhaled and let go. He dropped to the pavement, feet first. His right leg buckled and he fell onto his side. Gasping from the pain, he thrashed around on the cobblestones. The pain eased. Getting up slowly, he made for the gap in the wall near the tall hulking building on his left. Passing beyond the gap, he became aware of the faint musical sound of gurgling water.

About thirty yards away stood a large fountain, lit up with spotlights. Two soldiers dressed in khaki uniforms were leaning by its lip, their backs to him.

Ian immediately recognized where he was. In front of him was the famous Fountain of the Aquilone he'd passed by so many times before on his way to the library from his dorm. He calculated wearily in his head that he must have traveled nearly half a mile underground.

    The guards lounged around the rim, chatting to each other as they puffed away on their cigarettes. Ian turned and limped silently away. Passing between a gap in a tall hedge, he headed out in a westerly direction, passing beneath some large fruit trees.

    As he wound his way slowly through the lush plantings he tried to order his mind. What should I do?, he repeated over and over, his mind clouded by pain and fatigue.

    Suddenly, a vivid image sprang up before his eyes: his tefilin bag. Neatly folded inside one of the boxes was the slip of paper with the copy of the first manuscript he'd taken from the archives. What if they search my things and find it, he thought.

    Not paying attention, he nearly tripped over something lying in the grass at his feet. Looking down, he bent over and picked up a large coil of stout waxed cord. One of the gardeners must have dropped it or forgotten it. Testing the strength of the cord between his dirt-grimed hands, he came up with a plan of sorts.

    He'd pass by the Ethiopian College. If the coast was clear he'd try for his tefilin bag. If it looked too risky, he'd head directly to where he'd hidden the first pouch the day before under the tree by the radio tower. With the length of cord he had in his hand, he should be able to scale the outer wall right next to it and make his escape. Looping the thick coil around one of the straps of his knapsack, he limped forward on the damp soft grass.

    He made a wide circle, trying to avoid an empty open area that was brightly lit by spotlights. Sticking as best he could to the shadows, he arrived at the basketball courts, unnoticed. These were dark and silent. He crossed the dark open space. He stopped to rest a moment behind some trees, breathing heavily. The pain in his right leg had subsided to a dull ache but he could feel it starting to stiffen up. A strong burning sensation emanated from where the knapsack pad was rubbing against the gash on his left shoulder. Grimacing, he wiped his sweaty face. He was covered in filth and his clothes hung on him in tatters.

He crouched, fifty feet from the back of the Ethiopian college. Everything appeared normal. Still, he hesitated. Wincing, he crossed the short open space to the back doors. He tested one of the doors. It was open. He almost turned back then, but slipped inside instead. The hallway was empty. Climbing the back stairwell, he painfully ascended the two flights to his floor. He eased open the door a crack.

At the far end of the corridor stood a guard, a snub automatic rifle slung over his shoulder, leaning against the wall. Ian cursed under his breath. The guard stood up, impatiently glancing down at his wristwatch.

Looking about, the guard shrugged. He strode over to the bathroom and stepped inside, closing the door behind him. Ian opened the stairwell door quietly, limping down the corridor, to stop by the door to his room. He swung it open, closing it softly behind him. The room was almost pitch black. Only a faint light came from the small slit of the window at the far end.

He realized that he didn't have much time. The guard could be out at any moment and then he would be trapped. He reached up in the dark to the shelf over his bed, grasping the soft velvet of the tefilin bag in his hand. He heard a soft cough behind him.

Twisting around, he clenched his teeth, a wave of pain tearing through him. He fell down onto the narrow cot, and it creaked under his sudden weight. Catching the sob that threatened to bust forth from his lips, he peered into the dark. He could just barely discern the vague outline of a man sitting on the cot opposite him. His eyes slowly grew accustomed to the dark. He recognized by its characteristic shape who it was. It was Brother Michel.

They sat there, staring silently at each other in the dark, only a few feet separating them.

Brother Michel spoke first. In a hushed whisper he said, "Why did you take what they said you did?"

Ian was silent for a moment, waiting for the pain in his leg to subside. Then he whispered back, "They're important manuscripts. They don't belong hidden away in some cellar. They belong to everyone. Don't you see? You can't catalogue and then hide away the truth."

Brother Michel was silent.

Ian waited, numb with fatigue. Brother Michel sat there in the dark, staring at him. Then silently, the young priest nodded once and lowered his head. Ian understood. Getting up slowly, he clumsily wiped away the salty tears that ran down his cheeks.

"Thank you," he whispered.

There was no reply. None was necessary.

Limping over to the door, he opened it a crack. The long corridor was empty. He looked back one last time at the small figure seated silently in the dark, his head bowed forward. A deep throb of gratitude constricted Ian's chest. Stepping into the hall, he heard the toilet flush. Shutting the door quickly, he shuffled as quietly as he could to the door at the far end. Slipping into the stairwell, he closed the door behind him just as he caught sight of the guard exiting the bathroom. He heaved a deep sigh of relief.

Ten minutes later he had gained the shelter of the trees. Keeping to the shadows, and using whatever cover he could find, he made his way across the grounds to a grassy area where the large radio tower loomed high into the starry night sky. Coming close, he leaned his hand against one of the massive cold metal girders, panting. He was drenched in a cold sweat.

A powerful searchlight blazed out behind him from atop St. John's tower, illuminating a broad strip of ground, not three feet away. He lurched forward. The beam lanced away, brilliantly illuminating another wide swath of grass. Someone in the tower had seen something.

Loping forward at an irregular gait, Ian labored across the few remaining feet of stone path between him and the trees hard up by the perimeter wall. As he crossed the narrow strip, the beam caught him dead center. He didn't stop, passing into the circular shadows of the branches. A low wailing sound suddenly blared forth from high up in the tower.

Dropping to his knees by the roots of the fifth tree, he began to dig frantically with his bare hands into the soft earth. His fingers closed thankfully around the smooth clear plastic. Pulling it clear, he stuffed the pouch inside his shirt. He rose up onto his feet and pulled out the coil of rope from where he'd looped it under one of the straps of his knapsack. Uncoiling it, he hastily tied one end around the trunk of the tree.

The wailing sound of the siren increased in volume, spurring him on. He could hear voices shouting way off to his right, but to his ears they sounded confused. He realized that he had only minutes before they found him.

Pulling off his knapsack, he quickly tied the other end of the stout cord to it. Setting himself, he tossed it high. It soared upward, only to fall back to the ground a foot away. He gathered up the cord. Cocking his arm, he heaved mightily, lips drawn back, the skin on his face stretched tight.

The weighted knapsack sailed high over the lip of the wall. Ian grabbed hold of the cord between both hands. He tugged hard. Luckily, it seemed to catch on something on the other side.

He scrambled upward, driven by adrenaline. He no longer felt any pain. All that mattered was putting one hand in front of the other as he pulled with all his might. His chest heaved, his breaths came in gasps. He lifted himself hand over hand up to the lip. Hooking his good leg over, he straddled the wall and then began climbing down the other side. He dimly heard shouts and the sound of running feet on the other side. He let go of the cord and dropped the few remaining feet.

Pain tore through his right side again. He nearly fainted. Shaking himself, he crawled back to the wall. He had just finished untying the knapsack when he felt a hard tug. An instant later it shot back up the side of the wall and disappeared.

He rose unsteadily to his feet. His head was spinning. Shouldering his pack, he limped across the street, and disappeared into an alley between two run-down tenement buildings.

# CHAPTER 17

Glory is the eighth attribute, for the eight days
of circumcision followed by the covenant which
is the Tzaddik, Foundation of the world…it is
the Glory of the eight days of the Feast of Lights.

Tikunei Zohar 13

---

It was late. Jonathan regarded his surroundings through heavy-lidded eyes. A pleasantly relaxed feeling settled over him. Here I am sitting at the shabbos table of a great sage, and I can't even keep my eyes open, he thought. He forced himself awake. Someone started singing an ancient Hebrew song. The others seated around the large table picked up the tune. Jonathan lapsed into a reverie. It was Friday evening and he had been invited to eat the traditional Friday night meal at Reb Yossl's house. The house was located in the heart of Mea Shearim.

Reb Yossl, who was of the priestly line, could trace his ancestry back to the great Rebi Yishmael ben Elisha, a

Torah sage of the Second Temple period. Centuries later, his descendants had ended up many thousands of miles away, in the frozen wastelands of the Ukraine. Reb Yossl's father, Reb Levi Isaac, had been one of the leaders of a small religious Zionist movement at the end of the nineteenth century. His family had traveled under the most difficult conditions, finally arriving in the place of their dreams, the Holy Land. Settling in and around Jerusalem, they never left it.

Jonathan had gone to see Reb Yossl that morning at the synagogue he usually prayed in. After morning services, he had summoned his courage, and approached the small white-bearded man. The tzaadik stood, tefilin still on, studying a religious text. Jonathan spoke in Hebrew.

"Excuse me, Rebbe. I heard you give a shiur a few months ago at my yeshiva on the tractate of Ketubot."

Jonathan waited for a reply. Reb Yossl gave no sign that he had heard him. His gaze still rested upon the open text on the small wooden stand in front of him. Jonathan nervously took a deep breath and continued.

"I wanted to speak to you on another matter."

Reb Yossl looked up wordlessly, his clear blue eyes piercing into him. Jonathan felt his throat constrict. Swallowing hard, he plowed on.

"I recently heard a strange story from someone about the Menorah and I wanted to ask your advice."

Reb Yossl had been staring at him the whole time. Now he spoke.

"What is your name?" he said. The words sounded like they came through a long tube.

Jonathan hesitated. "Yonatan Charosh."

"Charosh," Reb Yossl repeated in Hebrew. "To hew, to carve, to delve. In what yeshiva do you learn?"

"Aish Yosef," Jonathan replied.

Reb Yossl nodded. "Come to my house tonight for the shabbat meal."

Turning back to the text, Reb Yossl leaned forward. Jonathan beat a hasty retreat, pleased with what he had accomplished.

Now he looked around the table, not recognizing any of the other guests. He wished he could shake his fatigue.

His mind wandered, reviewing what he had learned of the history of the Menorah over the past few weeks.

The conquering Roman general, Titus, had brought the Menorah and other Temple vessels back to Rome, lavishly exhibiting them in his triumphal march through the city in the year 71 C.E. There they were prominently displayed by his father, the Emperor Vespasian, in a building he had erected for that purpose. He called it the Temple of Peace, and dedicated it to his glory in the year 75 C.E. This palace stood halfway between the present Piazza Venezia and the great Coliseum on the Via dei Fori Imperiali, built by the facist dictator Mussolini. The Menorah was moved somewhere else in Rome after the Temple of Peace was destroyed by an earthquake, followed by a massive fire, in the year 191 C.E.

In the year 410 C.E., Rome was sacked by a Visigoth king named Alaric I. He took with him some of the other Temple vessels but for some reason left the Menorah behind. Forty-five years later, it was taken by the Vandal king, Gaiseric, who sacked Rome in the year 455 C.E. Gaiseric brought his cherished prize back to Carthage in North Africa, but he was not to hold onto it forever. In 534 C.E., Belisarius, general of the East Roman Emperor Justinian I, took Carthage from the Vandals on his way to reconquer Rome from the Ostrogoths. Belisarius had the Menorah transported to Constantinople, seat of power of the great Justinian I. Then a curious thing happened.

A Jew living in the city approached Justinian and warned him to relinquish the Menorah, as it had brought bad luck to whomever held it. If Justinian were wise, the Jew warned, he would heed his words and have the Menorah sent immediately to Jerusalem before his fair city was destroyed as well. The tale ended with Justinian, who was said to have been impressed by the warning, giving orders for the Menorah's transport back to Jerusalem.

Another tale he'd found in an obscure text, said the Menorah was then hidden in a Greek Christian Church in Jerusalem, where it remains to this day. Still another legend related that the boat which was carrying it back to Jerusalem sank in the Mediterranean in a freak storm that suddenly rose up to engulf it. A slightly different version, one that Jonathan had found the most intriguing, ended with Justinian ordering the Menorah to be sent back to Rome and hidden there underground.

In Kings I he found a passage that tells of King Solomon having King Hyram of Tyre make for him ten copies of the Menorah for the first Temple. Maybe, Jonathan surmised, it might be one of these copies and not the original Menorah, made by Bezalel in the wilderness, that Titus bore back with him in triumph.

To support this theory, he'd come across a paper where a biblical scholar had noted that the Menorah carved on the Arch of Titus in Rome shows a base wholly inconsistent with the Talmudic interpretation of the scripture. The base carved on the arch contradicted numerous engravings of the Menorah, which depicted an entirely different base. He'd found an article in an archeology periodical that had a color photo of one such engraving, uncovered only recently on the wall of an ancient synagogue in the Galilee.

In those sources, the base was described and drawn with three legs or feet, not the thick, solid base depicted on the arch of Titus. To make matters worse, the base on the arch has dragons carved on it. These were pagan symbols prevalent at the time, and would surely not have been placed on an authentic Jewish Menorah. A legend he'd just come across the day before popped into his head.

At that moment the singing stopped. The table became instantly quiet. Reb Yossl turned to Jonathan.

"What are the thoughts that occupy your mind?" he said.

Jonathan almost fell out of his seat. Nervously, he straightened himself back up in his chair and cleared his throat.

"I was just thinking about an old story I recently read."

"Tell us this story."

Jonathan spoke, acutely aware that all eyes were upon him.

"It was a story about Rabbi Shimon bar Yochai and Rabbi Eleasar ben Jose. According to the story, they traveled to Rome when Marcus Aurelius was emperor to see if they could persuade him to revoke or at least soften the harsh laws against the Jews that the Emperor Hadrian had enacted before him. They asked first to be taken to see the Menorah and the other holy vessels that were in the Temple of Peace before seeing the emperor. They were shown the Menorah and the other vessels after which they were brought into Marcus Aurelius' presence. The emperor received them with honor, and having been told of the two rabbis' great wisdom, he asked them to cure his daughter, who had just recently succumbed to an incurable disease.

"Rabbi Shimon approached her and spoke one word into the girl's ear. She immediately rose up from her bed, fully recovered. The emperor was so impressed that he allowed them to destroy any document they chose from the imperial archives. They took Hadrian's anti-Jewish laws."

Reb Yossl had listened quietly to the story. Now he spoke. "The holy master Yochai truly knew His Ineffable Name."

He paused for a long span, staring into the small flames of the Shabbos candles in the center of the table. All remained silent, waiting for the kabbalistic master to continue, as thin wisps of smoke rose from the flickering flames.

"You come as a messenger of a story I have not heard for many years. I was taught by my grandfather Reb Shalom, of blessed memory, that the messenger always comes in his appointed time."

A bearded fellow across from Jonathan, Reb Yossl's son-in-law, spoke up. His name was Aharon. In his late fifties, he was an imposing figure in his own right, bedecked in the traditional garb of the Bobover hasidim.

"Abba, what do you mean?" he said.

Reb Yossl replied with a parable. "What is it like? A king had slaves, and he dressed them with garments of silk and satin according to their ability. The relationship broke down, and he cast them out, repelled them, and took his garments away from them. They then went on their own way.

"The king took the garments, and washed them well until there was not a single spot on them. He stored them away, bought other slaves, and dressed them with the same garments. He did not mind, since they were at least worthy of garments that he already had, and which had been previously worn.

"So too our garments have been stored away and their stains have been washed clean with the blood of all our sacrifices. Their time has come to be revealed."

An old man with a long gray beard seated to the left of Jonathan spoke. "Blessed is His Name of glorious majesty forever and ever."

All at the table intoned, "Amen."

Reb Yossl closed his eyes and began to sing a beautiful poem written in Aramaic by Rabbi Israel Najara, one of the most prolific Hebrew writers of the sixteenth century. He was inspired by the kabbalistic school of Rabbi Isaac Luria (The Arizal) at Safed, Palestine. The poem is chanted on Friday evenings in Jewish homes all over the world. Its five stanzas describe the wonders of God's creation, concluding with a prayer that God may redeem Israel and restore Jerusalem in the End of Days.

Their voices rose, filling the stone walls of the room, bursting out the open windows into the summer's night air. A bitter-sweet longing filled Jonathan's heart with such poignancy that tears sprang to his eyes. He marveled at the urgency of that longing, even as it flittered away, to be replaced by a deep sense of majesty. It was as if a great chasm had suddenly opened before him, revealing new vistas and horizons stretching far beyond his view.

Reb Yossl's eldest daughter brought in the ritual water used at the meal's end. The bowl and laver were passed round the table as Reb Yossl's son-in-law Aharon led them in the 126th Psalm, the Song of Degrees.

The ancient silver kiddush cup was filled and Reb Yossl made a sign. To Jonathan's surprise, the brimming cup was placed in his hand. The psalm ended. All were quiet.

Lifting the heavy cup, Jonathan recited the blessing in a clear, strong voice. All at the table gave the appropriate response. They recited the Grace after meals and at the end Jonathan recited the blessing over the wine, drinking deeply from the dark sweet liquid. The table had been cleared during the Grace. As if by magic, the already crowded room began to fill with a large group of men, until it seemed that no more could possibly fit in. Yet still more streamed in. They were of all ages, dressed in different garb, though most wore the long black kapotot and shtreimels of Eastern Europe.

The heat in the room became oppressive, yet no one seemed to notice. The heavy smell of sweat came to Jonathan's nostrils. They began singing a tune that he had never heard before. It swelled and diminished and then swelled again even louder. Abruptly, it tapered off to a low hum, finally dwindling. The moment had arrived.

All eyes focused on the small frail figure seated a few inches from Jonathan. The sage spoke, and all ears strained to catch each syllable.

"In the Menorah the final path to victory over Esau begins. Their kingdom now covers the earth in the darkness of Falsehood. It is through the material world that Esau damaged the Voice of Jacob, weakening the pillar of Truth. It is only through the rejoining of Joseph, the righteous one, to Judah, who is the king, that the pillar of Torah will be made firm. As it says, 'The Righteous One is the foundation of the world. The eight days of circumcision, which is the Foundation of the Tzaddik, are equal to the eight days of the Feast of Lights.'

"The Unity of His Holy Name has been broken. Through the covenant and the lights of the Menorah It will be restored. As it is written, 'On that day God will be One and His Name One.' The final steps to the coming of the Messiah are here, my friends. The last in-gathering has begun. The blood of the covenant has washed away our sins. The time has come to restore the Light of Truth. The flame of the Menorah must be lit once more, to spread its

Light over the whole world. As it is written, 'And the house of Jacob shall be fire. And the house of Joseph flame. And the house of Esau like straw.' My friends, the time for proclaiming the Unity of His Name is here."

There was silence in the room. A strange hush lay over the crowd. Suddenly, Jonathan felt an electricity pulse through the air as the words of the tzaadik penetrated the hearts and minds of all those present. Aharon, Reb Yossl's son-in-law, spoke.

"How can we light the Menorah, Abba? It is lost."

Reb Yossl sighed. "God reveals all, Aharon. First there must be an awakening from below. Only then can we merit the blessing from on high."

"What must we do?" Aharon said, and Jonathan could sense all in the room lean forward to hear the Rebbe's next words.

At that moment the lights cut off, plunging the room in near darkness. There must be another brownout, Jonathan thought nervously. Over the last week there had been problems with the power due to the unusually hot weather.

One lone sabbath candle still sputtered on the table, casting with its feeble light an ever-changing chiaroscuro on everything and everyone. Reb Yossl was in darkness but then the small flame bent towards him, illuminating his lined face.

"The contraction of the Divine Presence is at an end. It comes even now from the East. The time of Its Revelation is upon us. Only through the Wisdom which is Torah can we merit the Final Redemption with the coming of the Messiah. Perform acts of loving-kindness, and gird yourselves for the battle to come. Make your will His Will, and he will surely make His Will ours."

Again, there was silence. Then a stooped-over old

man in the back began to sing in a thin, reedy voice. Jonathan knew the words well. It was a song of faith. It was a song of joy and redemption. It was called, "Here is God my Redeemer."

All began to join in, and as the sound of their voices rose upward in a great rumble, Jonathan felt the hairs on the back of his neck stand on end, his body tingling with goose bumps. They repeated the song several times, each time a bit louder in a state of near ecstasy.

Jonathan closed his eyes, the sound of the words surrounding him, lifting him up. He felt like a surfer, riding the crest of a mighty wave, the deep dark ocean far below, silent, waiting.

The singing quieted. Those who had come filed out. On the street below, Jonathan could make out their voices as they discussed what the Rebbe had said. There was an obvious note of excitement in their words as they debated their meaning, their voices dwindling into the night as they walked back to their own homes.

Jonathan lifted his hand to wipe his eyes. He felt a hand on his arm. Turning in the now total darkness, he felt a shudder of fear. Then Reb Yossl spoke, and a wave of relief washed over him.

"Come, tell me the other story."

"Which one?" Jonathan said.

"You know," was the answer.

"Oh," he said, pausing. "I was on an airplane...."

# CHAPTER 18

...and sovereignty will devolve upon the Gentiles for many years, while the children of Israel will carry a heavy yoke in the lands of their captivity, and they will have no Deliverer, because they have rejected My Laws, and their soul has scorned My teaching. Therefore I have hidden My face from them until they have filled up the measure of their sins. ...In those days a blasphemous king will arise among the Gentiles, and do evil things...Like the shooting stars that you saw, thus will be their kingdom. They will rule for a given period of years upon the earth, and crush everyone.

Dead Sea Scroll.

---

May 22

Dear Jonathan,

Of course, I must begin this letter with an apology. Events have been rushing forward so quickly I've been remiss in writing you (still that's no excuse). I'm writing to let you know that I looked into what you asked me to look up for you.

Before I tell you about that, I have some other news I thought I should mention first. I've sort of been adopted by a Jewish family whom I met in the synagogue in the old Jewish quarter of Rome. Their family name is Fragnini. They've been absolutely marvelous, and I've spent practically every Shabbos at their home. As luck would have it, besides a young son, they have a beautiful daughter named Arianna. She is a wonderful girl, and I am totally entranced. I may be falling in love with her, but it's still a bit early to say for sure. At least not just yet.

Anyway, back to your subject. I've found something that I can only categorize as, highly intriguing. I just read over that line and I know it doesn't sound too clear. What I mean to say is, I've stumbled across something that might be unbelievably important! I'm sure no one was meant to find it. I happened upon it by pure chance.

What I found is an original manuscript of a work by a man named Hegesippus, an early Church historian. In it, he gives an account of James from the New Testament. I don't know if you know who he was, but in the New Testament he's described in many places as being Jesus' brother and the head of the original Church in Jerusalem after Jesus' death. In describing him, Hegesippus states: "…he drank no wine…no razor came near his head. He alone was permitted to enter the Holy of Holies in the Temple, for his garments were not of wool but of linen, being of the priestly line. He used to enter the sanctuary and light the seven lights of the Holy Candelabrum. Because of his unsurpassable righteousness, he was called the Righteous One, the Moreh Zadok." Later he describes his death as follows: "So they went up and threw down the Righteous one, the blood brother of the Christ. They said to each other 'let us stone James the Righteous,' and began to stone him, as in spite of his fall he was still alive…While they pelted him with stones, one nearby called out: 'Stop! What are you doing…' Then one of them took the club which he used to beat clothes, and brought it down on the head of the Righteous one. Such was his martyrdom. Immediately after this Vespasian began to besiege them."

A note was attached to it. Someone had scrawled in French, "Remove to heretical section with Temple scroll." Beneath that it was signed only with the two letters, "O.S." I found this most intriguing and sinister. That started my mind spinning. You know how I love a good mystery! So I looked up the known version of the text in the library. It was missing some very important parts of the original.

I couldn't remember for a while where I had seen the term Moreh Zadok (Teacher of Righteousness) before, but finally it came to me. It's used many times in the Dead Sea Scrolls to describe the leader of the Community at Qumran.

Anyway, in the original text that I found, Hegesippus describes James as being the Teacher of Righteousness. His violent assassination by some group (probably the Sadduccean priesthood that were the puppet rulers under the Romans) was tied to the Revolt against Rome by the Zealots in 66 A.D. that eventually led to the destruction of the Second Temple four years later. I think I've figured out why they wanted to put this uncensored version away with some other "Temple scroll" in the heresy section. They were trying to hide documents that might be damaging to church theology. You see, if James really served as the High Priest at some point, and he really was Jesus' brother, then that means that Jesus was also a priest of the

House of Aaron, since they definitely had the same father, Joseph. How then can the Gospels claim that he was the Messiah of the House of David? By the way, I know there exists at least two more packets on your subject, but I haven't had the time to try and get them, yet. That's how fast everything is happening.

I almost forgot to mention it, but on my first day here I somehow ended up down in that place that your friend on the plane spoke of (you know who). I wasn't able to go into a certain area that looked interesting (if you know what I mean) but I'll see if I can try again some other time.

On an entirely different topic, I'm having a great time. Rome is truly a beautiful city. These past few weeks have been unbelievably exciting!

I thought you'd be happy to know that I've been putting on tefilin almost every morning and that I've been going to the synagogue in the old Jewish ghetto every Shabbos. That's how I met the Fragnini's. I'm not really sure why I've started to keep the Sabbath and such; all I can tell you is that it makes me feel good inside. Anyway, I hope all is well with you. I'll write again if I find out anything more. I'll include my address if you want to write back.

Love,
Ian.

Jonathan poured over the letter. Ian might be in danger and not even realize it, he thought. He had to figure out a way to warn him without tipping off anyone in the Vatican who might intercept his letter. After all, he thought, he had to consider the possibility.

Pacing back and forth in his room he muttered, "I need some kind of a code that only Ian will understand."

His eyes fell on the siddur on his desk. Of course,

he thought, I'll write an acrostic.

Sitting down at his desk, he began to compose a letter. An hour later he sat back, surveying his work. It was conceivable that Ian wouldn't get it. It was also conceivable that some censor in the Vatican might also figure it out. Well, it's a chance I'll have to take, he thought.

He had no other way of reaching him, and he didn't have the money to go to Rome and warn him. He could wire his mother for the money, but he figured he should wait a little before resorting to that. Who knows? Maybe there's really nothing to worry about. Maybe I'm just becoming overly paranoid. He read over his own letter one more time. It was filled with innocuous statements and tidings of how he was doing in yeshiva. Near the end he had written:

I hope you are saying the Lecha Dodi every Friday night. You remember, it was written by Shlomo Halevi. I love his style of writing!

Love,
Your younger brother,
Jonathan.

He had written the name, "Shlomo Halevi" in bold characters. He was hoping that Ian would remember that the Lecha Dodi, one of the prayers said every Friday night to usher in the Sabbath, was actually written by the great Rabbi Solomon Alkabets. His first name, Shlomo Halevi, was only known because he had used it as an acrostic at the beginning of each stanza of the famous poem. Jonathan had used the same acrostic style in his letter. If you took the first letter of the first word of each line it spelled out:

"Be careful. Trust no one."

He checked it over one last time. Satisfied, he sealed

the letter and hand-delivered it to the post office nearby.

As he left, he silently mouthed in Hebrew, "Lord protect him from all evil, protect his soul."

Jonathan waited. And waited. Finally, another letter arrived at the yeshiva almost three weeks later. It was slightly mangled. He had been anxious, unable to concentrate on his studies. He was almost at the point of calling his mother for funds for a plane ticket. Not even waiting to go up to his room, he tore open the letter and read:

May 25

Dear Jonathan,

I'm okay. Some terrible things have happened. Whatever you might hear, know that I am innocent. I've found the other two things I mentioned in my last letter. I am in hiding. I'm going to try to get this stuff out. No one will believe me unless I show them tangible proof. This has to be truly explosive stuff. I'm sure of it! But that's not all. I also found what you asked me about! I know it sounds incredible, even to me. I hope you get this letter soon. I'll try to get another letter to you when I can. Don't worry, I'll be alright. I regret nothing.

Love,
Ian.

Jonathan felt sick. Cold sweat broke out on his forehead and upper lip. He stared at the date on the letter, noting uneasily the shaky form of the script. There was no return address. He re-read the last few lines in amazement. Could it be, he thought, stunned. Could he really have found it?

Running up the stairs, he ran over to his desk and

pulled open the drawer. Frantically, he found Ian's first letter and opened it. He compared the dates. The second letter had been written just three days after the first. For whatever reason, it had been delayed all this time. Ian, obviously, had never received his letter.

Racing down to the lobby, he darted into a vacant phone booth and dialed. The phone rang several times, Jonathan's heart hanging on each ring. Please God, let her be home, he prayed. Someone picked up the phone on the other end.

"Mom, is that you?"

"Yes, it's me."

Jonathan sighed in relief. "Hi, it's Jonathan. I can't fully explain, but I need you to wire me some money as soon as possible."

"Why, what's wrong?"

"Look, don't get upset. I just need to go to Rome."

"Is something wrong with Ian? Jonathan, tell me what's going on."

"Okay, okay," he said, swallowing hard. "I asked Ian back in New York to see if he could find anything for me in the Vatican library on the Menorah and the other vessels of the Temple when he got to Rome. You remember that story I told you before I left about that fellow on the plane?"

"Sure, I remember. But what does that have to do with Ian being in trouble? And what kind of trouble are you talking about?"

"Well, I got a letter from Ian over three weeks ago. He wrote me that he'd found a secret document hidden somewhere in the Vatican. I wrote him right back and warned him to be careful. Then today I finally received another letter from him. He writes that he found some very important things and that he's in hiding. He says in the letter that something terrible happened but that he's okay."

"Read me the letters."

He read them to her. There was a long moment of silence, except for the hiss of static on the line.

"How much money should I wire you?" she finally said.

Jonathan took a deep breath. "Send me, I don't know, two thousand dollars? I don't know how much the airfare is and I'll need some money to get around with when I get there."

"Okay, I'll wire you the money right away. Call me as soon as you get there. And call me regularly to let me know what's going on. I'll have the money wired to the post office near your yeshiva, you know which one."

"Yes, of course. Don't worry, Mom. I'm going to find him. I'll call you as soon as I can."

"I love you. Please be careful. I'll say special prayers for both of you every night."

"I love you, too. Don't worry, I'm sure he's okay. You know how tough Ian is. Speak to you soon. Bye."

Jonathan hung up the phone and sat for a moment, thinking. Jumping up, he ran into the Beis Medrash, or Hall of Learning, to speak to his friend Shmuli and obtained the name of a relative who was a travel agent. Running back to the bank of phone booths in the lobby, he reached the agent on the phone, asking him about that day's flights to Rome.

"You missed the only two flights today. The next earliest flight is...tomorrow morning at 9:00," the agent said.

"Okay, put me on it."

"No problem. What is your return date?"

"I don't know. Can you make it an open ticket?'

"Okay. That will be, 1,260 shekel. I need the money today."

"I'm having the money wired over from the United States today, but I'm not sure when I'm going to have it."

"Bseder. You are Shmuli's friend. I'll buy you the ticket myself. I'll be in the office, at least until, eh, 19:30, maybe even a little later. Bring the money with you."

"Thank you. I'll be there."

Jonathan hung up the phone and looked at his watch. It was too early to go to the post office to see if the money had arrived. He ran back up to his room and packed a bag. Restless, he ran out to the post office. He waited over an hour, pacing back and forth. Finally they called his name. He showed his passport and signed for the money. After the clerk stamped some forms, he handed over a thick envelope containing the money, but not before counting it twice. Jonathan was ready to explode. Trying to calm himself, he ran out of the post office, the packet of money placed securely in his front trouser pocket. He dashed down the narrow stone streets of the ancient Jewish Quarter, finally reaching a bus stop. Another yeshiva student was standing there. He asked him how long he'd been waiting.

"Almost ten minutes," was the reply.

Jonathan nodded, wiping the sweat from his face with a tissue. He patted the money to check that it was still there and felt the reassuring thickness of the wad pressing against his leg.

He was a little nervous carrying around so much cash. He readjusted his black hat, tucking his long payos behind his ears. It was a typical hot, dusty, summer's day and it was almost one p.m. The blazing sun beat down on their heads.

Jonathan was dressed in his usual black wool suit, white short-sleeved dress shirt, black socks, and black dress shoes. He was also wearing a white cotton tee-shirt, and a pair of large heavy wool tzitzit under his shirt. A black felt yarmulke peeked out from under the back of his hat.

By the time the bus arrived five minutes later, Jonathan was sweating profusely. After the driver punched his bus card, Jonathan grabbed hold of one of the straps along the aisle. The air-conditioning was out. Thankfully, the driver had opened all the top windows on either side, and as the bus picked up speed, a refreshing breeze fanned Jonathan's face. He stood up straight to better catch the breeze.

Jonathan realized the bus would take him right through the outskirts of the Mea Shearim section. After I get the ticket, he thought, I must go see Reb Yossl. If he was lucky he might be able to find him in the synagogue where Reb Yossl usually prayed. It was nearing the time of the afternoon prayer service.

The bus veered to the right at a major intersection and headed into the commercial district. Jonathan got off. Getting his bearings, he headed down the street. At the corner, he turned right and started to scan the storefronts for numbers and names. He pulled out a small scrap of paper.

Looking down at the address, he walked across the street to the bottom of a flight of stairs. On a half-crumbling post were taped the names of several businesses, including that of the travel agency.

Climbing the stairs, he found himself on a dingy landing, a naked bulb starkly illuminating the shabby interior. Shrugging his thin shoulders, he headed down the narrow corridor, passing several blank doors along the way. Continuing on, he found a small yellowed placard affixed to the next door down. In flowing capital letters were printed: TRAVEL-TOURS EXPRESS.

The door was open. He walked hesitantly inside. Computer print-outs covered the floor. Two men in their thirties sat behind two desks, both speaking non-stop into the phones cradled under their chins as they stared into the computer screens in front of them.

One of them cupped his hand over the mouthpiece and spat out, "What do you want?" in rapid-fire Hebrew.

"I'm looking for Menachem," Jonathan said.

The man pointed to the fellow by the other desk and continued his conversation. Jonathan walked over.

"Excuse me," he said, "I'm Yonatan Charosh. I'm Shmuli's friend from the yeshiva. I spoke to you earlier about a ticket for tomorrow's flight, to Rome?"

Menachem held up his index finger and continued his conversation. Jonathan waited patiently. A minute later, Menachem paused, cupping the mouth of the receiver.

"Flight to Rome…oh yes, Shmuli's friend. Now, where did I put them," he muttered, rummaging through the layers of paper on his desk.

Something fell to the floor. He picked it up. "Ah, here it is," he said.

Looking it over he said, "It was a little more. I told you 1,260 or 1,270 shekels. Well it was 1,320 shekels. There was a surcharge I wasn't aware of. I figured you wanted it anyway and I had no way to reach you."

"No, that's fine," Jonathan said.

"Bseder, how do you want to pay?"

"I have dollars."

Menachem nodded as he pulled over a small calculator and pressed some buttons. "I'm giving you the black market rate," he said as he showed Jonathan the number.

Jonathan pulled out the envelope from his front pant pocket and counted out the crisp bills. He handed them over to Menachem, who counted them quickly, tucking them into his pocket.

"All the information is right on the ticket. It's an open ticket like you wanted." He lifted his hand and said, "Lehitraot," as he uncupped the receiver and continued his conversation.

Jonathan said, "Thank you."

Slipping the ticket into the inner pocket of his suit jacket, he hurried back down to the street. He looked at his watch. They probably finished the afternoon service, but maybe I can still catch him, he thought. Wending his way through the crowds, he headed a few blocks over, into the Mea Shearim section.

Immediately one could detect a difference. Here the women were all modestly covered and almost all the men were dressed either in dark suits and hats or the traditional kapotos and shtreimels of the various Hasidic sects. A few of the men and boys were dressed in short-sleeved white dress shirts and pants or shorts, colorful knitted yarmulkes perched atop their heads.

Jonathan strode swiftly down the familiar narrow streets to a small stone sanctuary butted up against a larger building. He was sweating as he climbed the shallow steps. Wiping his brow, he stepped inside.

The afternoon service was over. Sitting around several tables piled high with different religious texts sat a few knots of men dressed in black, immersed in learning. Jonathan threaded his way past the tables to an alcove. On the wall hung a large intricate picture depicting a great circle. The circle was made up of many concentric rings, each ring consisting of many tiny Hebrew words. Above the circle in large capital letters was written the single Hebrew word, "East". Seated beneath it was Reb Yossl, his small bent-over frame facing away from Jonathan. Approaching him respectfully, Jonathan waited in silence.

Reb Yossl opened his eyes. The piercing blue eyes of the tzaadik stared straight through him. Reb Yossl opened his hand. Not a word had been spoken.

Jonathan sank down onto a small chair next to the aged Torah sage. Reb Yossl placed his hand on Jonathan's arm. He spoke softly. The words seemed to emanate from somewhere other than his mouth.

"Whatever comes to your hands to do, do it with all your might!"

Jonathan recognized the words; they were from Ecclesiastics. Reb Yossl paused. The sage spoke, his voice a dead whisper.

"I have seen a vision. Letters of white fire from the Merkavah. They took form. Before me lay a piece of wood, broken in two. Suddenly, the two pieces joined into one, and it was as whole as if it had never been broken. It sank into the ground. Time passed. Then from the bare earth a green shoot sprang forth. And from the shoot sprouted a rose and letters of black fire flew before my eyes. And the words spoke to me, and they said, 'They shall no more be two nations, nor shall they be divided into two kingdoms...They will be My people and I will be their God. And David My servant will be king over them—they will have one shepherd.'

"A great fear came over me, and seized by bones. The true fear of God. And I wept with joy to feel the truth of that fear. And I ascended in my vision into a great hall. And there an angel greeted me. He took my hand and led me upward into the inner-most heavens, where I saw two great hairy red hands. And the hands were gripping the legs of the Throne of Glory.

"The angel then spoke to me, 'His hands are strong, but the flames of Yosef will burn them like straw.'

"And I said, 'Where is this flame to be found?'

" 'Rome.' "

Jonathan's face had drained of blood. Had Reb Yossl's hand not been holding his arm he would have fallen. He tried to speak, but his throat had gone dry.

Finally he was able to croak out, "My brother is in Rome. In the very heart of the Vatican. I asked him to look for evidence of the Menorah and the other vessels of the Holy Temple. He has written to me twice. I just received his second letter today. He writes that he has found the Menorah! He says that he is in hiding. I bought a ticket for tomorrow's flight to Rome. What should I do?"

Reb Yossl had been listening intently. Now he asked, "What is your brother's name?"

"Ian."

"No, in Hebrew."

"Yosef. Yosef ben Yisrael."

There was a sharp intake of breath. Reb Yossl said, "You must go and seek out your brother. You must go to Rome. Your brother is in great danger. Save him if you can. The last struggle has begun. The spiral has come full circle. Remember to be true to yourself as was Pinchas and not to fall into the trap of Zimri."

"Give me a blessing," Jonathan pleaded.

The old man sighed. He placed his frail hands on Jonathan's head.

"May God make you like Ephraim and like Menashe," he uttered.

Jonathan rose up. He felt a great strength flowing through him. It was as if he had shed back the layers of time and stood now as some ancient Hebrew warrior. He stood erect, a steely glint flashing in his eyes as he looked deep into the clear blue eyes of the tzaadik. In the Rebbe's eyes he saw mirrored a long corridor. The corridor was lined with the faces of many men, his ancestors. Their faces were serene, but the light that burned deep within those eyes was an unquenchable fire, and a spark of that indomitable spirit passed to him, igniting his soul.

The sage spoke again. "Fear not. The whole world is a narrow bridge." Picking up a small slip of paper he scrawled a name on it in Hebrew. Looking up he said, "Should you need help, place a letter in the hands of this man. He is at our consulate in Rome. Remember the words of the prophet, 'Not in power and not in strength, but in my spirit says the Lord of Hosts .' Now go in peace and God will be with you."

Jonathan's hand closed around the slip of paper. Not looking back, he walked out into the bright sunlight. Behind him, bent over, sat the tzaadik, swaying back and forth, his eyes closed. His lips moved silently in prayer.

## CHAPTER 19

When King David had dug the foundation for the Temple, he found a stone resting on the mouth of the abyss with the divine Name on it. He put this stone into the holy of holies in the Temple. The sages of Israel began to fear lest some young men might learn the divine Name and destroy the world. To prevent this, they made two brazen lions which they placed on iron pillars by the door of the holy of holies, one on the right and the other on the left. If anyone entered and learned the divine Name, these lions would roar at him when he came out, so that through terror and fright, the Name would be driven out of his mind and forgotten.

Jesus of Nazareth went secretly to Jerusalem and entered into the Temple, where he learned the holy letters of the Divine Name. He wrote them on parchment, and uttering the Name to prevent pain, he cut his flesh and hid the parchment therein. Then, again pronouncing the Name, he caused the flesh to grow together.

As he left the door, the lions roared and the Name was erased from his mind. When he went outside the city, he cut his flesh again and drew out the parchment, and when he had studied its letters, he learned the Name again. Thus was he able to perform all his miracles and wonders.

                                  Legends of Jerusalem.

# Menorah

Undersecretary Maglione was in a vile mood. Dark storm clouds, blocking out the mid-afternoon sun, colored the sky a dull green hue. Thin gray clouds raced beneath them. The air was charged with the distinct smell of ozone. A strong breeze wafted through the tall narrow windows. Getting up out of his plush leather chair, he strolled across the polished inlaid marble floor to stand beside the tall casements, gazing down at the courtyard below. Two young priests dressed in dull black robes scurried across the broad flagstones, darting into one of the many doors that led into the vast structure that comprised the headquarters of the Sacred Office.

From this building orders went out to the four corners of the globe, directly affecting millions of lives. And I can't even locate one cursed Jew, he thought darkly. Thick wet drops began to fall on the dry flagstones below. He watched in detached fascination as they created a pattern on the dry courtyard stones. That cursed Fragnini must be helping him, he raged inside.

He had known for some time now that the young Jewish scholar had been seeing the daughter. Ever since his nephew had reported to him about the house with the gold lion by its door, he'd had them watched. The reports he'd received said that she was as beautiful as her mother.

I am not the second son of a pastry baker now, he thought with malicious glee. You took away my beloved Gabrielle without a second thought. You brushed me aside as if I didn't even exist. We shall see.

A delicious scene leapt unbidden into his mind. He sat on an ornate throne. Beneath his feet was laid out a magnificent rug of astounding intricacy, each color glowing with rich and subtle fervor. Kneeling upon it, as beautiful as ever, was Gabrielle. She threw herself at his feet, sobbing.

He shook his head in annoyance, astounded at his own thoughts.

Gazing down at the courtyard, he knit his tall brow. His small features creased in a scowl. He wondered, what has that wretched thief actually taken? His keen mind grimly realized that whatever it was, it must have been of sufficient importance for the young Jew to have risked stealing it.

The clouds finally broke, letting loose a heavy downpour. He remained standing by the opening. The drops finally reached him, spattering across his face as they glanced off the outer metal edges of the casements.

CHAPTER 20

He said: The world was sealed with six directions. As it is written: (Psalms 104:2), "He wraps Himself in light as a garment, He spreads out the heavens like a curtain."

*The Bahir 30*

---

The flight touched down on schedule. Jonathan checked his watch. It was almost two p.m. He'd spent most of the flight praying. He was fasting and a little weak. Out of his inner suit pocket he pulled the two letters from his brother, re-reading them again. There must be more clues here to help me find him, he thought. He had made up a short list the night before in his dorm room. Pulling out a small sheet of paper, he stared at the few lines he had jotted down:

Places to look:
1. Fragnini house
    (Arianna Fragnini)

2. Vatican
    a. dormitory(roommate?)
    b. library (archives?)
    c. officials
3. Police
4. American Embassy

He looked over his list. Thoughtfully, he pulled out his ball-point pen and wrote: 5. Synagogue of Rome (Jewish Ghetto).

Satisfied, he folded the paper and tucked it back inside his jacket. He got his suitcase from the baggage claim and cleared customs after exchanging some dollars for liras. Coming out of the busy main terminal into the afternoon heat, he was immediately accosted by a taxicab driver.

"Come, I take you," he yelled heartily, grabbing for Jonathan's suitcase.

Jonathan held onto his bag. "How much to get to the center of the city?" he asked.

The taxicab driver grinned. "For you, only eighty thousand lira."

Jonathan calculated mentally. That sounded like too much. He turned away.

The cab driver shifted to the side, waving his hands excitedly as he yelled, "Okay, for you, sixty five thousand."

Jonathan shook his head and walked off. The cab driver followed him.

Turning around, Jonathan stopped. "Thirty thousand," he said, lifting up three fingers.

The cab driver rolled up his eyes and threw up his hands.

"Okay," he muttered.

"Take me to an inexpensive hotel in the center of

the city, okay?" Jonathan said.

The driver turned his head, and Jonathan could see he was grinning broadly. "Sure, but such information in not cheap!"

Jonathan frowned. "How much?" he asked.

Five minutes later they had decided on a price.

The cab deposited him in front of a decrepit building. He entered the stark lobby through a large door. At a desk against one of the walls sat a bored attendant. Inquiring after a room, the older man lazily directed him over to a set of elevator doors. Dragging his suitcase over to the elevator, he pushed the button and waited. A moment later the doors opened. He stepped inside, dragging his suitcase along with him. The elevator rose to the top floor.

Stepping out, he entered a large public room, charmingly decorated with numerous pieces of carved wood and displays of dried flowers. Jonathan was favorably impressed. Heading directly to the front desk, he asked for a room.

A bellhop led him down the hall. Producing a key, the bellhop opened the door. Jonathan followed him inside. The room was quite small and the furnishings were on the austere side.

Satisfied, Jonathan stowed away his luggage, making sure to lock the door behind him. Back in the lobby, he pulled out the sheet of paper with his list. He looked at the date on his wristwatch. The two letters from his brother had been written over five weeks ago. The trail might be very cold by now, he realized.

Going back to the front desk, he inquired from the clerk about making a long-distance collect call to the United States. He looked at his watch and asked for the correct time.

The clerk answered, "Five minutes to four, sir."

He'd set his watch correctly. In New York it was almost ten o'clock in the morning. His mother would be in school, teaching. He'd have to wait until late that night to try and reach her.

Back down on the street he bought a map in English from a small kiosk on the corner. Quickly orienting himself, he set off on foot for the Jewish ghetto.

Almost a mile later he reached his last landmark, the Piazza Venezia. He was hot and weak from the lack of food and sleep. Ever since yesterday, when he'd received that fateful second letter, he'd been under a tremendous strain. Resting briefly beneath the massive white marble monument to Italy's first king, he got up and walked past the Teatro di Marcello. Following the map, he turned onto the Lungotevere Cenci. Directly in front of him stood an imposing structure, the Synagogue of Rome. The majestic Tiber flowed by to his left.

He looked at his watch. It was twenty minutes to five. Taking several long strides, he crossed the street. He climbed the steps leading up to the entrance, two at a time. Breathing heavily, he pulled open one of the massive doors and entered the vestibule. Off to one side stood a tour guide with a group of tourists, cameras at the ready.

Surprised, Jonathan stood there, watching. Next to the guide stood a small, wizened old man with a beard, a large black yarmulke covering his head. Jonathan hung back, waiting for an opportunity to approach the man he assumed was the sexton. The group moved on to the next display. Frustrated, Jonathan trailed behind them. He felt a tap on his arm. At his elbow stood the sexton, a puzzled look on his face.

The sexton said, "Desidera?"

Jonathan smiled, a pained look on his face. He

didn't know any Italian. "Do you speak English?"

The sexton replied, "No, no too good."

"Ata medaber Ivrit?" Jonathan said.

The sexton smiled. "Yes," he replied in Hebrew.

Jonathan drew out his list from his jacket pocket. In Hebrew he asked, "Do you know of a family named Fragnini?"

"Yes, of course. Don Fragnini is the president of the synagogue."

"Did you happen to notice a young Jewish man, very tall, with him?"

"You mean the American student, studying in El Vaticano?"

"Yes, him," Jonathan replied.

"Of course. He was here several times with the Fragnini family for the Sabbath services, though he hasn't come in a while."

"I am his brother. I came from Israel to find him. Do you have any idea where he might be?"

The sexton shook his head. "You might go to the Vatican or better yet, go to the Fragnini house. I'm sure Don Fragnini would know where he is," he said.

Jonathan got directions to the house. "Thank you so much. Also, when do you start the afternoon service?"

The sexton sighed. "We no longer have enough men to make the minyan in the afternoon."

"Would you mind if I went in to pray?" Jonathan said.

"No, of course. I will make sure no one disturbs you," the sexton assured him.

Jonathan entered the main sanctuary. Standing by one of the pews, he pulled out the small siddur he always carried on him. He looked up front. A massive marble ark stood there, flanked by two large Menorahs. Carved deeply into the pale marble lintel above the ark were the words, "Know before Whom you stand." Swaying back and forth, feet together, he closed his eyes and prayed silently.

Ten minutes later he walked out of the massive edifice. He'd wanted to say good-bye to the sexton, but he was nowhere to be found.

Reading off the sexton's directions, he followed the street signs through the narrow cobblestone ways until he came upon a small open court. There at the far end stood a large house. Hurrying across the open space, he ascended the steps. At the massive door, he kissed the large gold mezuzah in the shape of a lion affixed to the door-post. He knocked on the thick wood door.

He waited a moment. The door opened. Staring at him was a maid, a large white apron tied to her front. She said, "Buonasera. Desidera?"

"Hello," Jonathan replied. "I am looking for my brother Ian, Ian Charosh. Is Don Fragnini home?"

Marta frowned. "No parla inglese. Come si chiama Signore?"

Jonathan shook his head, smiling. Marta frowned again. She took a step back. The door slammed shut in his face. He stood there, staring at the door. Shrugging, he knocked again. After a long pause the door opened. Marta stood in the doorway, an annoyed look on her face. He noticed out of the corner of his eye someone pass behind her, inside the house.

Putting his foot in the door he yelled past the surprised Marta, "Hello. I'm looking for my brother Ian. Is Don Fragnini home?"

Marta tried to shut the door but was blocked by his foot. Just then the door opened wide, to reveal Signora Fragnini. She smiled gently, her beautiful face lighting up.

In perfect English she said, "I'm sorry. Don Fragnini is not home at the moment. I am Signora Fragnini. Can I help you?"

Jonathan removed his foot from the door.

Straightening up he said, "Yes, thank you. My name is Jonathan Charosh. My brother's name is Ian. He wrote me recently, and in his letter he mentioned that he had met your family."

Signora Fragnini cut him off before he could continue.

"Please come in," she said softly "Of course we know Ian."

She ushered him into a magnificent room. Speaking sharply to Marta, she gave her instructions. Marta quickly departed. Signora Fragnini led Jonathan over to a plush white couch. Sinking down into its soft cushions, he leaned forward on its edge. Signora Fragnini seated herself nearby on an antique chair.

She spoke. "Ian is a wonderful young man. My husband brought him back from the synagogue one Sabbath several months ago. My son Eli looks up to him so much."

Jonathan smiled awkwardly.

She continued. "I don't know if he wrote you about it in his letter, but he was also seeing our daughter Arianna. Both my husband and I approved. In fact we were delighted. There aren't too many suitable young Jewish men these days, and we have been worried about Arianna."

Jonathan said, "Yes, in his first letter Ian mentioned your daughter."

Signora Fragnini sighed. "Yes. We've been so upset. Ian was supposed to come to us for the Sabbath more than a month ago. Since then we haven't heard a single word from him."

Marta appeared, carrying a silver folding tray. As

she set it up next to him, Jonathan shifted uncomfortably on the couch.

"Please, eat something," Signora Fragnini implored him.

Jonathan looked over the plate of assorted cakes arranged before him. Embarrassed, he shook his head politely. Besides not wanting to break his fast, he didn't know what kind of a kosher home the Fragnini's had and so was afraid to eat anything.

Signora Fragnini said, "Don't worry. It is all from my own kitchen. We keep a strictly kosher home."

Jonathan's face flushed slightly. Not wanting to insult her, he nodded his head. He picked up a piece, biting into it. It was delicious.

Signora Fragnini signaled to Marta. She poured out a tall glass of milk and handed it Jonathan. He reached forward to snag another piece of cake, washing it down with some of the cold milk. He was starved. Signora Fragnini watched him eat, smiling. He finished the glass. Marta, hovering nearby, took the glass away and handed him a lace napkin before leaving the room.

Signora Fragnini asked politely, "When did you arrive in Rome?"

Jonathan, dabbing his mouth with the napkin, said, "Just this morning."

"Where are you staying?"

"At a hotel not far away. It's called the Bertoli."

She nodded. "You must stay with us. We insist," she said in a tone of finality.

Jonathan tried to protest.

"No," she said. "Give me the key to your room. I'll have our driver Angelo go over and pick up your things. No brother of Ian's is staying in a hotel when we have plenty of empty rooms here."

Jonathan tried to object one last time, then decided to give in.

"Good," she said, taking the hotel key from him. "You must be very tired from your trip. My husband should be back home within the hour and you can speak to him then. Marta," she called.

Marta hurried into the room.

In Italian Signora Fragnini said, "Take our guest up to the corner guest bedroom please."

Marta bowed slightly and said, "Si, Signora Fragnini."

She led a reluctant Jonathan up the stairs to a huge bedroom with a massive four-cornered canopied bed carved out of polished dark timbers. The entire ceiling was frescoed with a colorful scene of an idyllic Italian countryside. Marta left quietly, closing the door behind her. Looking around, he thought, I guess I should get some rest.

Going over to the tall set of windows beside the bed, he pulled aside the soft silk curtains to gaze down upon a beautiful atrium garden. Letting go of the curtain, he seated himself on the soft bedspread. Taking off his hat and jacket he placed them on an intricately carved wooden chair. He slipped off his shoes, laying down on the bedspread. A moment later, he was fast asleep.

# CHAPTER 21

A time is coming—declares my Lord God—
when I will send a famine upon the land: not a
hunger for bread or a thirst for water, but for hearing the words of the Lord. Men shall wander from
sea to sea and from north to east to seek the word
of the Lord, but they shall not find it.

Amos 8:11

---

Undersecretary Maglione stood before his superior. The office was far more splendid than his own. Its lofty ceiling, soaring high above, was frescoed by one of the great masters. Upon the walls hung several priceless works. Underfoot, an exquisite soft Persian rug stretched out in all directions. Secretary Karocyz sat behind a large gilt-edged desk inlaid with marble, ebony, and teak. A dour expression animated his corpulent features.

"What news do you have to report? I pray there is nothing worse," he said, rolling his eyes heavenward.

Undersecretary Maglione cringed inside. To the Secretary he maintained a calm demeanor. He spoke. "A letter was sent to the culprit from the Holy Land. I have it here in my hand," he said, revealing a thin blue envelope from a fold in his robe.

"What does it say?" Secretary Karocyz said.

"It appears to be a letter from the thief's brother, your Grace. I have several good people puzzling it out to see if it contains any hints as to his current whereabouts, but so far they have found nothing."

"So, he has a brother in the Holy Land," Secretary Karocyz mused aloud.

---

There was a knock on the door. Jonathan rose up into a sitting position. Opening his eyes wide to wake himself, he stared blearily around the shadowy room. I must have conked out, he thought. There was another knock.

Clearing his throat, he called out, "One minute," as he got up off the bed.

Locating his shoes, he slipped them on, reaching for his jacket. He opened the door.

Marta stood in the hallway, waiting. He straightened his black felt yarmulke on his head. She beckoned him to follow, heading down the grand marble staircase.

She led him through the living room and under a marble archway to the formal dining area. A large heavy-set man sat at the head of a massive stone table. The table was set for dinner. To his immediate right was seated a teenage boy. At the near end of the table Jonathan recognized Signora Fragnini.

The large man got up, waving his hand to the chair next to him, as he boomed heartily, "Come. Sit here by me."

Jonathan took the seat that had been proffered to him.

"I am Don Fragnini," the heavy-set man said, a great grin splitting his broad features. "This is my boy Eli, and of course you've already met my wife Gabrielle."

Jonathan nodded. "Yes. It's a pleasure to meet you Don Fragnini."

Eli couldn't contain himself any longer. He burst out, "Do you know where Ian is?"

A pained expression came over Jonathan's face as he said, "No. That's why I've come. To find him."

Don Fragnini gave Eli a stern look. "Don't bother our guest. He's as worried as we are about Ian, probably more so. Let us all eat, and then we will talk. Marta," he said turning to the maid, "bring out the food please."

They ate quickly. As Marta began clearing off the table, Jonathan quietly recited the short grace after the meal.

Don Fragnini waited until he was finished, and then said, "Come. Let's go into my office and talk."

Eli said, "But, Papa, I want to talk to him also."

Gabrielle turned to Eli and said, "Let your father talk with Jonathan first. You'll have plenty of time to speak to him later. He's going to be staying with us until we find Ian."

Eli tossed his head and stomped away. Don Fragnini led Jonathan into the wood-paneled office that was his private den. Seating himself behind a large desk, he leaned back in a chair. Jonathan sat down in a soft leather and wood arm-chair in the middle of the room.

"Don Fragnini, please tell me what you know," he said simply.

Don Fragnini leaned forward in his chair, the leather creaking under his weight.

"Not much, actually. As my wife told you, almost five weeks ago, Ian was supposed to come to us for the

Sabbath as he has almost every Sabbath since we first met him. Late that Friday afternoon, my wife Gabrielle received a phone call from our daughter. She said she wasn't feeling well and to tell Ian that she was sorry she couldn't make it."

Don Fragnini got up to pace the thick piled carpet by the side of his desk. Leaning his bulk against the front of the desk, he continued.

"Well, he didn't show up that night. We were a little concerned, and of course Eli was very disappointed, but we figured that he couldn't make it in time and that we would see him the next morning in the synagogue. We waited for him after the services, but he never showed up.

"Eli wanted to walk right over to the Vatican that afternoon and see if anything was wrong. But I told him to stop being foolish. Maybe Ian had decided not to come for some reason and wouldn't appreciate us bothering him." He paused to scratch his head.

"Go on," Jonathan said.

"Well, after Shabbat was over that night, Arianna called. She said she was feeling better and asked to speak to Ian. I told her that he hadn't come to us for Shabbat. She got very upset, and I asked her why. She said she was worried about him. I told her not to worry, that I was sure everything was fine. You see," he said, getting up again, "I didn't want her to know that I was starting to be concerned myself.

"The next day, I had my driver take me over to el Vaticano. I made some discreet inquiries with someone I have had some business dealings with there in the past. He promised to look into it for me. I received a call from him that same day at my warehouse. He told me that, yes, there was an American student studying in the Vatican on a scholarship. He fit the description I had given him perfectly. He said that no one had seen him since the Wednesday or at the latest, the Thursday before. He also told me that he had the distinct impression that there was more to it than that."

"What do you think he meant?" Jonathan said, leaning forward.

"He said that he just had a feeling that something unusual had happened in connection with the American, but he didn't know what. And then he told me something even more disturbing."

"What!" Jonathan exclaimed, almost jumping out of his chair.

"It appears that a certain Vatican official may be mixed up in Ian's disappearance," Don Fragnini reluctantly replied.

"Really?"

Don Fragnini sighed. "Yes. You see, many years ago, before we were married, my wife became friendly with a young Catholic boy at the University." Looking Jonathan straight in the eye he said, "I can assure you it was purely platonic."

Jonathan nodded his head. Don Fragnini plowed on.

"Well it seems that at the time this Catholic boy was interested in my wife in a serious way. Gabrielle, of course, had no idea. This went on for some time. Several months later I was introduced to Gabrielle by a member of her family who was a friend of mine. We began seeing each other regularly. After a time, we decided to marry. The day after our engagement, I was walking to one of my classes, when who should I see, but Gabrielle and this Catholic boy standing under a tree. He was shouting and waving his arms wildly. I thought he was going to hurt her. Naturally, I rushed over and knocked him to the ground."

"He jumped up and made like he was going to attack me. I stepped forward to knock him down again but

Gabrielle rushed in between us and held me back. She spoke quietly to him to calm him down.

"He nodded and walked away, but not before he gave me a look that I will never forget. Gabrielle told me his name." Don Fragnini pushed himself away from his desk to pace the floor again. Stopping, he turned to say, "Several years back, in the course of one of my dealings with my business contact in the Vatican, I learned that this same young man had entered the Church and risen to a position of considerable power and influence. My source mentioned the name of this Vatican official in connection with your brother."

"I see," Jonathan said. "What is his name?"

"Undersecretary of the Sacred Office Alberto Maglione."

Jonathan nodded, digesting the information.

"I didn't leave it at that," Don Fragnini continued. "I contacted a friend in the police department and told him about Ian's disappearance. He said they would have to wait a few days, but if he had not turned up by then, they would list him as a missing person and begin a search. I asked him if he could look into it for me himself. He assured me he would.

"The next evening I received a call from the inspector here at my home. He said that he'd heard of nothing unusual going on in the Vatican. He asked me to be more specific, but what could I tell him? He told me that Ian hadn't been seen at the Vatican since the week before, but that his dorm room was still full of all his things. He asked if I wanted them to be sent here, and I said yes. Two days later the police listed him officially as a missing person. I get a weekly update from my friend in the department. So far they've found nothing."

Jonathan stood up. "Where are Ian's things?"

Don Fragnini nodded and took him over to a door set flush into the paneled wall. He opened it and turned on a light. Gesturing with his hand, he moved aside to let Jonathan look in.

"Here," he said.

Jonathan looked down. On the floor of a closet was a large green canvas duffel bag. He dragged it out slowly onto the carpet. It was very heavy. Five minutes later, he and Don Fragnini stood over the assorted items spread out on the thick carpet.

Jonathan looked them over one more time. Rubbing his chin with his hand, he turned to Don Fragnini. "Are you sure this is everything that was in his room?"

"Yes," was the definite reply. "I was assured of that by my friend in the police department."

"Well," Jonathan remarked with a note of triumph. "I don't see his tefilin bag. In his letter he said that he was putting them on again every morning, and they're not here. Unless someone else took them, that means that he must have gone back to his room at some point to get them, since he wouldn't normally be carrying them around. Tell me, have you spoken to your daughter recently?"

"Yes, of course. Why?"

Jonathan nodded. Pulling out his sheet of paper he said, "Can you give me her address and telephone number? I'd like to speak to her."

"I'll call her right now," Don Fragnini said, pulling over the phone on his desk. He dialed the number and waited. Shaking his head, he hung up the phone.

"She might be in the university library studying," Don Fragnini said. Thinking silently a minute, he turned and asked, "You mentioned a letter that Ian wrote. Can I see it?"

Jonathan pulled out the letters and handed them to Don Fragnini. "There were two."

Don Fragnini read them carefully. Looking up, he said, "Can I hold these for a while?"

"Sure, I guess so."

Placing his large meaty hand gently on Jonathan's thin shoulder, he said, "Come. You need to get some sleep. Tomorrow I'll have my driver take you over to Arianna's apartment. You can't expect to find Ian if you're exhausted."

Jonathan reluctantly allowed himself to be led back up to his bedroom. At the door he turned to ask, "What do you think happened to my brother?"

Don Fragnini was clearly concerned. "I don't know."

His suitcase was waiting for him in the center of the bedroom. Opening it, he changed wearily into his pajamas and lay down on the soft bed. He closed his eyes, relaxing. His eyes shot open. *I forgot to call Mom*, he suddenly realized. He was about to get up and look for Don Fragnini, when he paused to reconsider. *I'll call her as soon as I have something definite*, he thought, closing his eyes.

Bright sunlight streamed through the silk curtains as Jonathan finished putting away his tefilin. Having spent many years in yeshiva, he was used to getting up early. Slipping his siddur back into his jacket pocket, he picked up his hat and closed the door behind him. Walking downstairs, he followed the delicious smell of cooking food. He felt a little awkward walking around a strange house, but his hunger won out over his timidity. Near the entrance to the kitchen he hesitated.

Sticking his head in, he saw Marta busying herself with some pots. The kitchen was the biggest one Jonathan had ever seen. Looking up, Marta noticed him. Smiling, she waved for him to come in. At the far end of an island were several leather bar stools. She motioned for him to sit down. Place mats with settings were neatly set up on the marble countertop in front of him. As Jonathan seated himself, Marta brought over a skillet, a delicious smelling omelet sizzling in it.

Tilting it towards him she asked, "Si?"

"Si," he replied, his mouth watering. He got up to wash his hands. As he came back to the stool, Marta brought over a small basket of fresh steaming rolls, straight from the oven. Jonathan, reciting the blessing over the bread, broke open one of the rolls. Marta smiled appreciatively as she continued her work, one eye on Jonathan.

Half an hour later he leaned back, stuffed. He'd eaten so many of the rolls he'd lost count. Getting up slowly from the table, he smiled at Marta and said, "Thank you. It was delicious."

She nodded, smiling broadly. Leaving the kitchen, he nearly collided with Eli.

Eli smiled brightly as he said, "I wanted to talk to you last night but you went to sleep right after talking to Papa."

"Sorry," Jonathan said. "Actually I'd like to talk to you now, if you don't mind. I'll keep you company while you eat."

"Okay."

Jonathan spent the next twenty minutes talking to Eli but learned nothing new.

As Eli got up to leave, Jonathan asked, "Where is your father and mother?"

"Mama is still sleeping. Papa was out of the house hours ago. He gets up before dawn to go to the warehouse."

Jonathan frowned. "Your father said he would have his driver take me over to your sister's apartment. Do you know how I can reach him?"

"I can do better than that," Eli said. "I'll call the

driver for you myself."

"Thanks."

Ten minutes later, seated in the back seat of a large hunter-green Mercedes sedan, he leaned forward to ask the driver a question.

"Excuse me, but did you ever meet my brother Ian?"

In halting English, Angelo said over his shoulder, "No, but I see him once."

Jonathan leaned forward on the leather seat. "When?"

"With Signorina Fragnini."

Jonathan leaned back. They drove on for several minutes. A startling thought popped into his head.

Leaning forward again he said, "When was this?"

Angelo turned around for an instant and said, "About two weeks ago."

Jonathan sat there, stunned. Stumbling on the words in his excitement he said, "Where?"

Angelo answered matter-of-factly, "In Ostia Antica. Of course, I no bother them. They no see me. Too busy look at each other, if you know what I mean," he finished, turning his head to give Jonathan a sly wink.

Jonathan said, "Have you told anyone else about this?"

"No. You first to ask."

"Please don't tell anyone else. It's very important."

"Va bene."

Jonathan took that for a yes. "One last thing," he said. "Where were they when you saw them?"

"At a cafe', by the sea."

Jonathan leaned back into the plush leather cushions. One thing was certain. Don Fragnini's daughter Arianna was definitely the next person he should see. He pulled out his sheet of paper and added to his list:

6. Ostia Antica (Cafe?)

# CHAPTER 22

"What have you to report?" Undersecretary Maglione barked, fixing his nephew with a harsh glare.

Brother Michel, shifting his feet uncomfortably on the cold marble, said, "Just this morning we traced one of the items that was taken."

"One of the items?" Undersecretary Maglione's voice rang like steel being pulled from a scabbard. "What do you mean, one of the items? Are you telling me that more than one manuscript was stolen?"

Brother Michel's face flushed red. A single bead of sweat rolled down his face. In a pleading voice he replied, "We don't know. Anything is possible."

The Undersecretary tapped his upper lip with his thin index finger. "Well, what was it?"

Taking a deep breath to calm himself, the young priest said, "We traced the missing pouch to the heretical section. It appears to have contained a scroll of great antiquity. It was donated to the collection by brothers of the

Dominican order affiliated with the Ecole' Bibliot. That is all we know about it."

Undersecretary Maglione had leaned back in dismay as his nephew was speaking. Pursing his lips, he pointed his long thin finger at him.

"Continue your search. Perhaps there are other items missing. If so, they might shed further light upon the matter."

"Yes, your Grace," Brother Michel said.

Undersecretary Maglione grunted once, waving his hand in dismissal. Brother Michel hastily departed.

Waiting for the heavy inlaid wood door to close behind the back of the young priest, the Undersecretary paused a moment before picking up the phone. He dialed a coded number and was presently connected to the office of his superior. After a momentary pause, a silky smooth voice came on.

"Yes?"

"Your Grace, I am pleased to report some progress in the case. We have traced a missing document to the heretical section."

The voice on the other end took on a slight edge. "The heretical section? My God, what was it that he stole?"

Grimacing, the Undersecretary said, "All we know is that it appears to be a scroll donated by Dominican brothers of the Ecole' Bibliot."

The voice on the other end had regained some of its smooth texture. "Interesting. I will make certain inquiries of my own." The voice suddenly took on a distinct edge. "What a fiasco this is." There was a slight pause. "Report any further developments to me at once."

Undersecretary Maglione quickly said, "Yes, your Grace" before the line went dead.

Jonathan peered out the tinted window as the car pulled up to the curb. Angelo, coming around the back, opened the door and Jonathan stepped out.

At the entrance stood a doorman dressed in a smart uniform. Angelo walked straight up to him and whispered something in his ear. The doorman nodded, performing a slight bow. Angelo headed back to the car in a hurry.

Jonathan turned to thank him, but Angelo had already taken off. Turning back, he smiled at the doorman.

"Signorina Fragnini?" Jonathan said, gesturing ahead with his hand.

"Si, si. Scusi," the doorman said, ushering Jonathan across the ornate marble lobby into an old style elevator cage.

Pulling down the gate, the doorman shoved over the go-lever. The elevator rose slowly and finally reached the top floor. Escorting him down the hall, the doorman left him by a door.

He was alone. Staring at the blank door, he hesitated a second. He lifted his hand and knocked twice. There was a muffled response. Waiting a minute, he knocked a bit louder. Suddenly, the door was flung open. In front of him stood Arianna Fragnini.

She yelled, "Che cos`e`," staring at him.

She was dressed in a thin pale silk camisole and nothing else. Jonathan averted his eyes to the floor. Arianna stood there, a puzzled frown on her piquant face. Then, looking down at herself, she realized what was wrong.

"Uno momento," she said as she dashed away.

A moment later she was back, wearing a thick terry cloth robe. She stared at Jonathan, whose gaze was still studiously riveted to the floor.

"Va bene," she laughed.

Jonathan didn't take his eyes off the floor.

Reaching forward, she touched his arm as she repeated, "Bene."

At her touch, Jonathan jumped back in startled amazement. Arianna placed her hand over her mouth, trying to control the laughter that bubbled forth as Jonathan leapt away, almost tripping over himself. Jonathan straightened his black felt hat back on his head and risked a quick peek.

Arianna said in English, "Sorry, you surprised me."

Summoning what was left of his dignity, he introduced himself. "Hello, My name is Jonathan Charosh. I'm Ian's brother."

Wiping away the tears from the corners of her eyes she said, "I'm sorry. Come in. I just wasn't expecting you to jump away like that."

"That's alright," Jonathan said.

Letting him in, she motioned him over to the couch. He sat down. Standing ten feet away, she stared unconsciously at the thick payos that grew on either side of his face.

Jonathan felt uneasy under her gaze. He said, "What's the matter?"

She said, "I was just thinking how much the two of you look alike."

Jonathan smiled. "You're one of the only people besides our mother to say that."

Arianna smiled back. Jonathan looked up.

"I came from Israel yesterday to find my brother. I know he's in some kind of danger and," he paused to say softly, "I know he trusts you."

Putting her finger over her lips, she opened her eyes wide in warning, beckoning silently for Jonathan to follow her. Getting up, he followed her over to a side table. She gently lifted the phone off the table. Turning it carefully upside down, she pointed to a small black plastic microphone stuck to the bottom.

Jonathan nodded, comprehension dawning on him as she carefully placed the phone back down. Arianna tip-toed over to her bedroom. Beckoning again, she walked through the open doorway.

Jonathan walked over to the door of the bedroom. Arianna stood by a set of silk drapes that covered a tall bedroom window. Lifting them slightly, she crooked her finger at him.

Jonathan hesitantly came over. He looked down to the street below. At the corner stood a non-descript man in his late fifties, wearing a conservative gray suit. He seemed to be in no hurry, and appeared to be engrossed, reading a large magazine of some kind.

Arianna whispered, "I don't think he's a policeman. I walked right by him one day. He wears a gold ring with a large ruby set in it on his left hand. Also, I noticed that he was wearing very expensive leather shoes. I don't think the police pay so well."

Jonathan nodded.

Arianna let go of the curtain, and turning to Jonathan said softly, "Why don't you go back out to the living room and let me finish getting dressed. I'll only be a few minutes and then we can go somewhere and talk, okay?"

Jonathan nodded. Five minutes later Arianna emerged from her bedroom dressed in a cream blouse and a short pleated navy-blue skirt with matching flats. Jonathan averted his eyes.

Arianna looked down at her outfit and said, "Scusi, do you want me to change?"

Jonathan got up off the couch and said, "No, no, it's fine, really."

Pulling her hair back in a beret, she walked over and grabbed her keys and a small purse from the table by the door. The door slammed behind them. They boarded the elevator and began to descend.

Jonathan was fascinated by the antique lift. It was open on all four sides and ran on a central shaft into the middle of the lobby. Leaning over the side railing, he gazed down at the opulent marble floor that appeared to be rising up slowly to meet them. He noticed two men standing off to the side, staring up at them. The doorman was nowhere in sight. That's odd, he thought. Looking down again, he noticed that one of the men was extremely burly. The other was older and was dressed in a gray suit. With a rising sense of excitement and fear, he recognized the older man. He was the one Arianna had pointed out a few moments before from her bedroom window.

"Look," he yelled, pointing down. "Isn't that the guy on the corner?"

Arianna looked over the side. "Yes," she cried, noticing the men for the first time.

They had already descended more than half way down. Arianna pulled on the go-lever. It was stuck. She slammed down the red emergency button. The ancient elevator shuddered. The cable groaned. Grabbing hold of the sides, they held on as the elevator ground to a stop a few feet later.

The two men rushed toward the elevator well in the center of the lobby. Arianna pulled on the lever with all her might. A grinding sound issued from the motor. Suddenly, the elevator began to ascend.

Jonathan leaned over the side. Far below, he watched

the older man push the younger burly one toward a stairwell before rushing out of the building. Jonathan looked over to Arianna where she stood, leaning her body hard on the lever arm, trying to coax the machine to rise faster. She smiled back, a thick strand of her silky hair covering her face.

Tossing back her head, she said, "As soon as we reach the top, pull open the gate and run to your left."

Jonathan nodded. The elevator finally reached the top. Leaping forward, Jonathan pulled open the gate. Arianna dashed out, Jonathan following at a run. Racing down the hall, Arianna skidded to a halt by a door at the far end, Jonathan close behind her. Yanking it open, he followed her into a stairwell. A short flight of stairs on their right led up to a thick metal door. Leaning over the rail, Arianna spotted a large meaty hand on the railing, two floors below. Hearing their footsteps, the burly man leaned out, catching a glimpse of her. Letting out a loud bellow, he surged forward. Without thinking, Arianna grabbed Jonathan's hand and dragged him up the short flight of steps. Pulling open the door, they rushed out onto the sunny roof. Arianna slammed the door closed behind them, sliding a large metal bolt home.

"Come on," she yelled, sprinting across the roof.

Racing behind her, Jonathan tried to catch up. He had a hard time keeping his balance on the uneven surface. They ran around several large glass skylights sticking up on the surface. Suddenly they came upon the edge. Arianna skidded to a halt. Jonathan, taken by surprise, nearly fell off the side. Righting himself at the last moment, he heaved a sigh of relief. Stepping gingerly over to the edge, he peered over the side. It was a long way down.

"How far can you jump?" she said.

Jonathan looked up, to stare at her in disbelief. Leaning over the side once again, he tried to gauge the distance to the next roof-top.

It was well over six feet across. He looked at her and shook his head. "I have a bad knee. I don't know if I could make it."

Just then they heard loud pounding sounds coming from behind them.

Arianna smiled tightly and said, "I don't think we have a choice."

Jonathan, a grim look on his face, nodded silently. He watched as Arianna took a few steps back. Setting herself, she rushed past him. She soared over the edge, landing on the other side. Behind Jonathan came the terrible sound of metal being torn apart.

Arianna eyes widened as she screamed, "Hurry!"

He didn't look back. Backing up several steps, Jonathan whispered a silent prayer. Rushing forward, he leapt over the edge just as he felt his knee give out. His black hat flew off, caught in the swirling air. Hooking his arms out, he slammed into the opposite wall, frantically grasping. Someone bellowed something behind him. He held on.

He felt firm hands grasp his arms, pulling him upward. Straining his body, he managed to hook one leg over the lip. Hands grabbed him by his suit jacket, pulling him onto the black rooftop. They sat there a moment next to each other, panting.

Getting up, they ran towards the roof door. The burly man yelled something behind them in frustration, but it was lost in the wind. Gaining the door, Arianna slammed it shut.

Jonathan shook his head in amazement, happy to

still be in one piece.

Grasping the metal rail she said, "Come, we have to leave before the big one on the roof lets the other one know where we are."

She galloped down the stairs. Jonathan painfully followed. Exiting through a back way, Arianna hustled him around the corner. At a bus stop stood two older women and a tall man in dirty coveralls. Hiding behind him, they waited for the bus, eyes peeled to the corner.

Arianna pulled two tickets from her purse. Somehow she had managed to hold onto it. Several agonizing minutes passed. They nervously watched the corner, expecting the two men to come rushing round it at any moment. Finally, the bus pulled up.

Jumping up through the rear doors, they got on just before the doors shut behind them. Arianna went forward to hand the driver the tickets. Coming back down the aisle, she dropped down into a window seat. Jonathan sank gratefully into the seat beside her.

As the bus picked up speed, Jonathan leaned back against the molded plastic, rubbing his knee. Arianna opened her small purse, pulling out a moist cleansing tissue. She gently dabbed Jonathan's cheek. He jerked back from the unexpected sting of the alcohol.

"Hold still," she chided, wiping the blood off his face and neck.

In all the excitement, he hadn't even realized that he'd scraped himself. Gritting his teeth, he allowed her to clean the cuts on his cheek. He waited to make sure she was finished. Looking around again, he noticed that the closest people to them were the two old ladies from their stop, and they were busy chattering away to each other in Italian.

Turning to Arianna, Jonathan said, "I know that

you know where my brother is. Take me to him."

Arianna leaned back, a surprised look on her face. "How did you know?"

Jonathan smiled, his eyes crinkling up. "Your father's driver Angelo spotted the two of you by accident about two weeks ago in a cafe´ holding hands. Don't worry," he added, seeing her worried expression, "I told him not to tell anyone else."

Arianna leaned back. Staring out the window, she said softly, "I don't know what I would do if something were to happen to him. I love Ian very much. You must believe me."

Jonathan nodded his head, momentarily at a loss for words. Finally he said, "Tell me what happened."

She stared earnestly into Jonathan's eyes. "There's so much to tell." She licked her lips and began.

"Late one night, over a month ago, I woke up. I heard a strange scraping noise coming from the front door of my apartment. I got up and went to the door and called out. I heard a faint voice say, 'It's me. Open up.' I didn't recognize it. Opening the door, someone fell inside onto the floor. It was Ian. He had been leaning against the door. I half dragged him across the apartment and onto the bed. I couldn't believe it. He was in terrible shape. His clothes were all ripped up and he was covered in dirt. I managed to get his knapsack off. That's when I noticed that the whole back of his shirt was caked with dried blood. I almost panicked. You wouldn't believe how much blood there was. I cleaned him up and found a long gash that went from his shoulder to the middle of his back.

"He was groaning and almost delirious. I was crying; I couldn't help it. I told him that I was going to call a doctor. Suddenly, his eyes snapped open and he grabbed my wrist hard, hurting me. His eyes were all red and there was a wild look to them.

"He groaned, and yelled, 'No. No doctor. Don't tell anyone, not even your father. Promise me!'

"Crying and shaking, I promised not to call anyone. As soon as I said that his eyes rolled up in his head and he let go of me, collapsing back onto the bed. I tell you, I was so afraid for him, I almost called the doctor anyway. I finally got the wound on his back cleaned and dressed with a bandage. He was feverish. I turned him back over on his back, but he kept moaning. He started mumbling, 'My leg, my leg.' I looked at his legs, but I couldn't see anything wrong with them. I tried to move his right leg and his whole body shuddered. I rolled him gently onto his side and cut off his pants. That's when I saw it. I almost fainted.

"On the back of his right thigh was a huge black welt. It was so big. It pulsed a little, you know, like it was alive. I was afraid to touch it. I got him to swallow some pain killers, but he still thrashed and cried out for a long time. Finally, I got him to go to sleep. He tossed and turned and babbled at times. He kept repeating one word over and over. His fever finally broke in the early morning and then he slept more peacefully."

Arianna jumped up at this point to pull the cord. Looking down she said, "We have to get out here."

Jonathan lurched up painfully out of his seat. Stepping out of the open doors, he followed Arianna.

At the curb, she turned to yell over the sounds of the departing bus, "Before I take you to see him, we have to make sure that no one is following us. Do you think you're up to it?"

Jonathan grinned. "Sure," he said. "My knee's feeling better already."

"Then follow me," she said.

What followed was an hour of non-stop movement that made Jonathan's head spin. They jumped into cabs, ran down into the Metro, dashed in and out of crowded stores. Finally, they ended up in the Metro again. They boarded a train, and half an hour later, pulled into the Termini station.

Arianna led Jonathan over to an empty bench by a wall. "I'll be right back," she called over her shoulder. She headed over to one of the many ticket counters.

Coming back over, two tickets clutched in her slender right hand, she said, "Our train doesn't leave for another twenty minutes."

Jonathan grunted. "Where are we going?"

"Ostia Antica. My roommate's family has a beach house there."

"Where are they?"

"Oh, they live in Brussels. My roommate finished her class work early this semester, so she went back to spend the summer with them. The house is empty." She smiled. "She lets me stay there whenever I want." Looking around the station, she said, "I'll be right back, I'm just going to get a paper."

"Wait, I wanted to ask you a question," Jonathan blurted out.

"What?"

"You mentioned on the bus that Ian kept repeating a word over and over that night in your apartment. What was it?"

"Oh," she said. "It was the word, 'menorah.'"

# CHAPTER 23

The nations shall come to your light…
The wealth of the nations shall come to you…
They shall bring gold and frankincense

> Isaiah 60. 1-6

---

They arrived at the villa late in the afternoon. The house was situated on a slight rise, directly on the beach. Jonathan could taste the salt in the air. Pulling a key from her purse, Arianna quickly opened the door and stepped inside. Jonathan followed her into the cool interior. He felt like he was moving in a dream.

"Hello," he called out into the empty living room. "Is anybody home?"

Around a corner appeared a familiar face. Jonathan stood for an instant, frozen in shock. Then, unable to control himself, he rushed forward to hug his brother. Jonathan clasped Ian tightly, shaking from joy and the sudden release of pent-up tension. Ian held his brother close, fighting back the tears.

Looking up, Ian saw Arianna. He beckoned with his free hand, and she danced over to his side. Letting go of Jonathan, he clasped her tightly. Jonathan stepped back. He looked his brother over and was more shocked. Ian had lost a lot of weight. He was very pale. A heavy stubble covered his cheeks. His eyes were deeply set, surrounded by dark rings. Those eyes had a haunted look. To Jonathan, his brother seemed but a ghost of his former self.

Jonathan said, "Are you alright?"

Ian smiled. "I'm getting better."

Seeing the concern on his brother's face, he limped forward, and clasped his arm in a firm grip. They both laughed. Turning to Arianna, Ian kissed her on the lips.

"I missed you so much," he said.

She squirmed a little in his grasp, stroking his hair gently. Aware of Jonathan standing awkwardly in front of them, she pulled away, clearing her throat.

Ian looked at his brother and laughingly said, "Sorry, we haven't seen each other for over two weeks."

Jonathan gave an understanding nod. Waving his hand, Ian limped up three short steps and down a short hall to the kitchen. He eased himself into a chair by the kitchen table. Jonathan joined him.

"That limp is pretty bad," Jonathan said.

Ian raised his eyebrows. "Actually, it's much better now. The first two weeks I could barely stand."

Jonathan shook his head in sympathy, and waited for Ian to continue. "There's a lot to tell," Ian began.

"Actually I've been having an interesting time here too," Jonathan said.

Jonathan told him about the two men.

"I was wondering how you got that scrape on your face," Ian remarked at the end.

Glancing up at Arianna, he said, "Do have any idea who they might be, or who sent them?"

Arianna shook her head.

Jonathan said, "I think I might. Arianna's father told me about a Vatican official by the name of Undersecretary Alberto Maglione of the Sacred Office. He said that a long time ago, Arianna's mother was friendly with this man, in her University days. Well it seems that this fellow had certain feelings that your mother didn't reciprocate."

"But that must have been so long ago," Arianna said. "Surely this priest would have forgotten about that by now."

Jonathan and Ian looked at each other.

Jonathan said, "Does that name mean anything to you?"

Ian shook his head. "No. Not at all."

Jonathan said, "Do you know who was in charge of your scholarship to the Vatican?"

Ian shook his head but then stopped abruptly. Frowning, he said, "I just remembered something. My thesis advisor at Columbia, you know the one who gave me the scholarship, said he'd gotten it from an uncle of his who is an official at the Vatican. I'm trying to remember if he told me his name or what office he was in charge of. I wonder if that's the same guy."

"I'll bet he is," Jonathan said.

Arianna called over to them from the refrigerator, "Are you hungry?"

"Yes," they both chimed in together.

Arianna laughed. "Good," she replied. Sticking her head inside she called out over her shoulder, "You're almost out of everything."

Ian replied, "Sorry. I meant to go out today. I just forgot."

While Arianna busied herself, Jonathan said, "So, are you going to tell me what happened to you, or not?"

Ian grinned. "Okay, hold your horses. I'll tell you everything. Let's see…."

Before he had finished his tale, Arianna brought over two heaping plates of steaming pasta smothered in sauce.

She placed them in front of the two of them with a flourish, and said forcefully, "Manga."

Ian turned to Jonathan. "You know, she's the best thing that ever happened to me."

Arianna blushed. She said, "I bet you say that to all the girls."

Ian, suddenly serious, gazed deeply into her eyes. "No. I've never said that before to anyone."

Ian clasped Arianna's hand to his with a tender caress. Then turning back to Jonathan, Ian continued where he had left off.

"So, as I was saying, the secret tunnel leads right up into a tool shed in some kind of vegetable garden. I'm not sure exactly how long the tunnel is, but I'm almost positive it's wide enough to fit it through."

Arianna stared at the two of them in amazement. "Am I hearing you right?" she said. "Are you two planning on going back there to try and steal it?"

Ian turned to Arianna, a wide grin splitting his face. "Don't think of it as stealing. We're returning it to its rightful owners."

Jonathan grinned as well. Lifting a finger in the air, he stated, "The Talmud teaches us that it is a great mitzvah to return a lost object back to its rightful owners."

Arianna looked at their earnest faces. Throwing up her arms in defeat, she said in an exasperated tone, "I'd call it crazy."

"Don't worry," Ian assured her. "Just ask my brother. God is looking out for us, right?"

Jonathan nodded his head. "Very funny. I only wish you were more sincere."

Ian shrugged. "You want to know something? With everything that's happened to me over the last few months, I think I am starting to believe that God is behind all this." Becoming more focused he said, "So tell me more about this Reb Yossl. You said before that he told you about someone you could go to for help here in Italy."

Jonathan nodded. "That was pretty much it. He said that if I needed help, all I had to do was get a letter to someone in the Israeli consulate in Rome."

"Did he say what kind of help?" Ian said.

"No."

"Do you have the name on you?"

"Sure."

Ian turned to look at Arianna. Hesitantly he asked, "Will you help us?"

Looking into his eyes she said, "You're going to do it no matter what I say, yes?"

Ian nodded.

A smile brightened her face as she shot back, "Well in that case, what's the plan?"

They stayed up late that night, discussing everything for hours. Finally, they got up to go to bed. Arianna showed Jonathan to one of the guest bedrooms. They bid him good night.

Leaning on her a little for support, the two young lovers headed off to a large bedroom on the other side of the house. Letting go, Ian sat down on the side of the bed. Arianna leaned close, gently unbuttoning his shirt. She ran her fingers lightly over his strong arms and chest, caressing his skin. Stepping back, she slipped out of her clothes, revealing herself before him in the bright moonlight that streamed through a huge skylight in the center of the room. Ian drank in her beauty.

Slipping gently down beside him, she carefully removed the rest of his clothes, pressing close to him under the satin sheets. That night they made passionate love. Exhausted, they rested in each other's arms. Arianna tenderly stroked the edges of the terrible gash on his back. By now it had scabbed over, and was healing nicely.

"Hold me tight," she whispered.

Ian wrapped his arms around her. "What's wrong?"

"Nothing," she whispered, staring up at the bright moon.

In the morning, Ian awoke. Carefully disentangling himself so as not to wake her, he got up and quietly slipped on a pair of sweats Arianna had brought him on her last visit. Looking down at her peaceful face he thought, she's so beautiful.

Barefoot, he walked across the house with only a slight limp. Ian stepped into the spacious living room. At the far end, his back to Ian, stood Jonathan. Both his legs were placed firmly together. He swayed back and forth silently.

Ian approached, quietly easing himself down into an over-sized chair. He waited for Jonathan to finish. Jonathan took three steps back and then three forward. Turning around, he noticed Ian.

Smiling he said, "I hope you don't mind that I borrowed your tefilin. I found them in your knapsack on the coffee table."

Ian smiled. "No, of course not."

Jonathan went back to finishing the morning prayers. Pulling off the phylacteries, he wound them back into their boxes.

Looking over to Ian he said, "You know, you didn't tell me what you did with the manuscripts you found."

Ian grinned. "Well if you remember, I told you that I was able to get out all three of them. The first contained the manuscript I wrote you about in my letter. The second one had an ancient scroll in it. I tried to decipher it but I wasn't able to get very far. I'm almost positive that it was taken from one of the caves at Qumran, probably by someone on the dig."

"Really?"

Ian nodded. "Yeah. The parchment was pretty brittle and I was afraid of damaging it. I could make out the first column easily. It was written in some form of Aramaic. It seemed to be different from the Aramaic I remember seeing in the Talmud, but I'm no expert."

"Did you figure out what it said?"

"Nah, I didn't have enough time."

"What about the third pouch?" Jonathan said.

"That one was just a portfolio containing some artist's drawings of different candelabrums. They were by somebody named Savelli. It had nothing to do with what we're interested in."

"I wish I could see that scroll," Jonathan exclaimed.

Ian shook his head, pursing his lips. "I was too afraid to keep them on me, so I had Arianna mail all three pouches to you in Israel two weeks ago."

Two hours later, Arianna stood by the front door. They had all decided that it was best if Jonathan hid out at the beach house for the time being as well. Ian was filled with misgivings. He had been having second thoughts all morning.

He kissed her, going over her instructions one last

time. "Now remember, don't go back to your apartment. Make sure you give the letter directly to the man at the consulate. Are you sure you're going to be okay?"

"Don't worry. I'll be fine," she reassured him, patting his arm. "After I deliver the letter, I'm going to go straight to my parent's house and stay there. That's the safest place for me to be."

"Good," Ian replied, not wholly convinced. "How do you think your father's going to take it?"

"He's going to be very angry."

Seeing Ian's worried look, she added quickly, "But not at you. He doesn't take too kindly to people chasing his daughter. My father is very well connected. And my mother is from an influential family as well. They wouldn't dare do anything to us."

She leaned forward. Standing on her tiptoes, she kissed him. Waving good-bye, she walked down the path. Ian anxiously watched her lithe form recede. Reluctantly, he closed the door, but not before taking a quick look to see if anyone had seen them. The road beyond was empty. A seagull circled overhead, crying out on its way to the sea.

Three days later, there was a knock on the door. Ian, who had been puttering in the kitchen, walked slowly to the door. His leg had improved considerably over the last few days and he even seemed to be gaining back some of his weight. His left shoulder was still stiff but the scab on it was already starting to peel.

He motioned silently to Jonathan, who stood in the living room. In his left hand Ian held the hardwood walking stick that he had been using to get around. It had a battered brass bull's head for a handle and the end was tipped in brass as well. It was exquisitely weighted, despite the numerous nicks and scratches covering its entire surface. Unlocking the door, he took a step back, swinging it open. He held the stick loosely, ready to strike.

Framed in the doorway stood two athletically built young men, wearing dark shades. The hair on their heads was closely cropped, and they were clean shaven, with deep tans. One was fair, the other had jet-black hair. Large nylon backpacks were strapped securely to their backs.

Ian stared at them a moment in surprise. He said, "What do you want?"

The short darker one answered in a clipped tone, "We heard you needed a little help." He spoke with a distinct Israeli accent.

Jonathan, ignoring his brother, came forward to ask expectantly, "Did Reb Yossl send you?"

The short one replied in Hebrew, "Yes. He received your letter and we came as fast as we could."

Smiling broadly, Jonathan waved them in. Ian grudgingly lowered his stick, locking the door behind them. The two young men looked around a moment before stripping off their heavy packs. Jonathan led them into the living room, Ian cautiously trailing behind.

Ian said, "Do you think you were followed?"

"No," the taller one replied.

"How can you be so sure?" he prodded.

The shorter one gave Ian a hard look. "Don't worry. We know what we are doing."

The two of them looked to be in their early twenties, but they carried themselves with a certain air of competence that made them appear older.

He said, "Are you from the Mossad?"

The short one cracked a small smile for the first time, revealing his even white teeth.

"No," he replied. Extending his arm in friendship,

he clasped Ian's hand in a firm grip as he introduced himself and his friend.

"My name is Avi. And this," he inclined his head, "is Shuli. We recently completed our active service. We are both paratroopers and we were in the same unit together for the last year. We are here strictly on our own," he stated in a matter-of-fact tone.

Ian introduced himself and Jonathan. They all shook hands.

Avi said, "That's a good grip you've got, but what is with the cane?" he said, staring at the walking stick Ian had switched over to his left hand.

Ian turned a little red. Staring directly into Avi's eyes he replied, "Don't worry. I won't slow you down."

Avi gave him a hard look. "Good."

Jonathan, meanwhile, had returned with a tray of tall glasses and a pitcher of water. He set the tray down on the coffee table. Handing out glasses of water, he motioned for everyone to sit down. Striking up a conversational tone, he tried to ease the tension in the air.

"So how was your flight?" he said.

Avi grunted in reply.

Jonathan plowed on. "Did you speak with Reb Yossl before you left?"

"Yes," Avi said. "He has a message for you. He said to tell you, and these are his own words, 'Tehyeh Chazak. Al Tefached. Hashem yiftach haderech.' "

Jonathan nodded, suddenly too choked up to respond.

Puzzled, Ian turned to Avi and said, "How do you know Reb Yossl?"

Avi looked at him a long moment before replying in a clipped tone, "His grandson was in our unit. His name was Aryeh. He was our friend."

"What happened to him?" Jonathan said.

Avi didn't reply. Shuli smiled sadly and said, "He's dead."

There was a moment of pained silence. Ian broke it by asking the two Israelis, "Do you know why you're here?"

They both shook their heads.

Shuli said, "No. Reb Yossl thought it was best that we knew as little as possible in case we were stopped and questioned."

Ian nodded approvingly. Getting up off the chair, he left and returned a moment later with a large map.

Spreading it out on the coffee table, he glanced over to where the two Israeli young men sat.

"You're here to help us retrieve the Menorah that Titus stole from the Second Temple almost two thousand years ago. And," he paused for effect, a smile playing over his lips as he stabbed a finger down onto the center of the map, "it's right here, in the heart of the Vatican."

He noted with satisfaction the look of surprise on the two hard-bitten faces.

## CHAPTER 24

When you light the lamps, the seven lamps
shall illuminate the Menorah...

Numbers 8:1

God told Moses to tell Aaron, "The sacrifices are
offered only as long as the Holy temple exists.
But the lights will forever burn on the Menorah...

Midrash, Num.8:1

---

Two days later, all was in place. Avi and Shuli had left for Rome to look things over.

While leafing absentmindedly through the Italian newspaper Arianna had bought in the train station, Ian had come across an article in the entertainment section. On the top of the page was a picture of the Pope, shaking hands with someone in a tuxedo as they smiled warmly at each other.

He looked up excitedly and called the rest of them over.

"Look at this," he cried.

The others stared down at the picture and the caption beneath it. Jonathan jumped up and ran out of the room, shouting over his shoulder, "I'll be right back."

Two minutes later he returned, a thick book in hand.

Handing it to Ian he explained, "I saw you had one of these in your knapsack."

Ian grinned, opening the Italian-English dictionary. Half an hour later, they had puzzled out the article.

It appeared that the Vatican was getting set to hold a concert that very Saturday night in a large hall right next door to St. Peter's. It was to be a commemorative performance to honor the six million Jewish victims of the Holocaust.

The Vatican orchestra was to play several pieces from famous Jewish composers, and the world renowned violinist, Baruch Yacobi had been invited to perform. He was the man in the picture shaking the Pope's hand.

Also on the program that evening was a special recital by a Jewish boys' choir from Jerusalem. The boys were being flown in on a specially chartered flight right before the Sabbath, and according to the article, were scheduled to return to Israel right after the performance.

They immediately set their plans in motion. They would go in that very night, and unknown to all the dignitaries attending the gala only several hundred yards away, they would make away with the Menorah, literally from right under their feet.

# CHAPTER 25

This may be compared to a king who had a beloved friend, and told him one day, "I intend to come to your house for a meal… make preparations." His friend hurried to set up the house, arranging his simple table and lamp. The king came to visit surrounded by his entourage, preceded by a servant bearing a lamp of gold. When the friend saw all the honor of the king he became embarrassed, and hurriedly hid all he had prepared, for it was all so plain and common. The king entered and said, "Didn't I tell you I was coming—why is nothing prepared?" Said his beloved, "I saw all your honor and was embarrassed, for all I prepared for you was common and simple." Said the king "I swear to you! I reject everything I have. Out of love for you I want to share only your simple things."

So too — the Holy One is all Light,
yet He tells Israel to light the Menorah! And
as soon as they light the Menorah,
the Divine Presence arrives…

                                    Numbers Rabbah 15:8

———————————

## Friday, 10:00 a.m.

Looking up from the nearest pile of papers the Undersecretary snapped, "What progress do you have to report?"

Brother Michel swallowed hard. "Nothing new, your Grace."

"What? I sent you ten priests over six weeks ago. Are you telling me that in all that time you've found nothing else?" he screamed.

The young priest visibly withered under the verbal attack. Summoning up his remaining courage he replied, "There is so much to go through, your Grace. If only we had some clue as to what he was after, we could then easily discover what is missing."

The phone rang. Reaching over without looking, the Undersecretary picked up the receiver and held it to his ear.

He listened silently for a moment, his face turning slightly red. He nearly screamed into the other end, "Make sure you have enough seats set up for the Press. They hate it when they have to stand."

Slamming down the receiver, he looked up. The phone rang again. Irritated, he snatched it up. His face went through a sudden transformation, becoming totally flaccid. He listened silently to the voice on the other end for a long time.

Desperately, he managed to get out, "Yes, your Grace," before the line cut off.

Hanging up the receiver, he looked up at Brother Michel and screamed, "Get out of here and get back to work."

The young priest scuttled away. As he left, he

mentally shuddered, wondering what his uncle would do to him if he ever found out what he had done.

### Friday, 5:00 p.m.

A silver van with the markings of Fragnini Imports/Exports emblazoned on its side pulled into the narrow driveway. It rolled down a steep ramp and came to a complete stop. A heavy garage door opened silently. The van moved forward and was obscured from view as the door closed behind it.

The van doors slid open. Jonathan and Ian alighted onto a brightly lit cement floor. Arianna rushed forward to smother Ian with kisses. From the front cab stepped Avi and Shuli. Going around the two lovers, they began unloading their gear, Jonathan lending them a hand. Looking around, Ian realized that everything had already been unloaded.

"Sorry," he said.

Avi grunted. Grabbing one of the heavier packs, Ian followed Arianna through a narrow passage and then up a long flight of cement steps. The others trudged up behind them in single file.

In the marble foyer stood Don Fragnini. Beside him was his wife Gabrielle. Seeing Ian emerge behind their daughter, they came forward, beaming.

"How are you my boy?" Don Fragnini said, clasping Ian's right shoulder in a meaty grip.

"I'm well," Ian grinned.

Signora Fragnini waited till her husband had finished mauling Ian before stepping forward to give him a quick peck on the cheek. "We're so glad to see you safe and well," she said softly into his ear.

Ian blushed. Don Fragnini stepped forward.

"Welcome. It is a pleasure to have you all here in our house."

Avi and Shuli nodded their heads. Jonathan said, "Thank you for all your help."

"Where's Eli?" Ian said.

Don Fragnini laughingly replied, "We thought it best to send him to a friend's house for the weekend. Of course, if he knew what he was missing, we'd never hear the end of it." And then, "Come, let's all go into the den. I have been thinking about your plan and I have a suggestion to make if you don't mind…"

The Sabbath passed slowly. Don Fragnini went to synagogue as usual. When he returned, they all sat down to a lively Sabbath meal. The table conversation ranged over a broad array of subjects. The one topic that wasn't broached was the one that weighed most heavily on their minds. After lunch, Don Fragnini and his wife excused themselves and went upstairs to rest. Ian and Arianna strolled off into the inner garden, hand in hand.

Jonathan headed over to the family library. Surrounding himself with all the texts he had accumulated, he spent the afternoon memorizing the dimensions given in the Bible of the Menorah's different segments. Avi and Shuli ensconced themselves in the den, where they poured carefully over the detailed maps Don Fragnini had provided. Two days before, the two young Israeli men had spent the entire day touring the Vatican museums and St. Peter's, anonymous amongst the throngs of tourists who visited there daily.

## Saturday, 8:09 p.m.

The three of them stood nearby, waiting impatiently. He had insisted that they wait until the Sabbath was over. Taking the three steps back and three forward that signaled the end of the silent prayer, Jonathan opened his eyes. Nodding his head, he rushed over to change into the same dull black outfit the other three had on. Back at the beach house he had convinced them that he had to come along to check the authenticity of whatever it was that was down there.

The newspaper article stated that the concert was set to begin at 9 p.m. They were counting on the fact that most of the guards would be stationed either out front for crowd control, or in and around the concert hall itself.

The silver van, headlights on, slid quietly out from the driveway. Arianna sat behind the wheel. They had all strenuously argued against it, but since she was very familiar with the streets and they didn't have anyone else they could fully trust, she had finally convinced them. Heading off into the night, she drove through the narrow streets at a sedate pace.

Three blocks away, she hung a sharp right and came to an abrupt stop. Slipping into reverse, she slid the van into a dark alleyway and turned off the lights and the motor. An identical van slid quickly past in the opposite direction. As it passed, she waved silently to the grinning face of Angelo, hunched behind the wheel. The second van turned right and continued on. Seconds later, a long black Fiat sedan slid past, its windows darkly tinted.

They waited. Five minutes passed. Turning the ignition, she started up the engine. The van exited the alleyway and hung a quick left, heading towards El Vaticano.

## Saturday, 8:42 p.m.

Avi held the thin black nylon rope taut. The sky was overcast with a thick veil of clouds, but no rain was expected. Ian climbed down, his non-skid padded feet landing gently on the neatly manicured grass. He had gained back much of his strength over the last few days. Strapped to his back was the walking stick. Only Jonathan remained on the other side.

Ian called softly over the wall, "Come on, you can do it."

Looking up, he heaved a sigh of relief, seeing the thin form of his brother perched high above. He climbed halfway up, helping Jonathan down. Avi, who had been anchoring the line, shook his head. He jiggled it, then tugged hard.

The light nylon cord, a small sharp metal claw hooked on one end, came free. It fell onto the grass with a slight thud. Rapidly rolling the cord into a tight loop he whispered, "Are you okay?"

Jonathan nodded, rubbing his arms. Avi clipped the thick coil onto his belt. He looked over to Shuli, who stood alertly in the shadows of a nearby tree. Shuli lifted his hand in the all clear sign. Avi nodded. Peering into the dark, he lifted his hand.

They had decided to come over the north-west wall. Besides being one of the most direct routes to the tool shed, it had the added advantage of being opposite one of the most secluded spots in the Vatican City. Shuli took point, the other three trailing out behind him at spaced intervals. They advanced cautiously, darting from cover to cover. Passing just a hundred feet to the north of the Fountain of the Waterfalls, Shuli stopped.

He motioned silently. The others halted, waiting. Shuli pointed ahead. Four pairs of eyes turned to look in the direction of the fountain. They saw several guards hanging around the illuminated steps. The guards appeared not to have noticed them. Giving them a wide berth, the four young men crept silently away. Wending their way among the lush tropical foliage, Shuli jerked up his hand. They froze in their tracks.

Up ahead sat the illuminated shape of a large fountain, the famous Fountain of the Aquilone. This was a spot fraught with danger. Ian had seen guards here the fateful night of his escape. The area was wide open. If there were any guards about, they would surely be spotted.

Shuli motioned them forward to his position behind a large tree. Peering out together, the four surveyed the area carefully. It appeared to be deserted. Avi, leaning forward, whispered into Shuli's ear. He nodded. Creeping forward, Shuli darted across the well lit space, gaining the haven of the shadows of a triangular court. Leaning his head out in the warm air, he gave a signal. Avi tapped Jonathan on the shoulder.

Taking a deep breath, he dashed across at a run, to stand by Avi's side a moment later. Avi tapped Ian's shoulder. Without hesitating, he limped across at a trot, Avi following close behind him.

Racing forward on padded feet, they reached the shadow of a heavy iron gate. From Shuli's pack appeared a set of heavy bolt cutters. Avi held a few of the links taut. The chain cut easily.

Avi carefully let the broken ends rest on the thick metal bars of the gate. Opening the gate slowly, he held it open just wide enough for the others to pass through. Then passing through himself, he closed it, arranging the chain artfully so that to a casual observer it would appear that nothing was wrong.

## Saturday, 9:02 p.m.

The concert was supposed to have started by now.

From where they stood, all they could hear were the chirping sounds of crickets in the fragrant night air.

Ian led them quickly along the narrow gravel path. On either side, the tall stalks of corn swayed in the wind. Several thick raindrops began to fall. They all looked up. The clouds above were definitely thickening. Ian stood by the door to the tool shed. He turned the knob. It wouldn't budge. He tried it again. Turning to Avi, he whispered, "It's locked."

Avi shouldered past. Pulling out a small black case, he inserted a thin metal pick into the key-hole. An instant later, it clicked once. Turning the knob slowly, he eased the door open. Sticking his head inside a moment, he popped it back out and opened the door wide. The others filed in and Avi slipped in last, shutting the door firmly behind him. The shed was almost pitch black.

Avi whispered, "Lights."

Four powerful beams sprang out, brightly illuminating the tall columns of bagged fertilizer stacked up in rows from floor to ceiling. Ian played his beam on some gardening implements set on a rack. Walking away, he traced the beam further along the opposite wall, finding the heavy metal grate. It was set into the rock wall about four feet off the floor.

"I found it," he called softly.

The others crowded around, shining their lights through the bars and into the dark tunnel beyond. Ian crouched down, inspecting the bolts with care. He tugged at the bottom right bolt. It came away easily along with a little cement. He turned his head to look up at them, his face shining in the light. A broad grin split his handsome features.

"It's just as I left it," he exclaimed, his voice hoarse with emotion.

Avi grunted. Avi and Shuli crouched down beside

him to inspect the grate. Setting themselves, they each grasped a corner.

Avi said softly, "On the count of three. One, two, three."

They strained, pulling with their gloved fingers on the edges. It gave away easily.

Avi stepped forward to shine his beam into the open mouth of the tunnel. The tunnel slanted sharply downward after the first few feet. The young Israeli man got down onto his belly, and keeping the light in front of him, began to crawl down the tunnel, head-first. Ian put his arm on Jonathan's shoulder. Jonathan turned to look at him.

"Well," Ian said. "You're the one that got us into all this. Are you ready?"

Jonathan grinned. "Yes, big brother, I am."

"Then climb on in."

Jonathan crawled inside, Ian following right behind him. Shuli stood by the opening to keep guard.

About sixty feet later, the tunnel ceiling rose up sharply, the incline becoming less steep. Ian got up onto his feet. Avi and Jonathan were already standing by one of the rough rock walls, waiting for him.

Limping slightly, Ian moved up to take the front position. Turning his head back, he said, "Follow me, and watch out for rats."

## Saturday, 9:33 p.m.

The floor of the tunnel had leveled out. Ian stepped forward, out of the mouth of the tunnel. The others came out, close behind. Stopping to pan their powerful flashlights into the vast pitch-black space, they stared about them in wonder. Three beams lanced out into the black void, but in this immense underground cavern, they were pitifully weak.

Ian tried to orient himself. Last time, the torches in the crypt had lit his way, albeit feebly, to the tunnel's mouth. From where they now stood, he couldn't make out any landmarks. Shrugging his broad shoulders, he led them hesitantly forward in the direction he thought was right. They proceeded slowly, picking their way over the uneven surface of the cavern, tiny pieces of soft rubble crunching beneath their feet. Ian played his beam to the right and left. All he could see was the same rock-littered surface in all directions.

He trudged on, beginning to wonder if he was leading them the right way. Several minutes went by. Suddenly, his beam brushed across the stone face of a massive rectangular structure not a hundred yards away. Ian rushed forward to inspect it.

Jonathan, who had come up behind him said, "Is this the one?"

Ian stared at the carvings on its walls. Shaking his head he replied, "No. The one we're looking for has some strange birds carved on it, and I don't see any of them here." Walking away, he said, "Come, there's lots of them. I'm sure we'll find it. It's one of the bigger ones."

They walked past several smaller crypts, stopping only to inspect the larger ones. Off to one side, Ian noticed a big one. It looked strangely familiar. Heading over to it, he saw with a rising sense of excitement that it had been dug out deeply from the floor of the cavern. Now he remembered. The one that held the Menorah had also been at a lower level.

Scrambling down the rough rocks in the inky darkness, he shined his flashlight over the walls. A myriad of wicked eyes stared back at him, hooked beaks gleaming in the cold light.

Startled, he called over to them. "Over here."

The two others had been searching another large crypt fifty feet away. Avi and Jonathan hurried over, picking their way past the huge number of rocks strewn all around. Jonathan shined his beam on the carvings.

"This is it," Ian exclaimed.

They split up, searching for the entrance.

"I found the doorway," Jonathan called softly to the others.

"Don't move!" Ian whispered in his ear. Brushing past, he turned to whisper, "Stay here."

Avi followed Ian inside, one hand clasped to the long throwing dagger strapped to his side.

### Saturday, 9:56 p.m.

Undersecretary Maglione sat in the second row, directly behind the vast bulk that was the Secretary of the Sacred Office. He had been trying to avoid his superior all day. With all the arrangements for the evening's performance, he'd had ample excuse not to have spoken to him yet. He knew though, with a sense of fatalistic resignation, that after the performance he would be called aside to give his report.

Luckily, everything had gone smoothly. The event appeared to be a stunning success. Twisting his head to survey the immense crowd, he keenly noted the ample press in attendance. The evening should generate some excellent reviews, and a measure of the credit would ultimately be his. He shuddered involuntarily. *I wonder what the Secretary would have done had it been otherwise*, he thought. He recalled their last conversation.

"I have made inquiries," the Secretary had said. "It

would seem that the missing item is an original document of incalculable value. It was sent to the collection from an archeological site in the Holy Land under the supervision of brothers of the Ecole' Bibliot. It appears to have been a parchment scroll of some kind, originating in a cave somewhere in an area known as the Dead Sea. Apparently it was deemed to contain information best kept in the protective hands of the Holy Mother Church. I need not emphasize how critical it is that this document be recovered and returned to its rightful place."

Glancing forward to a special podium erected in front, Maglione stared in fascination at the back of a large ornate gilt throne. I wonder if he knows, he mused to himself. Heaving a deep sigh, he settled back into the plushly cushioned seat and pretended to enjoy the performance.

### SATURDAY, 9:59 P.M.

Their lights intersected in the center of the room, reflecting brilliantly off the polished gold. Framed in the doorway, Jonathan sucked in his breath. Stepping forward, he entered the crypt. Ian waved him back. Directing his beam onto the dusty floor directly in front of the stone pedestal, the cold light revealed the black folds of a voluminous robe. Avi advanced slowly, shining his beam on the puddle of cloth. With a fluid motion, Ian pulled out his walking stick.

Stepping cautiously forward, he pushed on the edge of the robe with the brass tip. He felt no resistance. Puzzled, he ran it through the folds, bunching up the cloth in a pile. Reaching down, he picked it up by one of its ends. It was empty.

Darting a glance in Avi's direction, he exclaimed, "I don't understand it. I left him here. I checked him. He was dead."

Avi looked down at the empty robe. "Maybe someone came and took the body away."

The three of them looked around. The four bare walls of the crypt stared back at them.

Avi turned to Jonathan. "Come here quick. We don't have much time."

Jonathan, shaking his head in wonder, stepped inside. In the light of the flashlights he gazed reverently at the large candelabrum. Moving closer, he peered intently at the gold balls and flowers on the arms and central stem, counting them. He checked its length carefully. He ran his eyes over it. He stopped at the base. There, where the base met the center stem, was a definite seam. He examined the carved figures and large rings set on either side of the base.

"Well?" Avi said.

Jonathan stood before the large seven branched candelabrum lost in thought.

Ian, unable to stand the suspense, cried out, "What do you think? Is it the real one or not?"

Jonathan turned to face his brother. Shaking his head first, he nodded slowly as he said, "I think it is." Squinting his eyes he added, "I think the base was soldered onto it by the Romans, but otherwise I think it is the original." His voice was filled with awe.

They all stared at it a long moment. Avi, reaching into his pack, broke the spell. Pulling forth a thin nylon sack, he reached further down and removed a specially designed cart. Positioning it carefully on the floor in front of the pedestal, he motioned to Ian. They quickly covered the Menorah with the sack.

"Be careful not to touch it," Jonathan's voice sang out in warning.

Ian and Avi stationed themselves on either side of the stone pedestal. Grasping the sack on either side under its arms, they took hold of it.

"Ready," called Avi.

"Ready," Ian replied.

"Okay. Now!"

The two men strained to lift it. It must have weighed more than half a ton. Grunting with the strain, sweat broke out on their foreheads. They shifted it slowly off the pedestal, placing it gently down onto the rolling cart Jonathan held steady on the dusty floor.

"Are you clear?" Ian called out hoarsely to his brother.

"Yes," Jonathan said.

Ian and Avi let go. The flat cart creaked alarmingly under the massive weight, but held. Breathing heavily, they lashed it securely to the cart.

"Okay, let's go," Avi called out.

SATURDAY, 10:22 P.M.

Undersecretary Alberto Maglione leaned forward, staring in fascination. On the stage stood the Pope and Secretary Karocyz, as well as several other high ranking officials of the Curia. Across from them stood the famous violinist, Baruch Yacobi, surrounded by the children of the Jerusalem boys' choir. In the center of the stage, on a specially built podium, were set six tall candles, three on each side.

As a finale to the evening, a young boy began to mount the podium. Clutched in his small fist was a thin taper, a tiny flame burning at its end. As he reached up on his tip-toes to light the first candle, the choir began to sing the beginning chords of the Kaddish, the prayer for the dead. Stepping down, the young boy handed the thin taper to the next boy in line. The Undersecretary felt surprise as he found himself touched by the scene.

There was a rude tap on his shoulder. Irritated, he reluctantly turned his head away. In the aisle stood a young priest in the simple robes of the Dominican order. The incompetent idiot, he thought. Why had his sister married that low class Frenchman? Scowling, Undersecretary Maglione pushed his way past those seated in his row.

Reaching the aisle, he leaned close to whisper, "What is it?"

Brother Michel managed to get out, "Uncle. We just discovered what else was taken."

The Undersecretary grabbed him by the arm, the scene on the stage all but forgotten. "What was it?"

Brother Michel swallowed hard. "There were two other pouches missing. One was a folio of sketches by Savelli. The second was a manuscript from the second century by the Christian historian, Hegesippus."

The Undersecretary rubbed his chin. "What would he want with those?" he muttered aloud.

Pulling Brother Michel along with him, he headed toward the back of the great hall.

Turning to the young priest by the exit he said, "Did you reference them on the archives computer?"

"Yes, your Grace."

"And what did you find, you idiot?" the Undersecretary hissed.

"I found that all three are listed in the computer under the same title."

"Which was?" the Undersecretary asked, about to lose his patience.

"Candelabrum, your Grace," Brother Michel hurriedly replied.

The Undersecretary repeated the word softly to himself. Then, distracted by the performance up front, his eyes were drawn unconsciously to stare back up at the center stage. There, the Jewish boys of the choir stood, ranked round about six tall candles. They blazed forth as the boys poured out the climax of the song.

The Undersecretary stood transfixed, staring at the six flames, three on each side. His eyes bulged out. How could he have found it, he thought wildly. Only a select few even knew of its existence.

Turning to Brother Michel, he shot out, "What were the sketches of Savelli of?"

Brother Michel stuttered out, "Why, ahh…candelabrums, your Grace."

His face flushing red, the Undersecretary ran out of the hall. Surprised, Brother Michel hurried behind, trying to catch up.

## Saturday, 10:24 p.m.

They had nearly finished. A steady warm rain fell from the sky. Only Ian remained, slowly paying out the thin wet cord as the massive object inched its way down the other side. The immense tension on the rope eased.

Off to his right, he heard the unmistakable sounds of hoarse voices calling out through the rain. Grasping the slick rope tightly, he pulled himself up. A spotlight played across the walls and finally found him, three quarters of the way up.

He heard several of the soldiers cry out to him in Italian, their voices muffled in the rain. Not bothering to turn around, he pulled himself to the top. Scrambling over, he spared a swift glance below. A squad of guards, only a hundred feet away, shouted at him, coming towards him at a run. One of them stopped to unsling his rifle, letting go a short burst.

Bullets sprayed the wall inches from where he lay. He let go of the rope, leaping to the ground. He tried to roll, but jammed his bad leg as he came down hard. Pain shot up through him like fire. Staggering erect, he allowed Jonathan to help him into the waiting van. On the other side, two of the guards were trying to climb the rope. Avi lunged forward. With a clean stroke, he severed the cord with his razor-sharp dagger.

They heard sounds of men cursing on the other side. Avi and Shuli quickly rolled the cart up the ramp and into the back of the waiting van. It peeled away, before they'd even had time to shut the back doors.

## Sunday, 12:47 a.m.

The van pulled up slowly, easing past the half-open doors of the quiet dimly-lit cargo hangar. Inside sat a large plain wood coffin. A hundred yards away, lit up by its own running lights, rested a plane. A large tanker truck was nearly finished fueling it up.

The boys of the Jerusalem choir were on a tight schedule. Their flight was due to take off in less than ten minutes. The back and side door panels of the van shot open. Out the back jumped Avi, Shuli and Jonathan. From the side panel stepped Ian, leaning heavily on his walking stick, one arm wrapped around Arianna's slender shoulder. The driver's door opened slowly. Out stepped the massive bulk of Don Fragnini.

Grinning, he came forward to clasp Ian's arm. "You'll take good care of her, I know," he said, a broad grin lighting up his face.

Ian grinned back. Arianna exclaimed, "Oh, Papa.

Don't worry."

"Whose worried? " he cried out, laughing jovially.

Avi and Shuli shifted the heavy coffin onto a large hand truck. They had just reached down to pull it forward when bright spotlights flooded the area, blinding them. No one moved, caught in the powerful glare of the beams. Undersecretary Maglione strolled forward, stopping a few feet in front of them. Behind him stood Brother Michel and a customs officer, with several other officials standing at a slight distance.

"Search them," Undersecretary Maglione said.

The customs officer gave the nod. Don Fragnini tried to protest as the customs men moved forward. Shading his eyes with a meaty paw he thundered, "I am a respected member of the municipal board. How dare you treat us in such a manner."

The Undersecretary cut him off. "Silence!" he screamed.

Eyes glittering malevolently, he said, "I'd hoped that you had involved yourself personally," a smile curling his upper lip.

"What are you talking about?" Don Fragnini sputtered.

The customs men drew back, having completed their search. They all shook their heads. The customs officer leaned over to whisper into the Undersecretary's ear.

Maglione frowned. Turning his gaze toward Ian he said angrily, "Where is the scroll?"

Ian returned his stare and replied, "Sorry, I don't know what you're talking about."

The Undersecretary's eyes blazed. He was about to respond, when his eyes, alighting upon the large wood coffin on the floor between them, lit up.

Pointing down he screamed, "Open it!"

Don Fragnini stepped forward to block their way. "You commit a great sacrilege by opening this coffin," he warned. "You will be desecrating the dead. I will have you publicly repudiated by the Church," he yelled, his face turning red.

The customs men hesitated. The Undersecretary turned to them and snapped, "What are you waiting for? Push this foolish Jew away. I am in authority, not him. He speaks lies."

The men stepped forward. Don Fragnini was forced to step aside. One of the customs men produced a crowbar. Working one end, he pried open the lid, and they lifted it away.

There in the coffin lay the wizened figure of the old sexton, dressed in a plain white robe, his hands resting peacefully on his chest. The customs men stepped back in surprised embarrassment. Undersecretary Maglione leaned over, to stare in disbelief at the still, bearded face.

Don Fragnini came forward, to stare down by the side of the coffin. "He died just a few hours before the Sabbath. His last request was that he be buried in Jerusalem. We received special permission to put him on this flight, since he must be buried as soon as possible according to Jewish law."

The customs officer signaled his men to close the coffin back up. Coming forward hesitantly to where Don Fragnini stood, he cried out, "Forgive us Dottore. We did not know what we were doing. We were only following the orders of the Undersecretary."

He finished his last words, casting a black look in the Undersecretary's direction.

Don Fragnini nodded benevolently. "Of course, of course. I understand completely. Now, if you would be so kind as to direct your men to help us load the coffin before the plane leaves, I will be forever in your debt."

The customs officer smiled gratefully. Springing forward, he rattled off a series of commands in Italian. The customs men darted forward, quickly carting the coffin out of the hangar. The Undersecretary stood rooted to his spot, his eyes unfocused, unable to speak.

They filed past, hurrying out onto the tarmac. As he passed, Ian winked at Brother Michel. Brother Michel smiled back.

The others had already boarded. Ian and Arianna reached the ladder, trailed by the bear-like bulk of Don Fragnini. At the bottom of the steps, Don Fragnini leaned forward to kiss his daughter on both cheeks. She leaned down to hug his thick neck. Waving down to him with tears in her eyes, she started up the steps.

Ian let go of her hand, holding back a moment. "How did you know they would be waiting for us?" he shouted over the sound of the powerful jet engines.

Don Fragnini leaned up to shout back, "I didn't. I just thought we couldn't take the chance." He turned to leave, but then turned back to shout, "Don't worry. My ship left exactly at midnight. It will arrive in Haifa in less than three weeks."

"You know, you never told me what it is you export."

Don Fragnini laughed. "Why, olive oil, my boy, olive oil!"

# CHAPTER 26

The work is not yours to complete, but neither are you able to rid yourself of responsibility for it.

Ethics of the Fathers 2:21

---

The room was a shambles. Jonathan slowly entered the small dorm room in a state of shocked dismay, stopping repeatedly to pick up numerous religious texts from the floor. He stared uncomprehendingly at his older brother who stood in the doorway, coolly surveying the damage. Ian answered the unspoken question on his brother's face in a somber voice.

"It would appear that the Church has a very long arm." As an afterthought he commented, "It wouldn't surprise me if we were being watched at this very moment." Seeing the startled expression on Jonathan's face he added, "Don't worry. I'm sure we're safe here." Looking about he said, "Do you think they took anything?"

Jonathan threw up his hands. "Who knows?"

The three young people sat in the small open air cafe, basking in the last rays of the sun. A cool breeze wafted past, fragrant with the scent of flowers. The wind gusted, lifting up the corners of the gaily checkered red and white tablecloth. Ian and Jonathan grabbed the flapping ends, placing salt and pepper shakers strategically at the corners. Arianna smiled at Ian as she slipped her arm into his.

Turning his head, he smiled back. "Are you sure the food is good?"

Jonathan grinned. "It's great. Unfortunately the service isn't."

Nuzzling her head on Ian's arm, Arianna asked in a worried tone, "Who do you think was in Jonathan's room, and what were they looking for?"

"I'm not sure who they were, but I sure know what they were after." Ian asked his brother, "You're absolutely sure no one picked up any of your mail while you were away?"

Jonathan said, "You were there yesterday when I picked up my packet at the post office."

Enjoying an inexpensive bottle of wine, the three sat back, relaxing in the cool evening air. Small globes of warm light sprang on, swaying gently in the branches nearby.

A tall thin man, his arms knotted with muscles, kept close watch on them from the rooftop of the opposite building. A slim set of binoculars rested snugly between long confident hands. A taut muscle around his mouth jerked once.

They parted company a while later. Jonathan caught a bus back to the Old City. Ian and Arianna waved good-bye. Walking arm in arm, they strolled a few blocks to the small apartment they had rented nearby.

It was midmorning, two and a half hours after the time they had agreed to meet the night before. Cursing under his breath, Ian hurried through the tall doors. Not surprisingly, Jonathan was nowhere in sight.

The travel alarm clock he had placed on the night stand the night before had been set properly. Unfortunately, he had failed to turn the alarm on. They had both slept late. He had awakened to the blaring sound of a car alarm on the curb below their bedroom window. Hastily jumping into his clothes, he'd kissed Arianna before dashing out of the apartment with a quick, "See you soon."

Striding over to the main counter, he stood impatiently in line. Five minutes passed. Finally his turn arrived. Stepping up to the counter, he asked in halting Hebrew, "Do you have any packages for a Jonathan Charosh?"

The mail clerk nodded lazily, disappearing behind a partition. He returned a few moments later. In a bored voice he said, "No, sir."

Spinning around, Ian bumped into a large Hasidic man who had stepped up behind him.

"Sorry," he called out as he raced out the doors, making a bee-line for Jonathan's yeshiva. Jogging nimbly past the more sedate pedestrians strolling the already hot and narrow stone-paved streets of the Jewish Quarter, he sprinted towards his destination. Taking the steps in front of the yeshiva three at a time, he flew through the doors and down a long corridor. Up two long flights of steps, he skidded around a corner and came to an abrupt stop. The door to his brother's room was wide open. Sticking his head in, he cursed softly under his breath, "Damn."

He spun around, about to head off to the Hall of

Learning, when he collided full force with a slight yeshiva student coming the other way.

"Sorry," Ian cried out, hastily reaching down to help the young man up. Ian ran over to pick up the young man's black hat. Dusting it off, he smiled apologetically, handing it back to the yeshiva student.

"Sorry again," he said.

Turning around, he took several steps before stopping in mid-stride. Twisting his head, he noted that the young man appeared to pause for a brief instant by the door to his brother's room before continuing on down the hall. Racing back, Ian stopped short. Placing his hand on the shoulder of the yeshiva student, he said, "Were you by any chance looking for Jonathan?"

The startled yeshiva student spun around almost losing his glasses. Readjusting them on his thin face, he said with an Israeli accent, "Yes, I was."

Smiling broadly, Ian held out his hand. Grasping the thin hand in his own powerful grip he said, "I'm Jonathan's brother. Have you seen him today?"

"No," Shmuli replied, shaking his head. "I've been on vacation the last two weeks. I just got back today."

Nodding politely, he turned to leave. Remembering something, he stopped to say, "Oh, I almost forgot. The day Jonathan left, a package came for him. I was in his room at the time, so I signed for it. I hope that's alright."

"You bet," Ian exclaimed. Unable to control his excitement, he said, "Where is it?"

"Oh, I left it in my room. It's just a few doors down. Do you want me to get it?"

"Sure. I'll come with you."

Ian followed the slight yeshiva student down the hall and into an identical room. Shmuli leaned over a narrow cot and pulled a large thick brown package from a shelf crammed with religious books.

Handing it to Ian he said matter-of-factly, "Here it is."

Ian stared down at the brown package resting in his hands. His mouth had suddenly gone dry. He couldn't believe it. This is what I risked everything for, he thought in amazement. Well, I hope it was really worth it.

Finding his voice, he looked up and said, "Thanks. Uh, if you see Jonathan, could you tell him to call my number to let me know he's alright?"

Shmuli nodded.

---

The phone was ringing. Seated just a few feet away, Ian didn't notice. Arianna ran over to pick it up on the last ring. Shaking her head in annoyance, she spoke into the receiver.

"Hello."

There was a short response on the other end. Tapping Ian on the shoulder she said, "It's Jonathan."

Ian looked up for the first time. "What?"

Then focusing on her words he said, "Oh, Jonathan. Thanks."

Handing him the phone, she smiled, ruffling his hair. Since he had come back early that afternoon, he hadn't budged from that spot. Spread all around him on the table were several texts. In front of him lay a large half-opened scroll and beside it, a small notebook. On the pad were jotted a fair number of lines.

Lifting the receiver up to his mouth he said, "Hi. I'm glad you called. I was a little worried. Are you okay?"

Hearing the reply, he nodded. "Yeah, I'm sorry I missed you too. I forgot to set the alarm." Taking a short breath, he said in a hushed tone of barely concealed excitement, "I've got it."

There was a yell at the other end.

"Yeah, I know. I can hardly believe it. I've been working on it all afternoon. And if what I've translated so far is correct…well, you'll just have to see it for yourself."

Listening a moment, he said, "Okay. I'll be there as soon as I can."

Hanging up the phone he looked up at Arianna, grinning sheepishly. "Look, I'm only going to go over for an hour or so."

"But I thought we would go out to eat soon," Arianna pouted.

Ian looked at his watch in amazement. It was almost nine p.m. Getting up, he stretched his tall frame. He drew her slender body against his broad chest.

"Sorry, love. I totally lost track of the time. I promised Jonathan I'd be right over and I don't want to stand him up twice in one day."

Running her nails affectionately through his hair, she sighed. "Okay. I'll run out and get a bite myself. Just promise me you'll get something also!"

"Don't worry," he said, grinning. "I'm sure I can grab something on the street."

Twenty minutes later, he alighted from the bus. Hitching his battered old knapsack squarely on his shoulder, he headed across the brightly lit parking lot. He entered one of the narrow, dimly lit, stone paved lanes of the old Jewish Quarter. Two pairs of eyes tracked his progress.

He wore open leather sandals in the Israeli style. The slap of the leather on the smooth cold stones echoed softly from the tall chiseled stone walls that rose high above on either side. Behind him came the barely perceptible pad of feet.

Turning a corner, Ian darted into a dark entranceway. Seconds later, two silent shadows walked past. Thirty feet away, a street lamp cast a feeble light. As they approached the light, they paused to look about, confused. Ian could now see them more clearly. The first was tall and gaunt, the other squat and burly. They turned to mutter to each other.

Sauntering back in his direction, Ian tensed his body into a tight coil. The two passed by his hiding place and continued on. Ian didn't move, breathing softly. The soft pad of feet faded in the distance. Relaxing, he let out a long breath. Stepping from the shadows, he peered once behind him and then continued on.

Turning the next corner, he felt thick hands grab his arms from behind, pinning them behind his back. His knapsack fell to the ground. In front of him stood a tall angular figure. The faint light shone behind the figure, highlighting his shape. The man's face was still in semi-shadow. The figure turned its head slightly. Ian recognized him. It was the waiter from the restaurant in Rome. A muscle twitched in the man's cheek.

Ian lurched and kicked, wrenching his arms from the heavy grip. He crouched, driving his fist into the stomach of the tall man. It was like striking a tree. A thick meaty arm clamped around his throat from behind, jerking him up. His vision blurred. He began to black out. Thrusting his head back convulsively, he felt bone crush beneath it. The man behind him let out a soft wailing sound. The thick arm fell away. Ian gasped for air.

The tall gaunt man seized his left arm, the hands gripping with numbing force. Ian shifted, clamping his right hand around the other's rock-hard arm, seeking a lock.

For a moment the two stood immobile, straining silently.

Ian squirmed, heaved, kicked. He hacked with the back of his hand at the tall man's neck. The hand-grips loosened. Lashing out with his foot, he landed a crushing blow to the side of his attacker's head.

He was buffeted by a powerful blow to his back. Falling to his knees, he felt an explosion of pain. Falling and twisting, he rolled and swung out his leg. The short squat man fell with a heavy thud, his head slamming against the stone paving with a sharp crack. A short metal bar clanged to the stone. It rolled several feet over the uneven surface, coming to a rest a few inches from Ian's head.

Ian tottered erect. He seized the bar. A rushing figure leapt toward him. Swinging the bar, he struck a solid blow across the angular face of the gaunt man, crushing bone and teeth. Blood spurted, spraying onto Ian's arm. The tall man let out a keening wail, falling to the side. As he fell, he struck out viciously with his arm. Barely avoiding the blow, Ian swept the bar down. He swung again and again, with all his force. The man fell to the ground. Panting, Ian let the bar fall with a sharp clang. Staggering forward, he limped over to pick up his knapsack.

He stared down at the dark form that lay nearby. The short squat man was out cold. Turning around, a horrid bloodstained face rose up in the feeble glow. The tall man tried to grab Ian's ankle but his arm appeared to hinge on three joints instead of two and he couldn't control the motion.

"Who sent you?" Ian spat out, stepping safely out of reach. He wiped some blood from his mouth and said, "Do I have to break more of your bones?"

The man was silent. Ian shook his head in disbelief. His right shoulder throbbed slightly. He felt it with his left hand. Nothing appeared to be broken. Turning his back on his attackers, he limped along the deserted lane.

Ten minutes later, sitting in his brother's room, he related the night's events to a horrified Jonathan.

"My God, I can't believe they attacked you right on the street," his brother said.

"I think they suspect or even know that I have the scroll."

"What's so important about this scroll?"

Opening his knapsack, Ian drew out the clear vinyl pouch. Unzipping it, he carefully removed the scroll. Pointing down to the second column he said, "This is when I realized just what I had uncovered. You have to understand. From an archeological perspective, this is the find of the century. But that's not why they want it back so badly. Here, let me read to you what I was able to translate so far."

In a ringing voice he read: "I am Jaacob, the righteous teach(er) of the community…those who are zealous for the la(w). I am blood brother of Yeshua the nazirite, the chosen Messiah of the house of Aaron. He who led the zealot revolt on the Temple Mount. He who was betrayed by Judas Ish Cariot. He who died at Golgoth(a) by the hands of the kittim on the Cross of Wood. What I speak to you I saw with mine own eyes. Hear my words all men and know by them the truth…."

# CHAPTER 27

And to Jerusalem, Your city, may You return in compassion, and may You rest within it, as You have spoken. May You rebuild it soon in our days as an eternal structure, and may You speedily establish the throne of David within it.

The Shmoneh Esrei

---

Reb Yossl's frail figure stood before the menorah. They had brought it here secretly, in the dark of night. They stood now in the bomb shelter of Jonathan's yeshiva, only a stone's throw from the Western Wall and the Temple Mount. Reb Yossl turned away. Walking over to a toolbox someone had left on a shelf, he rummaged through it, pulling something out.

The others stood around, watching Reb Yossl curiously. He lifted his feeble hand, and in the harsh light they saw a heavy hammer clasped tightly in his upraised arm. They all cried out. Reb Yossl brought the hammer crashing down onto the base. There was a loud metal clang. The hammer dropped to the floor with a heavy thud.

They all rushed forward. Jonathan turned and said, "Why, Rebbe?"

Reb Yossl smiled weakly, pointing with a shaky finger. They all followed it. Gathering around, they carefully examined where Reb Yossl's hammer blow had landed. A deep dent had appeared and the golden surface had flaked away as well, revealing a dull brass color beneath.

Avi bent down closely to inspect the dent. "It's definitely hollow."

Reb Yossl said, "Cut it open."

Three hours later, Avi carefully finished cutting the base in two. Shuli and Ian, thick towels in their hands, rushed forward to pull the two pieces apart.

A small torrent of dark brown sand poured out onto the floor. The young men jumped back in surprise, sand spilling out over their shoes. Reb Yossl shuffled forward, falling to his knees. He sifted the sand slowly through his aged fingers. Reaching into a tall pile heaped at the center, his hand closed around something. Tugging feebly, his hand emerged.

He held the object up to the light. Twelve precious stones in four rows, three to a row, were set in a plate of pure gold. The stones caught the light, flashing out brilliantly in their many colors. Below each stone was the clear inscription of a Hebrew name.

"Rebbe, can it be?" Jonathan said.

Reb Yossl nodded, tears in his clear blue eyes. Turning it around, he carefully searched its back. Pressing gently on a spot, they all heard a soft click. A secret panel opened.

Reb Yossl stood frozen, staring at the Hebrew letters inscribed on the inside panel. There were seventy-two letters inscribed in the precious gold. A sudden wind passed through the still air of the bomb shelter, ruffling their hair and clothes. They all turned to stare at each other in wonder, knowing they were in a sealed room.

Jonathan turned fearfully to Reb Yossl. The sage stood as if in a trance. In a strained voice Jonathan said, "What is it?"

Reb Yossl looked up, his face radiating with a pure light. He made no answer, quickly closing the secret panel. The air in the room was still once more.

Ian said, "We must show this to everyone."

Reb Yossl turned to him slowly. In a quiet voice he said, "No, my son. The time has not yet come to reveal all this."

"But when will that time come?" Ian said.

"When the Messiah of David is revealed and anointed."

"When the Messiah comes?" Ian exclaimed. "We've waited over two thousand years for him."

"Be patient my son. He lives and breathes as do we."

They all stood silent, contemplating the words of the tzaadik. Jonathan had been sweeping away the rest of the sand. The three individual feet of the true base of the Menorah were now plain for all to see. The descriptions by the commentaries had been right after all, Jonathan marveled.

The broom pressed against something hard trapped beneath the sand. Jonathan fell to his knees. Groping about, his hands closed around two small objects. Pulling them free, he held up two small clay pots, one in each hand. Their seals were still intact. Rising up on his feet, he brought them over to the tzaadik. Reb Yossl examined the seals.

Turning to Ian, he said in a still voice, "The time is approaching more quickly than you can imagine!"

# EPILOGUE

When the Holy One showed Adam, the Primal Man, all the generations to come, he saw that David had no lifetime granted him at all. Adam gave him seventy years of his own life, and the Holy One signed the contract with him.

Zohar Genesis 91b

---

## KIBBUTZ EN YA'AKOV BETHLEHEM, JUDEA

### Present Day

He heard it cry out in the dry, baked air. Jumping up from under the shade of the tree, he dropped his sandwich on a flat rock.

It was hot. Too hot. The air was full of dust and the smell of sheep dung. The hot air shimmered in a haze. Upon the bronzed youth's head sat a faded green army hat he'd gotten from a friend. It only partially protected him from the merciless rays. Racing across the semi-arid terrain, he leapt nimbly from one stone out-cropping to the next. The bleating took on a terrified note, a painful keening mixed in with it. Increasing his pace, he nearly fell into the hole.

Skidding to a stop with his open sandaled feet, he righted himself. A shower of pebbles rained down upon the small lamb, eliciting further cries. He looked down into the pit. The lamb had fallen to the bottom, wedging itself between two large rocks.

He called to it in a soft, soothing voice, "Sorry, little fella. I'll have you out soon."

In his right hand he carried a long olive-wood staff. He had cleverly carved its top end into the shape of a flute. He'd taken a lot of ribbing about it from some of the regular members of the kibbutz.

"Who do you think you are, King David?" they joked.

He'd come directly to the kibbutz two years earlier from America. Many of the older members still considered him a newcomer.

Placing his left foot down on the sharp edge of one of the rocks, he shoved the bottom end of his thick staff into the soft dirt and gravel, wedging it under the rocks. He bent down, leaning his whole weight against the staff. The cords in his neck and arms stood out. At 5 feet 10 inches, he was not very broad in the shoulders, but his biceps were strong and he had powerful forearms. He strained mightily against the staff.

The rock barely budged. Crouching down to stroke the coat of the young lamb, he tried to calm it. Abruptly, the bleating stopped. He looked down at the lamb. It lay there between the rocks, looking back up at him with its big moist brown eyes. Dropping down his other leg, he stood in the pit, straddling the two rocks.

Twisting the staff down further, he set himself to push once again. He closed his eyes, summoning up every ounce of his strength. He grasped the smooth wood tightly between callused hands. Exhaling once, he filled his lungs deeply, shoving hard. There was a low grating sound. The rock began to move. Suddenly, it shifted to the side.

Losing his footing, he toppled into the pit. He almost fell right on top of the lamb. Grabbing at the sharp walls to break his fall, he scraped his knuckles and elbows raw. He stepped down carefully, grasping the lamb around its belly and lifted it up. It struggled a moment. Holding it firmly against his chest, he spoke to it in a soft voice, gently stroking its head until it calmed down.

Heaving it up, he lifted it clear. The lamb scrambled away, no worse for the experience. Dusting himself off, he clambered up out of the pit and inspected his staff. Its surface was unmarred. Dragging over some large rocks, he shoved them along with some dirt into the deep hole, covering it up as best he could.

He wiped the dirt from his hands onto his pants, surveying the scrapes and bruises on his hands and arms. He didn't even bother to look at the scratches on his legs. Shaking his head, he wiped his sweat-soaked brow. Adjusting his hat, he picked his way across the rock-strewn field. Near the bole of the tree, he noticed one of the sheep finishing off the last bit of the sandwich he'd thrown down a few minutes before.

Grinning to himself, he sank down, exhausted. He twisted off the plastic cover of the small canteen he'd placed under a nearby rock. Raising it to his lips, he let the cool water trickle down his parched throat, before using a few of the precious drops to rinse off his knuckles and elbows. The mixture of blood and water ran into the parched earth.

    He removed his hat and raised the canteen over his head. The water dripped through the thick auburn hair and onto his face. Refreshed, he twisted the cap back on securely, placing it back under the rock. He wiped off the head of his staff with his tee-shirt, shifting into a more comfortable position. Lifting the smooth flute mouth to his lips, he began to play a tune he had made up that morning.

# GLOSSARY

---

**Abba:** Father.

**Amalek:** Grandson of Esau (The Red One). The nation that arose from his loins represent, on a spiritual plane, the forces of Evil and Darkness. The Twelve Tribes of Israel are the sons of Jacob, Esau's brother. They represent the forces of Goodness and Light. The Jewish people are seen as engaged in a titanic struggle with Amalek for the destiny of the world. According to the latter prophets, in the End of Days that struggle will reach its final climax.

**Bseder:** Alright.

| | |
|---|---|
| **Chag Semeyach:** | Happy holiday. |
| **Concordance:** | Reference text (by name of subject) of the entire Old Testament. |
| **Curia:** | Administrative arm of the Vatican. |
| **Divine Face:** | In Jewish mystical teaching the Divine Face is an aspect by which a transcendent God interacts with his creations. |
| **Ephraim and Menashe:** | The two sons of Joseph. There is a legend that prior to the coming of the Messiah of the House of David (who is a descendant of the tribe of Judah) there will come onto the world scene a Messiah who is a descendant of the two sons of Joseph. He will wage a mighty war, and will usher in the Messiah of David. |
| **End Time:** | A.k.a the End of Days. The time immediately preceding the coming of the Messiah. Usually depicted as a time of great turmoil, war and famine. |
| **Feast of Lights:** | More commonly known as the holiday of Chanukah. A |

candelabrum is lit for eight days to commemorate a miracle of ancient times. A small band of zealots, led by the priest-warrior Judah Maccabee, in the year 165 B.C.E. succeeded in freeing the Temple from the vastly superior armies of the Seleucid Empire. They rededicated the Temple and lit the Menorah. Unfortunately, only one small jar of pure oil had escaped the notice of the foreign invaders, and still retained the seal of purity of the High Priest. It held only one day's supply of oil, and it would take seven more days to prepare new oil pure enough to be used to light the Menorah. The Maccabees lit the Menorah with the oil contained in the single remaining vessel, and miraculously, it continued to burn for eight full days.

**Gadol:** Great One. Usually refers to a Talmudic sage of great learning and piety.

**Gemara:** Talmud.

**Hester Panim:** This refers to the mystical concept that God has removed or contracted his Active Consciousness in the world from Biblical times to the present. This is to allow Humanity greater free will to choose its own Destiny. As a natural consequence of this contraction, the Human Race is free, either to rise to great heights of Goodness or sink to the depths of Evil. According to the Prophets, God promises to reassert his Presence in the End of Days, passing final judgment on all Humanity on Judgment Day.

**Ineffable Name:** The Tetragrammaton. This is the four letter name of God. He who truly understands the mystical power contained within it can perform all manner of miracles, including the resurrection of the dead.

**Kabbalah:** Works of Jewish Mysticism. The best known of these is the Zohar, ascribed to Rabbi Shimon Bar Yochai of the Mishnaic period. (first-third century C.E.)

**Kapotot and shtreimels:** Traditional garb worn by members of various hasidic sects. These ultra-orthodox Jews followed in the traditions of a movement which swept through Eastern European Jewry nearly three hundred years ago. The founder of the movement, The Ba'al Shem Tov, (Master of the Good Name) emphasized the Omnipresence of God, the importance and significance of man in the Universe, and the influence man and his actions have even upon God himself.

**Merkava:** Divine Chariot. Metaphysical term denoting an aspect of Divine revelation.

**Mitzvah:** Commandment of the Torah.

**Circumcision:** The covenant between God and Abraham and his seed. According to Jewish tradition, a new-born male child is circumcised eight days after birth. By this act Man is seen as completing the act of Creation. The parents become partners with God in fulfilling the very purpose of Creation: the possibility of relationship between God and Man.

**Minyan:** Quorum of ten men over the age of thirteen.

| | |
|---|---|
| **Olam Ha-Emes:** | The true world. In Jewish mystical thought, the world around us is illusory. The true world is the world of spirituality, where all souls go after relinquishing their physical bodies. |
| **Payos:** | Traditional sideburns. |
| **Pesach:** | Passover |
| **Pinchas:** | Phineas of the Bible. The original zealot who risked his life to sanctify God's name. |
| **Rebono Shel Olam:** | Master of the Universe. |
| **Seder, Sedarim:** | A traditional family meal held the first night of Passover. It has its own liturgy called the Haggadah which relates the story of the Exodus from Egypt. The Last Supper in the New Testament was most probably a seder meal in which Jesus and his apostles partook immediately prior to the events leading up to his crucifixion. |
| **Sephardic:** | Jews originally from Spain. In the fateful year 1492 (the same year Christopher Columbus set sail for the New World), the large Jewish |

community of Spain, which had flourished there for centuries, was expelled by order of the king and queen. Only those Jews who converted to Christianity were allowed to stay. The vast majority chose exile and migrated across the entire known world.

**Shabbos, Shabbat:** The Sabbath.

**Shalom aleichem:** A traditional greeting. Literally, "Peace be with you."

**Shema:** First word of the prayer, "Hear O Israel, the Lord our God, the Lord is One."

**Shmoneh Esrei:** The Eighteen blessings. A silent prayer, recited standing, feet together.

**Siddur:** Hebrew prayer book.

**Succah:** Covered hut. Erected as a temporary dwelling by religious Jews for the week of Tabernacles, it signifies God's protection of the Jewish people throughout all time.

**Tablet of Truth:** A.k.a. the Urim Ve Tumim A gold breastplate worn only by the High Priest, it was inlaid with twelve precious and semi-precious jewels, representing the twelve tribes of Israel. The name of each tribe was inscribed beneath its own special stone. Hidden within a secret compartment was inscribed the longer version of the Ineffable Name of God. The High Priest would use the mystical power contained within the Tablet of Truth as an oracle to divine God's will.

**Tefilin:** Phylacteries. Two small black boxes with attached straps that contain portions of the Torah, inscribed on bits of parchment. They are donned each morning by observant Jews for the morning prayers.

**Tzaadik:** Righteous individual.

**Tzitzit:** Traditional garment with fringes on its four corners.

**Va'ad Leumi:** Jewish quasi-government in British mandate Palestine.

**Yarmulke:** Traditional head covering.

**Yeshiva:** School of Jewish learning.

**Zealot:** For almost two hundred years a movement, called the Zealots, grew in ancient Israel. They held that being the elect of God, they should accept no master except God. Eventually, they precipitated the fateful revolt against Rome in 66 C.E. One of Jesus' original disciples was a man called Simon the Zealot. Much controversy has been generated over the question as to whether Jesus himself was a Zealot or at least sympathetic to their cause.

**Zimri:** A prince of the tribe of Simon, he desecrated God's Name by committing an act of sexual misconduct. Phineas slew him in the act with a spear.
See Numbers 25: 10-15.